An Enchanting Dare

The Daring Daughters Book 10

By Emma V. Le

Published by F

Copyright (c) L

Editing Services Ma

Cover Art: Vict

ASIN No: B09S Z

ISBN No: 978-2-492133-41-1

About Me!

I started this incredible journey way back in 2010 with The Key to Erebus but didn't summon the courage to hit publish until October 2012. For anyone who's done it, you'll know publishing your first title is a terribly scary thing! I still get butterflies on the morning a new title releases, but the terror has subsided at least. Now I just live in dread of the day my daughters are old enough to read them.

The horror! (On both sides I suspect.)

2017 marked the year that I made my first foray into Historical Romance and the world of the Regency Romance, and my word what a year! I was delighted by the response to this series and can't wait to add more titles. Paranormal Romance readers need not despair, however, as there is much more to come there too. Writing has become an addiction and as soon as one book is over I'm hugely excited to start the next so you can expect plenty more in the future.

As many of my works reflect, I am greatly influenced by the beautiful French countryside in which I live. I've been here in the South West since 1998, though I was born and raised in England. My three gorgeous girls are all bilingual and my husband Pat, myself, and our four cats consider ourselves very fortunate to have made such a lovely place our home.

KEEP READING TO DISCOVER MY OTHER BOOKS!

Other Works by Emma V. Leech

Daring Daughters

Daring Daughters Series

Girls Who Dare

Girls Who Dare Series

Rogues & Gentlemen

Rogues & Gentlemen Series

The Regency Romance Mysteries

The Regency Romance Mysteries Series

The French Vampire Legend

The French Vampire Legend Series

The French Fae Legend

The French Fae Legend Series

Stand Alone

The Book Lover (a paranormal novella)

The Girl is Not for Christmas (Regency Romance)

Audio Books

Don't have time to read but still need your romance fix? The wait is over…

By popular demand, get many of your favourite Emma V Leech Regency Romance books on audio as performed by the incomparable Philip Battley and Gerard Marzilli. Several titles available and more added each month!

Find them at your favourite audiobook retailer!

Acknowledgements

Thanks, of course, to my wonderful editor Kezia Cole with Magpie Literary Services

To Victoria Cooper for all your hard work, amazing artwork and above all your unending patience!!! Thank you so much. You are amazing!

To my BFF, PA, personal cheerleader and bringer of chocolate, Varsi Appel, for moral support, confidence boosting and for reading my work more times than I have. I love you loads!

A huge thank you to all of Emma's Book Club members! You guys are the best!

I'm always so happy to hear from you so do email or message me :)

emmavleech@orange.fr

To my husband Pat and my family … For always being proud of me

Table of Contents

Family Trees

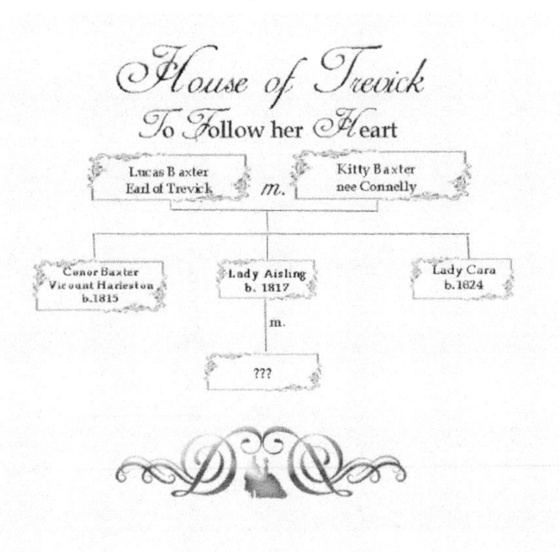

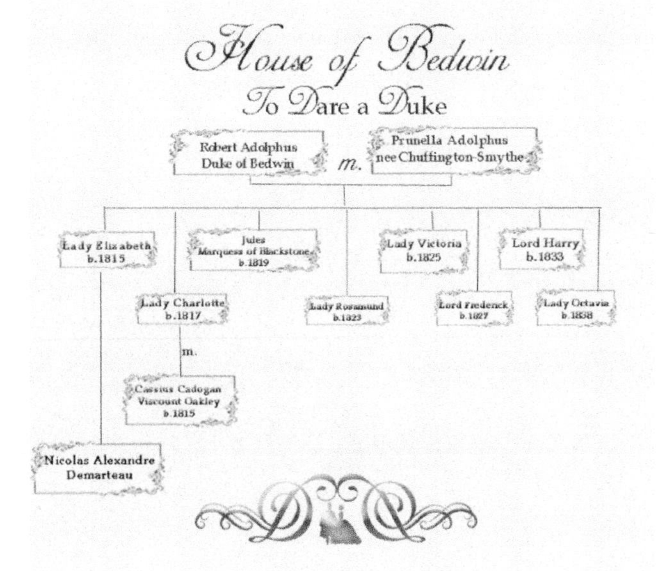

House of Cavendish
To Break the Rules
Silas Anson
Viscount Cavendish
m.
Aashini Anson
aka: Lucia de Feria
Twins
Ashton Anson
b.1816
Vivien Anson
b.1816
m.
August Lane-Fox
House of Hunt
To Steal a Kiss
Nathaniel Hunt
m.
Alice Hunt
nee Dowding
Leo Hunt
b.1815
Arabella "Bella" Hunt
b.1820
m.
Lawrence Grenville
Marquess of Bainbridge

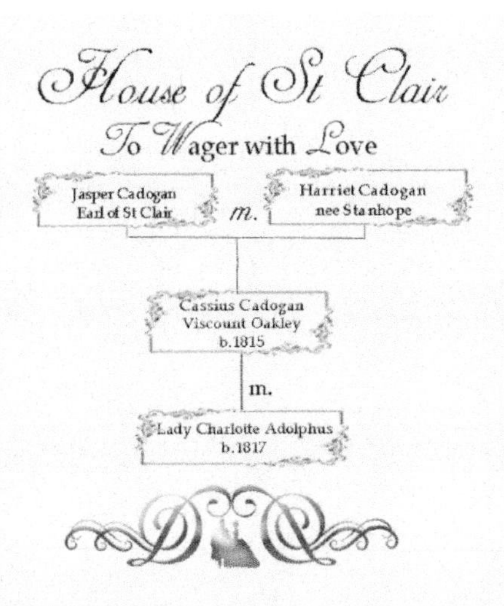
House of St Clair
To Wager with Love
Jasper Cadogan
Earl of St Clair
m.
Harriet Cadogan
nee Stanhope
Cassius Cadogan
Viscount Oakley
b.1815
m.
Lady Charlotte Adolphus
b.1817

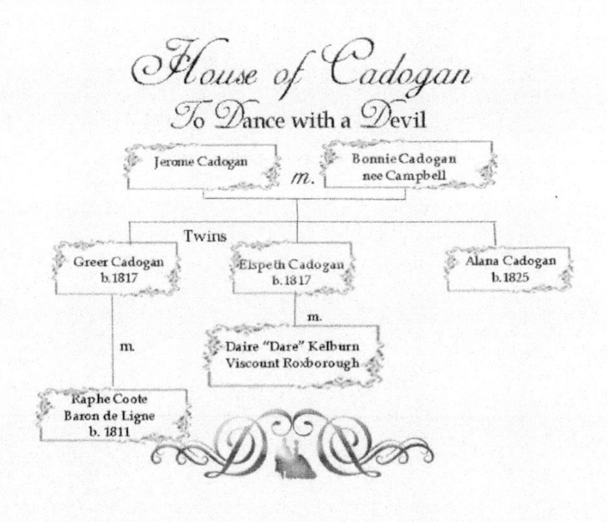
House of Cadogan
To Dance with a Devil
Jerome Cadogan
m.
Bonnie Cadogan
nee Campbell
Twins
Greer Cadogan
b.1817
Elspeth Cadogan
b.1817
Alana Cadogan
b.1825
m.
Daire "Dare" Kelburn
Viscount Roxborough
m.
Raphe Coote
Baron de Ligne
b. 1811

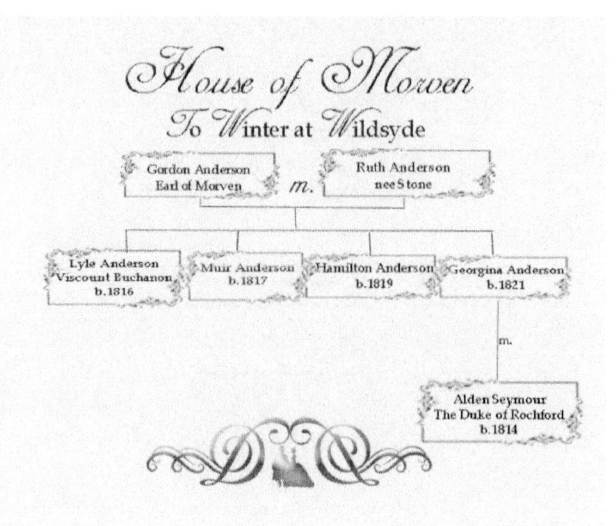
House of Morwen
To Winter at Wildsyde
Gordon Anderson
Earl of Morven
m.
Ruth Anderson
nee Stone
Lyle Anderson
Viscount Buchanon
b.1816
Muir Anderson
b.1817
Hamilton Anderson
b.1819
Georgina Anderson
b.1821
m.
Alden Seymour
The Duke of Rochford
b.1814

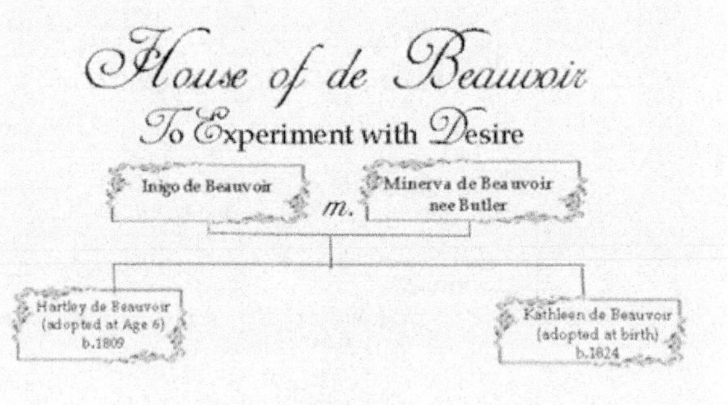
House of de Beauvoir
To Experiment with Desire
Inigo de Beauvoir
m.
Minerva de Beauvoir
nee Butler
Hartley de Beauvoir
(adopted at Age 6)
b.1809
Kathleen de Beauvoir
(adopted at birth)
b.1824

House of Rothborn
To Bed the Baron
Solo Weston
Baron of Rothborn
m.
Jemima Weston
nee Fernside
Larkin Weston
b.1816
Grace Weston
b.1821
m.
Mr Sterling Oak
b. 1813
House of Knight
To Ride with the Knight
Gabriel Knight
m.
Lady Helena Knight
nee Adolphus
Florence Knight
b.1817
Evie Knight
b.1822
Felix Knight
b.1824
Emmaline Knight
b.1826
m.
Henry Stanhope
b.1799

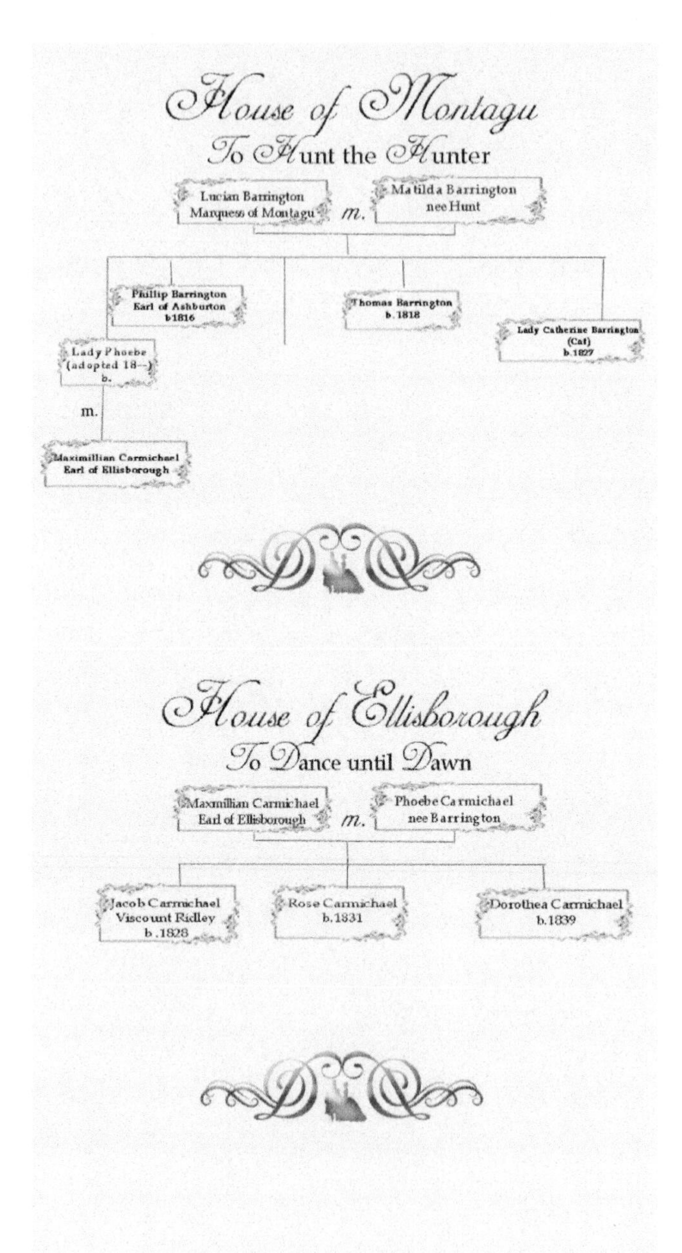
House of Montagu
To Hunt the Hunter
Lucian Barrington
Marquess of Montagu
m.
Matilda Barrington
nee Hunt
Phillip Barrington
Earl of Ashburton
b1816
Thomas Barrington
b.1818
Lady Catherine Barrington
(Cat)
b.1827
Lady Phoebe
(adopted 18--)
b.
m.
Maximillian Carmichael
Earl of Ellisborough
House of Ellisborough
To Dance until Dawn
Maxmillian Carmichael
Earl of Ellisborough
m.
Phoebe Carmichael
nee Barrington
Jacob Carmichael
Viscount Ridley
b.1828
Rose Carmichael
b.1831
Dorothea Carmichael
b.1839

Chapter 1

Louis,

Paris grows dull in your absence. I am bored and in need of distraction. Will you not return for a visit and see how your protégé goes on before he does something rash? My empire needs little of me, save for some growling and posturing on the rare occasion people forget with whom they deal. Our foes are all vanquished, on this side of La Manche, at least. I think I shall cross that narrow body of water and see what trouble I can stir up, for life is dull and I shall grow prematurely fat and old if I do not keep my wits and my weapons sharp. I should like to see the ladies gasp and whisper behind their fans. Will I spoil your newly shined and pretty reputation if I come? You think it is a joke, perhaps, but I will make good on my promise one day. I should like to see the place that was my birthright.

Do you think there are any remaining that would cut my throat for my father's crimes? My own are of little consequence across the channel, I think. My late, unlamented father's legacy is such I think I should sleep with one eye open on English soil. I believe I shall look forward to it.

Damn you, Louis, it is late, and I grow maudlin like a boy without his pa. You were always wise far beyond your years and I need your instincts and your surety to guide me straight, for my path becomes increasingly tangled. I do not truly wish to cause you trouble, but I miss you, and your too kind-hearted brother as well. I miss the days when we caused mayhem together. You are the only family I have known, and I wish to be reunited. Shall you come to visit me soon? Or shall I do something dreadful to demand your attention, like the wicked spoilt boy I know too well how to play?

—Excerpt of a letter to Louis César de Montluc, Comte de Villen, from Wulfric 'Wolf' De Vere.

27th April 1841, Cavendish House, The Strand, London.

"D'anam don diabhal!"

The words she'd thrown out with such frustration were still ringing in Aisling's ears. Wishing Sylvester Cootes' soul to the devil might be satisfying, but apparently it didn't actually *achieve* anything. The wretched man was still watching her as if she were some newly discovered species, as if he was determined to understand everything about her, to learn all her secrets. Well, he'd said as much, and wasn't that a terrifying thought? What might he discover, and how might he judge her if he knew? Her stomach twisted unpleasantly, and Aisling swallowed hard lest the meagre amount of food she'd forced past her lips curdled and her stomach rebelled.

All around her was merriment and celebration, and Aisling felt like a little dark cloud, hovering about and making everyone uncomfortable. She reached up and gently massaged her throbbing temples.

Why hadn't she told him to leave her alone? This, more than anything, troubled her. He'd offered to leave her be, and she'd felt certain the offer was a genuine one, yet she'd not taken it. Why? Why would she not snatch an opportunity to make him go away?

Because you don't truly wish him to, taunted a little voice in her head. She rejected it, irritated. Why would she not wish a man she could not stand to go away? Perhaps because she felt brave in front of him, in a way she never did with anyone else. Not any longer. He made her so furious she forgot her nerves, her doubts, and her own failings. She let her temper rule her and… and that felt good after so long. It was also dangerous. *He* was dangerous.

"Are you well, *mademoiselle*?"

Aisling turned to find a pair of startling blue eyes regarding her with concern. The Comte de Villen was too beautiful to sit comfortably beside and, much to her consternation, Aisling felt a blush climb her throat.

"Just a h-headache, *monsieur*," she managed, struggling to meet his worried gaze.

"Is there anything I can do? Should I fetch the countess to—"

"Oh, no, th-thank you. Some fresh air, I think, if… excuse me—" Aisling got up and hurried off, relieved to be away from the man, though he'd been nothing but kind and patient, trying his best to converse with her when he got little more than a word or two in reply.

Aisling pushed through the house, past busy servants bearing trays, and burst out into the garden to drink in the cool, sweet air.

Her temples throbbed harder, and she wished she could go home. Not to the elegant town house her parents owned here in London, but home to Trevick Castle. She wanted to walk and walk until her legs ached, to find her peace in the woodlands, to bury herself in the little corner of the world where she could be herself and shut out everything and everyone else. Soon, she promised herself. No one here would ever offer for her, and that would be another season over and done. In another year or two, maybe she could give up the pretence that she was even trying to find a husband, for it became increasingly difficult to keep up the facade.

"Aisling? Are you well?"

Aisling looked up, relieved to see Vivien's twin brother, Ash. She had loved Ash since she was a very little girl, and he was one of the few men she did not feel uncertain around. Once upon a time, many years ago, she had hoped he might offer for her, but he regarded her as a sister, nothing more, and she had long since come to terms with that. She could never marry, not now, and even if things were different, she could not imagine ever trusting another man enough to give herself into his keeping.

"Just a headache," she said, accepting the arm he offered her. "I needed some fresh air."

"Shall I take you to Nani Maa and have her mix one of her foul potions?" he asked, reaching out to tuck a stray curl behind her ear.

Aisling stared up into his handsome face, feeling some of her anxiety drain away. Ash always made her feel calmer, safer. "I don't think so. Just a turn about the garden and some quiet for a moment should do it."

Another male voice cut through Aisling's fragile peace and set her nerves jangling. "Then you ought to have a chaperone. I'm happy to oblige."

She turned, scowling, though she knew well enough who had appeared behind them.

"Mr Cootes, I do not require your chaperonage for a stroll in the garden in broad daylight with my friend, and you hardly qualify for the role in any case."

Mr Cootes shrugged and strolled closer. "When your friend is such a handsome and eligible young fellow, I'm afraid I must beg to differ, and I am better than nothing."

Ash beamed, the rat. "He has a point, Aisling," he said with mock gravity. "It seems unlikely any young lady could spend five minutes alone with me without wanting to tear my clothes off. It's for your own good."

"Ash!" Aisling exclaimed, mortified.

Ash only winked at her, a friendly, teasing smile at his lips before he turned to Mr Cootes. "Do join us for a stroll about the garden. The spring colour is very fine, and this poor lady has a headache and needs some air."

"With pleasure," Mr Cootes replied, offering Aisling his arm so she was sandwiched between them.

Aisling narrowed her eyes at him, but could hardly refuse. Reluctantly, she placed her hand on his sleeve.

They strolled around the extensive grounds, arm in arm, with Mr Cootes and Ash exchanging pleasantries whilst Aisling simmered in silence.

"This is a lovely spot," Mr Cootes observed as they came across a large ornamental pond. It was round with a three-tiered fountain at the centre and sheltered from the wind by hedges with openings that gave out onto prettily framed views of the garden. Aisling sat down on a bench, strategically positioned to give a glimpse of an antique statue of some naked male through the fountain's spray.

"My mother's favourite spot," Ash agreed. "Oh, and speaking of the same, there she is. Well, there are plenty of people coming out to enjoy the garden now, so propriety is served. If you'll excuse me."

Ash bowed to Aisling and hurried away before she could protest, leaving her alone with Sylvester blasted Cootes. Aisling glared at her friend's retreating back, wondering if she could be rude enough to follow him and abandon Mr Cootes without another word.

Before she could decide, Mr Cootes sat down beside her. "Is it true you are in love with him?"

Aisling gasped at the bold question. She glared at him, but he just watched her placidly. Deciding this might be a good way to be rid of his attentions, she didn't prevaricate.

"Yes. It's true," she said, chin up and defiance in every word.

He nodded, as if it were no surprise. "I thought as much."

"What is that supposed to mean?" she demanded, hearing the amusement in his words.

He sat back, crossing his long legs and stretching one arm along the back of the bench. He looked totally at ease, and she noticed his eyes were a light hazel, flecked with gold.

"Only that he is the kind of man you *would* form a *tendresse* for."

"How so?" she demanded, too irritated by the observation to tell him his opinions were of no consequence to her, which would have been the sensible thing to do.

His expression was serene, his gaze upon her unwavering. "You've known him a long time?"

Aisling nodded. "All my life," she admitted, for she saw no reason to deny it.

"He's been a good friend to you?" he guessed, and Aisling nodded again. That much was obvious.

Sylvester just smiled at her, his gaze direct, as if willing her to figure it out for herself.

"You think it's a childish crush, that I'm being foolish," she said, her voice curt, irritation simmering as it always did in his presence.

"I don't think loving a dear friend is foolish," he said, his voice surprisingly gentle. "I'm only pointing out the possibility that you have mistaken the love you have for a dear friend for something else."

"You do think me a fool!" Aisling folded her arms, her cheeks flaming. The arrogant devil. How dare he tell her what she thought, how she felt.

Sylvester sighed, shaking his head. "Perhaps I'm wrong. Only you can decide the truth, but I have watched you together on several occasions and I do not see any spark in you. You do not light up when you are with him as you might if you were deeply in love. I've had a chance to observe that emotion at close hand of late, and even you, as secretive as you are, might struggle to hide such a deep regard. You love him as a dear friend, as a brother, not as a man. There is no passion in your regard for him, no desire."

Aisling's mouth dropped open, but she was too stunned to say a word. She wanted very much to give him a scathing set down that would leave his ears ringing and his ego in tatters. The trouble was, she recognised the truth that rang in his words. Aisling knew why she had accepted the fact that Ash would never offer for her with such acquiescence. She just hadn't wanted to examine her own feelings. Her emotions had been too troublesome, so she had buried them deep, had become too used to ignoring them. Now, she took her love for Ash out and inspected it in the bright light of Sylvester's observations. It was so apparent she did not trouble herself to wonder how he'd noticed. It *was* obvious. She loved Ash very much, but it was not the passionate desire of a woman for a man she wanted to be her lover, her husband. Not that she was about to admit it to Mr Cootes, the arrogant devil, though she could admit it to herself. For she knew in her heart she could not feel that kind of passion for any man. Those feelings were dead and gone, and she was glad of it.

"You do not know what you're talking about," she said, once she had wit enough to speak again. "You know nothing of my feelings."

"Perhaps not, but I suspect I understand more than you think. You could trust me."

Aisling snorted. An unladylike sound, but the idea of trusting the man beside her was so outlandish she could not help her reaction.

He returned a smile that managed to be both boyish and wolfish at the same time. Oh, he *was not* to be trusted.

"I know you think that a ridiculous idea, but it is true. Why don't you just unburden yourself of whatever keeps you apart from the world, from life, even from your friends? Sometimes it is easier to confide in a stranger than someone close to you."

"From my friends?" she echoed, stunned by the suggestion. "What—"

He leaned closer, so close that her words snagged in her throat. His scent tickled her nose, shaving soap and freshly laundered linen, a trace of peppermint. No expensive, overpowering cologne, no waft of brandy, just clean male skin.

"Do your friends truly know you, Lady Aisling? Do they know the person you really are, the passionate woman you keep hidden and buttoned up and that makes you blush and stammer for fear people will guess what you are hiding?"

Aisling lurched to her feet, too unnerved not to react.

"Whatever it is you think you know, you're wrong," she said, her fingers curled into fists, too much anger in the words not to reveal he'd hit a nerve.

He sighed and sat back, watching her. "I would not betray your confidence, Aisling. Perhaps I could help you. I know you sneaked out of Rowsley House after midnight in nothing but your nightrail in the middle of December. Were you meeting a lover? Someone you feel real passion for, unlike your affectionate regard for Mr Anson? Are you in trouble, love?"

"How dare you," she whispered, so badly shaken she couldn't think straight. "How d-dare you suggest—"

He got to his feet, a lithe, elegant movement that brought him too close to her. Aisling took a step back, uncertain if her knees would support her much longer.

"Aisling," he said softly.

"No. I never gave you leave to use my name." Aisling grasped at that, at something tangible and simple she could be angry about.

"My lady," he corrected, his voice still gentle, persuasive.

"No!" she said, shaking her head. Aisling picked up her skirts and fled, unheeding of anyone watching her flight. She needed to be as far away from Sylvester Cootes as she could get, and she needed to stay away.

"Damnation," Sylvester muttered under his breath.

People were looking at him, their gazes speculative. Ashton Anson among them. And now the fellow was coming this way. No doubt to warn him off. He could hardly blame him, either. He'd made a spectacular mess of that when he'd only wanted to put Aisling at ease. Why he felt so certain she needed his help, needed *him*, he did not know. Perhaps it was arrogance on his part, and it wouldn't be the first time. Perhaps he'd convinced himself he was helping her when it was his own selfish desires at work, and he *did* desire her. He could not get the wretched woman out of his mind. She was an itch he could not scratch, and he was soon going to drive himself mad.

"She hates you," Ash said cheerfully, sitting on the edge of the fountain and trailing his fingers in the water.

"Must you look so pleased about it? It's not like you want her," Sylvester groused, folding his arms. He'd spent a little time with Ash in Brighton, but didn't know him well.

Ash smiled. "No, but I am her friend and feel a responsibility for her. I should not wish to see her made unhappy."

"And you think I mean to make her unhappy?" Sylvester demanded, irritation climbing.

"Oh, set your hackles down, Mr Cootes. I meant no insult. As a matter of fact, I think you're good for her. I've never seen her speak her mind or look so animated as she does in your company. You bring out the worst in her and it is a joy to see."

Sylvester regarded Ash with consternation, taking a moment to decide if that had been an insult or not. He decided it had not and relaxed.

"I mean her no harm. I would never—"

"Toy with her affections?" Ash suggested, smoothing his hand lovingly over his white waistcoat and admiring the way the sun glittered on the gold thread of the embroidery.

"Chance would be a fine thing," Sylvester muttered. "As you so kindly observed, she hates me."

Ash shrugged. "Perhaps hate is too strong a word, but she does not like nor trust you. She doesn't trust anyone, I think."

"Why not?"

Ash got to his feet and turned to look in the direction that Aisling had disappeared in. "I don't know. None of us do. Perhaps you can find out, but tread gently, Mr Cootes. I should hate to have to break your pretty nose."

Ash winked at him and sauntered off, leaving Sylvester to ponder how on earth he was supposed to gain Lady Aisling's trust.

Chapter 2

Wolf,

If you set foot on English soil, I will murder you with my bare hands. My reputation is shiny indeed, but it is only a superficial gleam and if you come and tarnish it, I will not easily forgive the harm you do. I am in pursuit of a wife, of a woman who means more to me than I care to consider, and if she slips through my fingers because of a scandal of your making, we will be at outs.

Once I am married, I will return to Paris to introduce my bride, or you may come to England with my blessing, but please, I beg you, not yet. The English have long memories and if you think your presence will not have people reaching for their weapons, whether with words or more tangible arms, you are a fool. Your father's name is still spoken as a curse here. You might keep that in mind.

Do not for a moment think I have forgotten you, troublesome boy. For all there is a scant three years between us, I knew you needed a father who was not a brute even more than I did. It bewilders me to discover you consider me in this light when Nic is far better placed for the position, but I should be proud if we ever came close to providing something of a family for you. Please do not force me to return and mend something you broke in a temper fit. We always guarded each other from the monsters, did we not, Wulfric? I always shall. Tell me what troubles you and I shall give what words of wisdom I can.

I miss you too, though I do not miss the mayhem you cause. I could use you at my back now, I think, for I have the strangest notion I am being watched. You are certain all our enemies were vanquished? For sometimes I get this sick sensation in my gut and – but I become fanciful. Ignore my foolishness.

For now, perhaps you should follow our example and find yourself a wife. Perhaps she could tame what I only ever held on a leash. Nic sends his best regards too and promises to visit you again soon. You are neither forgotten nor abandoned, petit loup, by either of us. Try to behave yourself for our sakes, and we will make it up to you.

—Excerpt of a letter to Wulfric 'Wolf' De Vere from Louis César de Montluc, Comte de Villen.

5th May1841, Lady Drummond's Spring Ball, Mayfair, London.

Aisling tapped her feet to the music, edging further behind a large potted palm. Her fingers curled about a glass of cool lemonade, welcome in the stifling room. She sipped it as she hummed to the music and watched the ladies and gentlemen swirling around merrily… and wished she were back at Trevick. Not too much longer, she promised herself. It would be summer soon and even the most determined of the *ton* would surely be gone by July. She could keep up the pretence until then. Even her brother Conor would champ at the bit to leave by June, so it might be earlier with luck. It was easier on nights like this when her brother escorted her to the dance instead of her parents. Mama would have noticed she was hiding by now, but Conor was too busy with his friends. Not that he wasn't an attentive brother. He was, but she could evade him in a way she would never have managed with her mother. Aisling leaned closer to the fern and gently bent one long frond down so she could get a better look at the dance floor.

"Are you a keen pteridologist, my lady?"

With a muffled shriek, Aisling jumped, launching her lemonade from her glass. A deal of it splashed over her gloves and narrowly missed staining the skirts of her gown.

"Oh! You blithering idiot. What do you mean by creeping up on me like that?" she said, huffing with irritation.

"My apologies, Lady Aisling though I did not creep to be fair. I called to you, but you were so taken by the music you must not have heard me," Mr Cootes replied, passing her his handkerchief. "And if you will lurk in dark corners, a fellow must take desperate measures to gain your attention."

Aisling took the hanky and mopped her gloves, which were damp and unpleasantly sticky. "Hold this," she said, thrusting her glass at him whilst she peeled them off and draped them over the side of the plant pot. "And no, to answer your question. I have no particular interest in ferns, other than their usefulness in offering me a hiding place. Sadly, this one is not as efficient as I'd hoped."

"I came to ask you to dance with me," he said, returning the glass to her when she reached for it.

"No, thank you," she said, sending him a dazzling smile and making little shooing motions with her free hand. "There you go. You have your answer and can run along now."

"Hmmm." To her annoyance he did not shoo as she had suggested, but leaned back against the wall, regarding her with that placid expression he always adopted. "But what would your mama say if she knew you hadn't danced all evening?"

"I danced!" Aisling objected, knowing better than to return home without having danced at all.

"Ah yes, with your brother, with Ashton Anson, and with Hart De Beauvoir, who looks like he wants to be here even less than you do."

"Are you spying on me?" she demanded.

He laughed at that. "In full view of the ballroom, yes, I suppose so. Come, give me your dance card. I wish to see how many of your other dances are spoken for."

Before she could protest, he'd caught hold of the little notepad dangling from her wrist, effectively trapping her hand too.

"My lady, tut, tut," he scolded her, giving a sad shake of his head. "Not one. Not one dance taken. Just how long have you been back here?"

"Not that long," she grumbled, tugging her hand free.

"Nonsense. If you'd been in plain view, you'd have to beat the fellows off with a stick."

"No, I should not," she returned coldly. "I am not popular, Mr Cootes, nor have I the desire to be."

"Why not?" he asked, looking genuinely perplexed. "You're beautiful, funny, and clever. Why would the men not flock to you?"

Aisling stared at him, an odd fluttering sensation in her belly in response to his words. He thought her beautiful and funny and clever? What nonsense. It was just the sort of thing men said to get what they wanted. He might look sincere, but men lied often and with ease. She'd not forget that in a hurry. Standing with him in this secluded spot was inadvisable too, for all they were in a crowded ballroom.

"Because I am not easy company, Mr Cootes."

"Ah, yes. Shy Lady Aisling, who becomes tongue-tied and stutters and blushes and can barely hold a conversation with a young man." His eyes glinted with humour.

Aisling clamped her lips together instead of uttering the crushing set down she wished to give, because it would only prove his point. She was neither shy nor stuttering with him.

"Young men of today are fools, my lady. They simply do not know how to go about bringing a timid young woman out of her shell. Whereas I have a singular knack, it appears."

"Oh, yes, to vex the poor creature so badly, she'll lose her temper and forget she was shy at all," Aisling retorted.

"Exactly." He beamed at her, looking as if he thought he deserved a reward for his cleverness.

"Except it wasn't a cleverly thought-out scheme, but simply your abrasive personality that had the desired effect," Aisling muttered.

He laughed then, a warm, rich sound that wrapped about her and made a frisson of pleasure skitter down her spine. Aisling shot him a glance, disturbed to discover she liked that she had made him laugh. Some people had a knack for it, like Evie, who was funny and clever with words without ever resorting to cruelty or sarcasm. Aisling had always rather envied her quick wit.

"Come. Won't you dance with me?" he asked again, his voice gentler now, holding out his hand to her. "I'll not persist if you refuse me again, but I truly should like to waltz with you."

Aisling hesitated. Waltzing with him was a bad idea, but if he would leave her be afterwards, perhaps it was worth it.

"If you promise not to ask me for another tonight and let me hide in peace. Your word on it," she said, studying his face for a hint of deception. She had long since realised that, for many men, their word was a worthless item and their honour nothing more than a façade.

"My word," he said gravely.

Aisling took the hand he offered. She was unconvinced he meant what he said, but it would be as well to test him. They strolled the edges of the ballroom as the dance in progress ended, and people took their places for the next.

"Thank you," Mr Cootes said, as he took her in hold for the waltz.

Aisling frowned up at him, her nerves skittering at the feel of his hand on her waist. His touch was light, but the sensation burned through her gown and her insides felt all muddled and stirred up.

"For granting me a dance," he said in response to her glower, before easing her into the waltz.

"Oh," she said, knowing she was being ungracious but too on edge to stop. Besides, if he didn't want a partner who was rude to him, there were dozens of other young ladies to choose from. Which begged the question, why her? "Why aren't you dancing with one of the more engaging young ladies here?"

He sent her an amused glance. "I *have* been dancing with the more engaging young ladies."

Well, she'd asked for that.

"I had to do something whilst I was looking for you," he added, his tone softer, as if easing her hurt feelings… which was ridiculous, because she had none. She didn't give a tinker's cuss who he danced with.

"Next time, I suggest you don't waste your evening looking for me. Find someone more agreeable."

"All the ladies are agreeable," he replied with a soft laugh. "It's very trying."

Aisling wondered what the devil he meant by that, and her perplexity must have shown, for he spoke again.

"I much prefer arguing with you. It's very dull when ladies agree with everything you say."

"What mad article agreed with you?" she asked in blank astonishment, the words flying out of her mouth before she could think better of them.

He threw back his head and laughed, causing several people to turn and look at them. Aisling blushed and wished she'd never agreed to dance with him.

"Not everyone finds me as objectionable as you do, my lady," he replied, his voice oddly gentle, as if he was trying to reassure her. "And stop worrying about what everyone else thinks. They are only jealous of the wonderful time I am having in such charming company."

To Aisling's everlasting relief, the dance ended, and she dropped his hand as if it had scalded her, stepping away from him.

"Stop it," she said, though the words she had meant to sound angry were edged with fear. "Stop trying to charm me. I don't know why you insist on doing so, but it won't work."

Mr Cootes stared at her, the concern in his eyes too easy to read. "What is it you are afraid of?"

"Nothing," she said, her voice cold and hard now as she stiffened her resolve. "I am afraid of nothing, and you would do well to stay away from me. You are right about one thing, Mr Cootes. I am not as fragile as I appear, not a damsel in distress, so go and rescue someone else. I don't want or need your help, or your trust."

Aisling hurried away, her nails digging into her palms to give herself something to focus on, so she would not cry. Her chest was tight, and her stomach twisted into a knot. A warm hand grasping hers made her spin around in shock and she had a bare moment to school her features as she realised her brother had come after her.

"Conor! Oh, you made me jump," she said, clutching at her chest and forcing out a startled laugh.

"What's wrong?" he demanded, glowering at her. "Did Cootes upset you?"

"What? Oh, no," she said, shaking her head, though he had upset her, only not in the way Conor meant. He had tried to be kind or pretended to be kind. "No, he's annoying, but he was quite the gentleman."

"Then why do you look so out of sorts?"

She returned a wry look and Conor snorted, well aware of her dislike of being in society. "If you need me to thump anyone, you need only say."

Aisling laughed and took his arm, relieved to have his reassuring presence close by. He was tall and lean and though he had inherited their mother's dark colouring as she had, his eyes were the blue of their father's and full of affection. She leaned into him, smiling now. "Isn't it unfair, Conor, there's poor Cara and Vi, desperate to be out, and here we are, dying to go home."

He snorted and gave a heavy sigh. "Too true, but no one ever said life was fair*, deirfiúr bheag."*

She smiled at him calling her little sister in Irish and jabbed him with her elbow. "Stop trying to sound old and wise. I know better."

"I *am* older and wiser," he countered, smirking at her.

"No, just older," she said, trying for humour and only sounding wistful.

She sighed inwardly. No one knew just how wise Aisling was, nor of the hard lesson she had learned by bitter experience, and the weight of guilt about her neck that she felt unequal to carrying. But that was simply cowardice. She had hardly made amends yet, but in a few years—as soon as her advanced age freed her from spending her time pretending to catch a husband—she would do everything in her power to cleanse her spirit of the wicked thing she'd done.

Chapter 3

Child,

You know how to get through this.

One green candle, one brown, one blue.

Amethyst, Citrine, and Jade.

Sandalwood.

Stop getting in a tizzy and remember yourself.

—Excerpt of a letter to Lady Aisling Baxter from Old Biddy Burke.

14th May 1841, Cavendish House, The Strand, London.

“Oh, do hurry, Aisling,” Cara fretted, jittering about in a most distracting manner.

“If you’d only stop harrying me, I might be able to think straight,” Aisling complained, shoving her bonnet on in such a haphazard way her maid tsked and hurried over to set her to rights.

“Well, it’s fine for you. You’ve been to a ball, a rout party, and a *musicale* this week, but this is our first outing and it’s only a dratted bookshop,” Cara said, looking as if she wanted to stamp her foot in frustration.

At sixteen, she was a whirlwind of a girl, with an extraordinary mane of fiery red curls, pale ivory skin, and freckles. Much to her own disgust she took after their father in colouring and no amount of soothing would reassure her that her unfashionable looks did not make her a pariah, but quite out of the ordinary. Aisling suspected she was going to be a remarkably beautiful woman, but she was tall for sixteen, already with a large bust and full hips, and she had all the usual insecurities that came with her age. Aisling worried for her, worried about the attention—and the kind of men—her curves would attract, and she did her best to prepare Cara for the ordeal to come. Not that Cara viewed it that way. She was bored, and chafed at being confined at home. Cara longed for society, for diversion and entertainment, and no amount of warnings from Aisling would dampen her desire for everything society would offer her.

By contrast, Lady Violetta was small and slender, a fragile blonde that men would no doubt fall over themselves to protect. A distant cousin, she had come to them as a little girl of six when her parents had died, and she was now a part of the family.

"We can visit the other shops, too," Aisling offered, hoping to placate her sister. The sooner her parents agreed Cara could come out, the better for everyone's peace, but she understood why they were holding back. Personally, Aisling wanted her out of the public eye as long as possible. The girl was far too reckless and outspoken. "But I thought you enjoyed visiting the bookshops most of all."

"Oh, I do," Cara said with a huff. "Only I'd rather be experiencing life myself instead of reading about it all the time."

"There, there, love," Aisling said. "It won't be long, truly. Just remember, your behaviour has a bearing on Mama and Papa's decision. If you hold up during this season with good grace, they might give in sooner."

Vi made a quiet choking sound, and Aisling bit her lip, quite understanding the girl's amusement.

"I heard that," Cara grumbled, giving Vi a look.

Violetta grinned and took Cara's other arm. "Sorry."

Cara let out a heavy sigh and shook her head, and a thick red curl tumbled free of her coiffure. "No. I can't pretend it isn't true. *Good grace* and Lady Cara are not words often heard in the same sentence," she said ruefully.

"Well, let us see if a shopping spree can't make us all feel better. I need a new copy of Culpeper's Herbal since Conor's wretched dog chewed mine to bits." Aisling tucked the ill-behaved curl back where it belonged, picked up her reticule and headed for the door, her sisters following behind.

Ransom's was a tiny bookshop, and an old one. It had become one of Aisling's favourite haunts when she was in town. Not that she didn't like Hatchard's too, but this tiny corner of London was a secret gem that she jealously guarded. It not only sold new titles, but antique books and collectibles and you never knew what treasure you might stumble upon by accident. She'd had to let her brother and sisters in on the secret, however, or visiting at all would have been difficult, as her parents had forbidden her to go out unescorted.

As usual, Conor availed himself of one of the few chairs in the place and sat down with a sporting journal to while away the time whilst they investigated the titles. The scent of paper and dust and leather was heavy in the air, and Aisling fancied she could smell the knowledge held between the pages of the overstuffed bookshelves. Happily, they appeared to be the only visitors today. Mr Ransom greeted her warmly, recognising a regular customer and immediately asked what she needed.

"Culpeper's Herbal? Yes, my lady. You are in luck. There is a very fine copy on the shelves at this moment."

Aisling nodded, pleased. "Excellent. I shall hunt down my quarry in that case."

"Actually, my lady, there is…." Mr Ransom hesitated and darted a nervous glance at her brother.

"Yes?" Aisling said, curious why he looked somewhat anxious.

He lowered his voice. "Well, I have had a curious volume come into my hands and I've not known what to do with it. However, what with your interest in medicines and… *unusual* titles—"

"Oh," Aisling said, perking up and glancing around herself much as Mr Ransom had done. "Yes, it might be something I'd find of interest. Might I see it?"

Mr Ransom nodded. "If perhaps you'd like to take Culpeper to the little reading nook, I could bring it to you."

Aisling nodded, understanding. The reading nook was a cramped corner at the far end of the shop and the farthest from any prying eyes. She lost no time in tracking down the herbal and making herself comfortable at the rickety table. The chair was little better, with lumpy padding and a spring that poked at her backside, making her sit at an awkward angle. There was still no better place in London and Aisling passed a happy five minutes inspecting the book, though she knew it practically off by heart already.

Quick footsteps announced the return of Mr Ransom, who handed her a small, but fat and well-worn book. "If it is of interest, I'd be willing to let it go cheaply rather than find another buyer. I must admit I…. It makes me uncomfortable to keep hold of such a thing. Silly, I know," he added ruefully.

Aisling bit back a smile and nodded her understanding. "Of course, Mr Ransom. I shall take a look and let you know." Though she already knew she would buy the volume. It had the feel of something old and precious, and she turned the pages reverently. The writing was neat, obviously in a feminine hand, and the drawings quite lovely. It was a grimoire and likely full of the most fascinating advice and information. Aisling was captivated and so absorbed in her perusal that she did not hear the tinkling of the shop bell. The dark shadow that fell over her might not have roused her attention either, if it hadn't made it hard to read. Irritated, she looked up and then swallowed an oath as she saw a familiar face staring down at her, curiosity burning in his tawny eyes.

"Is that a diary?"

Aisling slammed the cover shut and gathered up the copy of Culpeper's Herbal, so it hid the book from view. "Of a sort," she replied, pushing to her feet. "What are you doing here?"

Mr Cootes looked about the room, pursing his lips as though considering the matter. "Well, I thought I might buy a book. I rather assumed this was a good place for the endeavour."

Aisling frowned, annoyed that he should have found *her* bookshop, of all places. With difficulty, she manoeuvred out from behind the table and replaced the chair.

"Surely Hatchard's is more your style, Mr Cootes," she said, clutching her books tight to her chest. "Or are you a regular visitor to Mr Ransom?"

"No, actually. I've never even seen the shop before today, but I was passing, and it caught my eye. It's a fascinating little place, isn't it?" he added, looking about with obvious interest.

Aisling fought back a proprietary urge to tell him to find his own bookshop because this one was hers. "It is," she agreed.

"May I see what you've chosen?"

Aisling's hold on her book tightened a degree further. "Culpeper's Herbal. The dog ate my copy."

"Unfortunate," Mr Cootes replied, his lips twitching. "And the other title—"

Aisling felt a blush creep up her throat as she realised she would rather die than tell him. "None of your business," she replied, sticking her chin up.

His eyes gleamed with interest, and she silently thought a very bad word she'd once heard her brother say. Drat the fellow, now he was more interested than ever.

"My lady," he said, lowering his voice. "Not that I disapprove of such things, but you aren't buying, er—*naughty* books?"

Aisling blinked at him, momentarily nonplussed. "Naughty books?" she repeated. "Whatever do you—*Oh!*" She had once found a book with pictures in her brother's room when she'd been looking for a novel he'd borrowed and never returned. She'd only caught the barest glimpse of the *activities* illustrated within before Conor had snatched it from her, but she knew this was the kind of thing he must be referring to.

To her consternation, her blush increased. "Don't be disgusting," she retorted.

The devil shrugged, unimpressed. "I don't see what's disgusting about it. Some of the artwork is very fine indeed. You need not prevaricate with me, you know. I would not judge you for being, er… *curious* if it is something wicked."

"Well, of course it isn't! How could you think that I…." Aisling saw the amusement glinting in his eyes and wished she knew more bad words. She really must learn some new ones. "You are a—"

"Pestilential nuisance, yes, I remember," he said, grinning at her. "Might I call on you tomorrow?"

"Certainly not," she snapped, wishing he would move aside so she could pay for her books and get out of the shop.

Mr Cootes sighed and folded his arms. Unwillingly, Aisling's eyes drifted to his arms, and especially to the way the material clung to his broad shoulders and biceps. He seemed different since she'd last seen him at Christmas. She realised then that he had filled out and his clothing was of better quality than before. She had noticed when he'd stayed at Rowsley Hall that he was a little too lean for his build, his cuffs were fraying, and the fabric on some of his coats was shiny with age. Now he was impeccably turned out, and whilst he was hardly to be counted among those trend setters and fashionable gentlemen who turned all the heads, he looked… good. Very fine, actually.

"You are most unkind to me, my lady," he observed.

Aisling nodded, unperturbed. "Yes. So you really ought to bother some other young lady who will be nice to you."

"But I like bothering you," he said, his voice pitched lower now, far too intimate in the cramped confines of the bookshop.

A shiver skittered down Aisling's spine, and she took a step away, only to find the overburdened shelves at her back. She glanced down the aisle to the front of the shop, but they were hidden from view here and no one was in sight.

"You bother me too," he added, taking a step closer.

"Well, I don't do it on purpose," she retorted. Goodness, but he was large. He seemed to take up all the room, not that there was much to spare. Her gaze drifted to his mouth, which was wide and sensual, made for laughing and… *No.* She would not think about kissing. It would be utter madness. Besides which, she did *not* want to kiss the aggravating creature. His mouth curved upwards, and Aisling glanced at his face to discover him watching her staring at his lips.

Drat and bother and blast.

He leaned in, placing one hand on the shelf beside her. Aisling watched him as a mouse watches a cat settle in for a long wait outside its hidey hole.

"What's in the book, my lady?"

Aisling shook her head.

"You are an awful puzzle, you know."

"No, I'm not."

"I disagree."

"Well, I disagree with you," she retorted, aware that they were squabbling like children but quite unable to stop herself.

"I like you."

"No, you don't," she said at once, the words out before she could think better of them.

He looked at her with interest. "But I do, and why shouldn't I? You are intelligent, funny, and that sharp tongue of yours is fascinating. I adore the way you scold me, and besides all of that, you are quite extraordinarily lovely."

"Average," she said, wishing her words were not so breathless. Why couldn't she breathe? "No more than average. Passably pretty."

"What rot!" he exclaimed, looking at her in outrage. "False modesty is unbecoming in a lady."

Aisling glared at him, indignant. "I'm friends with Vivien Anson—I mean Mrs Lane-Fox—and Lady Rosamund Adolphus, and you've seen Greer and Elspeth, and—"

He pressed a gloved finger to her lips, silencing her. Aisling froze, galvanised by the touch of his hand against her mouth.

"Little fool," he whispered. "Don't argue when a fellow says you're beautiful. You are, you know."

Ridiculously, Aisling felt tears sting her eyes. She had been beautiful once, perhaps, but that was before. Now, whenever she looked in the mirror, she only saw the past looking back, and it was ugly. Her experience and her actions had tainted her, and no one would ever want her if they knew. He certainly wouldn't. Not that anyone would ever know. It was her secret to bear, hers to atone for.

His expression softened, and he dropped his hand, taking a step back.

"My lady?" he said, regarding her with earnest concern and sounding appalled. "Did I frighten you?"

Aisling shook her head, wanting only to be away from him.

"I would never… I did not mean—"

"You did not frighten me. I just want to buy my books," she said, forcing the words out and fighting for calm. If she did not get out of here, get away from him, she would scream.

"What is it?" he demanded. "Won't you tell me?"

"Nothing!" she exclaimed, but there was too much emotion behind the word.

"I wish you would trust me," he said softly. "I wouldn't let you down, you know."

Aisling stared at him, seeing sincerity in his eyes. She didn't believe it. Not anymore.

"Never," she said, making her voice as cold as possible. "I shall never trust you, so leave me be, Mr Cootes. I have no need of your gallantry."

She strode forward, and he moved lest she be forced to push past him. He was too much of a gentleman for that and he let her go, but she felt his eyes follow her as she hurried away to pay for her books.

Chapter 4

Dear Sylvester,

I hope you are having a marvellous time in town. Well, not <u>too</u> marvellous, for I want to interrupt your cavorting and ask a very great favour of you, which Greer and Raphe said I might, as you are my brother now.

I have been invited to stay with Lady Cara Baxter at Trevick Castle. I have my governess and my maid to accompany me, but I have been staying with my aunt and uncle, Lord and Lady St Clair, whilst Mama and Papa are away, but they have commitments and so cannot escort me. Gee and your brother are too busy with the restoration works at Marcross. Raphe said that he would be happy to give you more time off if you would accompany me to Trevick for my stay and see me safely returned home. I am to be there for two weeks, perhaps three. I have checked with Lady Trevick, who has extended the welcome to include you.

Please say you will come. I haven't seen Cara in an age and Trevick is a marvellous place to visit.

—Excerpt of a letter from Miss Alana Cadogan (youngest daughter of Mr and Mrs Jerome and Bonnie Cadogan) to The Hon'ble Mr Sylvester Cootes.

27th May 1841, Savile Row, Mayfair, London.

Sylvester stared down at the letter in his hand with something approaching disbelief. If he escorted Alana to Trevick at the close of the season, he would be in company with Lady Aisling every day. He'd never been much of a believer in fate or luck. Things were what you made of them, and a fellow succeeded or failed by his own efforts. Yet this was like a gift from the gods, as if they were encouraging him to go after her. Like the impulse that had taken him down the little back street and drawn his attention to that unprepossessing bookshop. Why he'd gone in that direction when it was completely out of his way, he could not say, but it had taken him to Aisling, and he wasn't about to complain about that. *She* would complain vociferously, he did not doubt.

An anxious sensation tightened his chest when he thought about that meeting. What was she hiding? Had she been afraid of him? She'd said she wasn't, but… she was afraid of something, or perhaps someone. All his instincts told him the young woman was full of secrets and not happy ones. She needed help, and if she had not confided in her brother or her parents, then the matter must be a delicate one. If only he could persuade her he was trustworthy. Ash had said she didn't trust anyone, and if that was so, it must be because someone had betrayed her confidence. If only he could hold his tongue and not rile her every time they met, he might stand a chance, but she was so deliciously easy to provoke, and he loved the way her eyes sparkled when she was cross with him. When she was irritated, she forgot her manners and her reserve and showed the passionate, forthright girl she ought to be. That was the real Aisling, he was certain. He wanted to know that woman, wanted to be the centre of her attention and all that fire she contained.

Sylvester sat and dashed off a quick reply to Alana, agreeing to escort her to Trevick before readying himself to go out. As his brother's estate manager at Marcross Manor, he was finally earning a decent wage. Of course, gentlemen ought not work at all, but he was not too proud to earn his keep. Those that didn't like it could mind their own business. That the Earl of Trevick would not like it one little bit was something he refused to dwell upon, though he knew he ought. A man with sense would consider the fact that Aisling was far out of his league before reaching for the moon, but he was too intent on knowing what it was she was hiding to be sensible. Besides, it was not like he was planning to marry her, only to be her friend.

His rented rooms on Savile Row were cramped, but it was a fashionable address and the kind of place a young man ought to spend the season. He had also begun replacing his decidedly shabby wardrobe, and the tailor down the street ought to have finished a new coat for him today. Snatching up his gloves and hat, he headed out.

The tailor's shop was not the most exclusive to be had in London, for such extravagance was above Sylvester's touch. However, Mr Howard was becoming known for fine quality tailoring and for not fleecing his clients, and had been recommended to him by his brother, who was always the height of elegance. Mr Howard looked up as he entered, greeting him, and promising to be with him shortly, as he was already in discussion with another client. A minion hurried to bring him coffee and some sporting journals to amuse him whilst he waited and so Sylvester made himself comfortable. A soft French accent caught his attention as two men emerged from behind the privacy screens, and he set the journal aside as he recognised the clients taking Mr Howard's attention were the Comte de Villen and Mr Barnaby Godwin.

"Non. Absolutely not," the comte said, clicking his tongue with irritation. He gave an irritated wave of his hands towards a selection of material laid out on a table before them. "The blue, or I wash my hands of you."

Godwin cast a last wistful glance at the bolt of dark maroon cloth that Mr Howard was holding out for him to inspect before giving a sigh. "The blue then, Mr Howard."

"Very good, sir. If I might say, it *is* an excellent choice," Mr Howard said, casting an approving glance at the comte, who, as usual, looked as if he'd just stepped out of a fashion plate. "Monsieur has an exquisite eye for detail."

"Better than mine, I daresay," Mr Godwin agreed affably. "It's why we're here, after all."

"Good day, Mr Godwin, Monsieur le Comte," Sylvester said, getting to his feet. "This isn't your usual haunt," he added, eyeing the comte with interest.

"No, it ain't," Godwin said with a laugh. "But I can't afford to beggar myself over one coat from his establishment. Reckon I couldn't afford to get my cravats there, let alone everything else he tells me I must have. Besides, I doubt Louis' tailor would have me. Would probably weep with distress if he was reduced to fitting the likes of me."

"My tailor only weeps if you do not pay him liberally, in both coin and compliments," the comte remarked dryly, holding out his hand to Sylvester. "Mr Cootes, how do you do?"

"Well, thanks. So, Mr Godwin is benefiting from your 'exquisite eye,' is he?" Sylvester said, wondering how on earth that had come about. The mysterious and elegant comte and the rather prosaic Barnaby Godwin seemed unlikely friends.

"That's right." Godwin replied, nodding. "Louis reckons he can get me leg shackled to the girl of my choosing if I follow his advice. First thing is to get me spruced up, you see."

"Barnaby," the comte protested, rolling his eyes. "I wish you would not. The world does not need to know your business. Or mine, for that matter."

Barnaby flushed, rubbing the back of his neck. "Well, it's only Cootes, not the world, but… right ho, won't breathe a word."

Sylvester grinned, amused. "Don't worry. I'll hold my tongue, especially if you fancy taking on another pupil?"

"Good God," the comte said. "One is enough. I regret to say that my nerves would not survive another."

"I've lamentable taste. That's the trouble. Offends his sensibilities. French, you know," Barnaby added in an all-too-audible whisper to Sylvester.

The comte snorted.

Mr Howard reappeared with Sylvester's coat.

"Ah, well. At least you can give me your opinion on this," Sylvester said as Howard helped him out of the one he wore and into the new. It was a very dark green frock coat, almost black, and fitted at the waist.

The comte eyed him critically as Mr Howard fussed about tweaking this and adjusting that.

"Oh, I say, very fine," Godwin said, before casting the comte an anxious glance. "It is, ain't it?"

"As you say, Barnaby. Very fine. The fit is excellent, Mr Howard, I commend you. Perhaps I might commission something from you in the future."

Mr Howard blinked in disbelief before rallying. "I-I should be honoured, monsieur. Truly. I am at your disposal…."

The comte nodded before the fellow began fawning over him, though it would be a hell of a coup for an unknown fellow like Howard to dress the *ton's* most elegant man.

"We will speak when we return for Mr Godwin's order. That is the two frock coats as discussed, the tails, the sack coat, and the trousers too. They will be ready when, precisely?"

"A week for the frock coats and trousers, a few days extra for the rest, no more. My word upon it," Howard said earnestly.

The comte appeared satisfied by this and turned back to Godwin. "Very good. Barnaby, are you done?"

"I am. I say, Cootes, we're off to my club for a spot of libation. Care to come along?"

Sylvester glanced at the comte, whose expression revealed nothing to suggest either pleasure or irritation at him being invited.

"Well, I don't wish to interrupt—"

"Not interrupting. Is he, Louis? You don't mind, eh?" Godwin said blithely, patting Louis on the shoulder in a convivial gesture.

"Not in the least," the comte said politely, and so Sylvester paid for his coat, arranged for it to be delivered to his rooms, and followed them to Barnaby's club.

Grants was an elegant gentlemen's club, but not one that aspired to the heady heights of Whites or Boodles. It had begun as a respectable establishment but was gaining notoriety of late. It catered more to young men with a hellbent desire for gambling and excess than the more illustrious haunts, which those with money but dubious reputations did not have a hope of joining. There were some infamous members who were giving the club a name for wildness and misbehaviour, and Sylvester admitted himself surprised to discover Godwin was a member.

"Been here for years, since before it became a fashionable venue for wickedness," Mr Godwin explained, though Sylvester had not asked aloud. "It's quiet during the day, though, as that sort don't tend to show their faces in daylight. There's only a few members who cause havoc, in truth, though they're bringing in a lot more eager young fellows wanting to follow in their footsteps, so the club holds its tongue about their, er… activities."

As they spoke, one such fellow entered the club and Barnaby lowered his voice.

"Ciarán St Just, Marquess of Kilbane," he said, though Sylvester knew well enough who the man was. "A hell-born babe if ever there was one and the worst of the lot. Don't ever play him at cards, he's got the devil's own luck. They say he's the wickedest man in London."

The man was tall and lean, with thick black hair that curled about his face, too long for fashion. Despite his youth, for he was certainly younger than Sylvester, there was an unmistakable air of menace and dissipation about the fellow; he was clearly someone best avoided. He glanced over at them as he walked past, perhaps aware of their scrutiny. Piercing eyes of a colour Sylvester could only describe as violet took them in and might have dismissed them until they settled upon the Comte de Villen and remained. The marquess' mouth tilted up a little at one corner. He inclined his head, very slightly.

"You're Villen," he said, apparently not caring for the rules and whether he was offered an introduction or not.

Louis nodded. Kilbane's uncompromising stare travelled over Sylvester and Barnaby, a somewhat contemptuous expression flickering in his eyes before returning his attention to Louis.

"If your charming friends have not already informed you, I am Kilbane. *Enchanté,"* he murmured, an amused glint in those strange eyes.

"As you say, delighted," Louis replied, holding his gaze. Sylvester glanced at Barnaby as the moment stretched out.

"If you fancy a drink, I have a superb Burgundy just begging to be opened. I should like your opinion of it. I believe you are something of a… connoisseur?"

Louis shrugged. "I enjoy fine things." "

Kilbane smiled broadly, showing even, white teeth. "I'm in the private rooms, but someone will show you the way."

"Perhaps later," Louis replied politely.

Kilbane chuckled and moved on without another word.

"Oh, I say," Barnaby said, looking unsettled. "You're not going, Louis?"

The comte shrugged, apparently unperturbed. Sylvester suspected he was used to such attention from both sexes. "Why not, he's interesting at least."

Barnaby frowned but held his tongue, though Sylvester thought it cost him to do so.

"So, what's the plan then, Louis?" Barnaby asked once the wine had been served and they'd given their orders.

Louis moved the glass idly between long fingers, making the wine swirl in the glass before raising it to his nose. "The Royal Academy exhibition," he said before taking a sip and closing his eyes.

He made a pleased sound and Sylvester fought an unpleasant stab of envy as he studied the fellow. Louis César looked like a damned angel fallen to earth. Would Aisling be so determined to keep him at bay if he looked like that?

"I know," Godwin said ruefully, catching his eye. "Life ain't fair."

"It is not," the comte agreed, opening his eyes and looking between them. "But why do you mention it?"

"Nothing," Sylvester said hastily. "What's happening at the Academy exhibition?"

"Mr Godwin is emerging from his, ah… *chrysalide?*" The comte snapped his fingers impatiently. "What is the word… for a butterfly before it is a butterfly?"

"Oh, chrysalis," Sylvester supplied. "He is emerging from his chrysalis. In the new wardrobe, I take it."

"*Exactement*," the comte agreed. "It is a good place to be seen, and to talk to a young lady about art."

"But I don't know the least thing about art," Godwin protested. "You can lay money I'll say something idiotic, and she'll think me a fool. I'm not sure this is the best idea, Louis."

Louis tsked, shaking his head. "I will teach you enough to get by. We have time."

Godwin looked doubtful, and the comte shrugged.

"Take my advice or don't take it. I promised to help you, but if you don't trust me—"

"It ain't that!" Godwin protested, going red in the face. "Course I trust you. I-I just don't want to let you down by making a muck of it."

The comte smiled, proving—if proof were needed—why so many women made utter fools of themselves over him. "You won't. I have confidence in you, Barnaby."

Godwin flushed harder and looked ridiculously pleased by the comment. "Well. Well, I mean to say. If you think so. I'll do my best. Swear I will."

"I know," the comte replied calmly and settled back with his wine.

"Who is the lady in question that you are trying so hard to impress?" Sylvester asked, curious now. "If you don't mind me asking?"

Godwin returned a somewhat sheepish smile. "I don't mind. As it happens, it's Lady Millicent Fortescue. A forlorn hope, no matter Louis' influence, I expect. She's above my touch and I know it, but a fellow must follow his dreams, I reckon. Even if they're out of reach. Louis believes he can help me win her, but the words 'pig's ear' and 'silk purse' keep going around and around in my brain until my head aches."

"The comte thinks you can do it. Looks ready to put money on it, I should say," Sylvester said, wanting to reassure the fellow, who seemed a good-natured sort.

He was right, though. Lady Millicent was destined for a duke or a marquess, an earl at the very least. Godwin didn't stand a chance. A depressing realisation, Sylvester had to admit, for he was likely worse off than Godwin. He too was a younger son, and with far fewer funds at his disposal. At least the fellow didn't dirty his hands by working for a living.

"You got a sweetheart?" Godwin asked him, the question taking Sylvester by surprise.

He opened his mouth to deny it, but then Aisling's image came to mind, with tears in her eyes when he'd told her she was beautiful.

"Yes," he said, the honest answer escaping him before he could stop it. "Yes, I suppose I do, but my hopes are probably worse than yours."

"Oh," Godwin replied gloomily. "Rotten luck. Parents don't like you, I suppose?"

Sylvester snorted and picked up his wine. "I've no idea. It's the lady that hates me."

"Dash it all! Well, that *is* awkward," Godwin said, his expression one of deep sympathy. "Not sure Lady Millicent knows I exist, but don't reckon she hates me."

Sylvester laughed and raised his glass in a toast. "It is certainly not the ideal situation, Mr Godwin, but faint heart et cetera, et cetera."

"I'll drink to that," the fellow said, and chinked his glass against Sylvester's.

Both of them looked somewhat surprised as the comte followed suit.

"To the pursuit of fair maidens," he said, his blue eyes glittering. "May we be worthy of victory."

Chapter 5

My Lord,

I write regarding your extraordinarily generous donation and the interest you have shown in helping my charitable organisation open another school.

The money you have gifted us is far beyond anything I had expected after our initial conversation, but is most gratefully received. We are looking for a suitable venue as I write this and will keep you appraised of our progress. I should be most pleased if you would be interested in viewing any suitable properties with us as it will be your money funding the project in its entirety.

In light of everything you have done and propose to do, I would like to suggest we name the school in your honour.

—Excerpt of a letter from Lady Elizabeth Demarteau (daughter of their graces, Robert and Prunella Adolphus, the Duke and Duchess of Bedwin) to Lord Maxwell Drake, Earl of Vane.

24th June 1841, The Royal Academy Exhibition, Trafalgar Square, London.

Much to his regret, Sylvester had to quit London to return to work at Marcross Manor for several weeks. The season was ending, however, and he was due to escort his sister-in-law Miss Alana to Trevick Castle. His brother, aware that he was anxious to return to town, but not the reason why, had told him to leave a few days earlier than planned. Sylvester had not needed asking twice. He had worried about Aisling in his absence, worried that whatever troubled her was a situation that might grow worse if he were not there to help her. Arrogance, he supposed, to believe she was a damsel in distress who could not manage without him. She'd told him as much herself, yet he sensed she was far more fragile than anyone realised. Besides which, he'd missed her, though he knew that was ridiculous. She was prickly and difficult and clearly disliked him, and yet he could not wait to see her again. Where she would be, however, he did not know, so he was on his way to visit friends and make some discreet enquiries.

"I say, Cootes! Over here!"

Sylvester stopped on the pavement and turned towards the road to see an elegant carriage coming towards him, pulled by beautiful, matched greys. Barnaby Godwin was hanging out of the window, waving his hat at him.

"Mr Godwin," Sylvester called back, raising his hand in greeting. "How do you do?"

"In prime twig," Barnaby called back, gesturing to himself and grinning.

"Oh, the great unveiling. The butterfly emerges. Is that today?"

"It is! Come along and see me make a twit of myself, why don't you? We're off to the Royal Academy."

Sylvester nodded and ran towards the carriage, dodging wagons and dogs and filth underfoot. The exhibition was as likely a place to bump into friends as any, and he enjoyed Mr Godwin's genial company. He climbed in to discover the Comte de Villen was also inside, and greeted the fellow with a friendly nod.

"I'm done up in my finery, Cootes, and I've learned my lessons by heart. His handsomeness over there thinks I'm ready," Barnaby said, winking at him.

Sylvester laughed. "Good for you. Give me some tips, will you? I don't know a damned thing about art myself."

Barnaby folded his arms, frowning with concentration. "Let me see what pearls of wisdom have I to share? One ought to identify the medium first. Is it a watercolour, or an oil on canvas, or whatever? How is it painted, laid on thick or delicate brush strokes? Does it appear chaotic or organised… er…. Oh, yes. Are the colours bright or subdued?"

The comte nodded approvingly and Barnaby beamed, looking pleased with himself.

"And…." the Frenchman prompted.

"And? Umm," Barnaby hesitated, an expression of intense concentration on his face. "No… No, don't tell me…. What is the meaning behind the painting? What is the artist trying to convey? Is there any obvious symbolism? Oh, and most important, how does it make you *feel*?"

Barnaby looked triumphant and Sylvester bit back a grin. "You'll sound like an expert all right," he agreed.

"So long as he does not get carried away," the comte cautioned with a smile.

"I won't, and if in doubt, ask the lady what *she* thinks of it," Barnaby added.

"That's certainly good advice," Sylvester replied, nodding.

"Providing you actually listen to the answer," Villen said dryly. "Ignore the lady's opinion at your peril. She likely knows a deal more about the subject than you do."

"Wouldn't be hard," Barnaby replied ruefully as the carriage halted. He peered out of the window. "Best get out here, my friends. Looks like the place is heaving. We'll be quicker on foot now."

As Barnaby had suggested, the gallery was a popular venue today, with the great and the good out to enjoy their fill of culture. The audience stared up and up at the myriad paintings sky hung all around the high walls, but the three men were more intent on their quarry than any art appreciation. It took them the best part of an hour to track down Lady Millicent, but she was here amongst the throng.

Sylvester regarded the lady with interest. She was a delicate, fair-haired creature, not beautiful by any stretch, but she had a sweet countenance. Her blue eyes shone with warmth, and she carried herself with such an air of good-natured amiability that he could see why Barnaby esteemed her.

"Dash it all. Now I'm nervous," Barnaby fretted, taking off his hat and running a hand through his hair so it stood up on end.

The comte tsked at him and made him smooth it down again.

"Do I look as I ought, Louis?" he asked, giving the comte an anxious glance.

Instead of brushing the question off impatiently, the comte looked him over, tweaked his cravat a little and gave a reassuring nod. "Very handsome, Barnaby. Exactly how you ought. You are ready, *mon ami*. Now, go over and bid the lady a good day and ask her how she is enjoying the exhibition. Ask her which is her favourite painting so far. If she has one, say, *Oh, I do not believe I have seen that one, where might I find it?* And with luck, she will offer to show you herself. Then, follow the rules which you have learned so carefully."

"How do. Enjoying the exhibition. Favourite painting," Barnaby recited obediently. "Right ho. I… I suppose I'll… er…."

The comte gave him a little push. *"Allez."*

"Yes. Yes, here I go." Barnaby swallowed hard, his complexion that of a three-day-old milk pudding. "Wish me luck."

The comte watched him go, looking quite as anxious as Barnaby.

"One raises them, does what one can, and then one day they're all grown up and ready to fly the nest," Sylvester said with a dramatic sigh.

The comte slanted a look at him but said nothing.

"She's smiling," Sylvester observed a moment later.

"*Oui*, but he's nervous. Wiping sweaty palms on one's trousers is not a good look," Villen muttered. "*Allez, Barnabé. Tu peux le faire*."

The two of them watched, with Sylvester feeling almost as anxious as the comte, who seemed to be deeply invested in the outcome.

"Do you have money riding on this?" Sylvester asked out of curiosity.

"Non!" The man looked indignant at the idea. "I am… a romantic. I wish to see him succeed."

Sylvester felt his mouth kick up in surprise. "A romantic?"

The comte gave a little huff of laughter, not taking his eyes from Barnaby and Lady Millicent. "This surprises you?"

There was a tone to the man's voice that urged caution, but Sylvester had never been much good at heeding that. "Yes, I suppose so. You're rather notorious among the widows and neglected wives of the *ton*."

"I have never interfered in a happy marriage, nor would I, and if ever I marry, I shall honour my lady and my vows. So, yes, a romantic. I believe in love, and I wish for my friend to have it as much as I wish it for myself. I am sorry if that does not fit with your view of my reputation."

His voice was icy, and Sylvester knew he'd touched a nerve. He hurried to make amends.

"I apologise, monsieur. I truly meant no insult. I hope you will forgive my clumsy interrogation. I was merely curious, but I am afraid I have never been adept at polite conversation. A lady once told me I was the most vexing man that ever lived," he added ruefully, hoping he had not caused a rift between them. He did not know the man well but liked him and would regret causing offence.

The comte turned back to him, studying him intently for a long moment. "Apology accepted. Who said you were the most vexing man that ever lived?"

Sylvester grinned. "Lady Aisling Baxter."

"Ah. The sweetheart, by any chance?" the Frenchman suggested, proving he not only paid attention but was as well versed in affairs of the heart as everyone said.

"The very same. Does that mean you believe I have cause to hope, Monsieur?" Sylvester replied. "I confess I have little else to go on for the lady does not appear to enjoy my company overly."

"It is a reaction, at least. Better than being ignored. *Oh!"* The comte clutched Sylvester's arm. *"Regardez ça!"*

The two of them froze, watching avidly as Barnaby offered Lady Millicent his arm and escorted her through the room. He glanced over his shoulder as he went and rounded his eyes at them, grinning broadly.

"He did it!" Sylvester said, clapping him on the back. "Well, done, old man!"

"It is only a first step, of course," the comte replied gravely, though he did not fool Sylvester. The man could not keep the glee from his expression. He looked as if he'd won the damned derby he was so pleased with himself. "I think a little drink is in order to celebrate, though. My nerves are shattered. What say you?"

Sylvester stilled as he saw Lady Aisling enter the room with her little sister, Lady Cara on her arm, and escorted by their brother, Viscount Harleston.

"Actually, monsieur, I don't suppose you'd give me the benefit of your opinion and your company for a moment. Lady Aisling is there, and I should like to speak with her. Perhaps you can deduce what her true feelings are, for I am all at sea."

The comte looked from him to the lady, his lips quirking. "Perhaps. Do you know her brother, though? We have not been introduced."

"A little, yes, though not well, but I can offer an introduction. Only…." Sylvester hesitated, belatedly wondering if this was the best idea.

"Only…?" The comte regarded him, that warning look in his eyes again.

With hindsight, Sylvester decided he would learn his lesson and didn't ask the man not to let Aisling fall in love with him.

The comte sighed, and apparently Sylvester was all too transparent despite holding his tongue. "I will restrain myself as best I can," the man drawled, quirking an eyebrow at him.

Sylvester cleared his throat. "Right. Sorry. This way, then."

The comte followed him over to where the ladies and their brother were admiring a painting by Turner of the Ducal Palace in Venice.

"My lord, ladies. It is good to see you. I hope you are enjoying the exhibition?" Sylvester asked, greeting them warmly and getting the usual frosty response from Aisling the moment she set eyes on him.

Viscount Harleston treated him to a critical once over. He was much like his sister, with the same black hair, though his eyes were blue. He gave a marginally more welcoming reception than Aisling, however, and Sylvester wondered how her warm brown eyes could contain so much ice. The younger daughter had apparently taken after their father, as her colouring was wildly different to her siblings. She had a riot of copper curls, and her pale skin was deeply freckled. Unlike her older sister her gaze upon him was frank and interested.

"Mr Cootes, how do you do?" Harleston said with a smile that was polite rather than overly friendly.

"Very well," he said, before turning to the Frenchman, who as Comte de Villen outranked the viscount. "Monsieur, might I introduce to you to Viscount Harleston? I believe you know Lady Aisling, and this is her younger sister, Lady Cara."

"Harleston," Villen said, giving a polite nod, before bowing to his sisters. "Ladies, a pleasure."

By now Lady Cara was gaping at the comte like he was a different species of man entirely, for which Sylvester could not entirely blame her. To his relief, Aisling seemed unaffected by his glorious presence and had rearranged her face, so she looked like the timid and unassuming creature she purported to be. Not that he believed it was entirely an act. She truly did hate being in society, and people made her nervous. She was on edge. Something or someone had knocked the confidence from her, but this shy, faded young woman was not who she truly was. Not when she could ring a peal over his head with such enthusiasm when he vexed her. He glanced back at Lady Cara and wondered if she was aware he was the man escorting her friend to Trevick, and if she had informed Lady Aisling.

"Will you be in town much longer, my lady?" he asked Aisling, knowing full well when she was departing town. She stood with her eyes downcast, but she looked up then, a glint of satisfaction visible as she answered.

"We leave tomorrow, Mr Cootes," she replied serenely.

Sylvester bit back a smile, doing his best to look crestfallen. "I am bereft, my lady. I had hoped you might remain for a day or two longer as I am only just returned to town."

"Oh, have you been away? I had not realised," she said, with such a guileless expression it was all he could do not to bark with laughter. The wretch. She knew damned well he'd been gone.

"Your brother is Lord de Ligne?" Harleston asked. "Who married Greer Cadogan recently."

"The very same," Sylvester replied. "I've just returned from Marcross, as it happens. They are both well. Blissful, I should say," he added with a grin.

Harleston laughed. "I wish the fellow luck. We know the lady well, don't we, Aisling? Greer is a handful. Never met such a creature with an aptitude for chaos," he said, his tone warm enough to ensure there was no hint of censure.

"I believe she keeps my brother on his toes," Sylvester replied, before glancing at Aisling again. "My brother is a lucky man, to have married such a woman."

Aisling stared at him, her eyes narrowing slightly. "Harleston, we had better find Mama and Papa, or they will wonder where we have got to. There is a great deal to do before we leave for home tomorrow," she said, taking her brother's arm. "Monsieur, Mr Cootes, good day to you," she said, giving her brother no choice but to guide his sisters away.

He turned to the comte, who was watching them go and looking thoughtful. "She hates you," Villen said, smirking.

Sylvester sighed. "That's it? That's the best you can give me?"

"Non, I am teasing you. I think it is not as simple as that," the comte said thoughtfully. "She did not even look at me. Not once."

"Well, perhaps you are not her type," Sylvester suggested, with no little satisfaction.

Villen returned a long-suffering glance, but didn't bite. "I am not so vain as to believe all women must fall at my feet, but to ignore me so avidly is not normal. I do not believe I have offended her, but I have noticed this before in her company, and it is not just me. She is not at ease with me, or in the company of any men, save Mr Anson, whom I believe she has known since she was a child."

"What are you saying?"

Villen shrugged, lowering his voice. "I'm not sure, but some women do not like men, as some men do not like women. Have you considered that?"

Sylvester frowned. He hadn't, in truth. "But would she hate me so, if that were the case? Besides which, I think it's more than that."

"She might hate you if you are trying to court her when she has no desire to be courted, but I must agree. I think perhaps she is distrustful of all men except those she has known since infancy, which suggests someone has given her reason to think that way."

"Yes." Sylvester nodded, and a spark of anger lit in his chest as the comte touched on something he had wondered himself. He stood, staring at the painting in front of him without really seeing it. Frustration gnawed at him, and he did not know what to do. If Aisling persisted in keeping him at arm's length, he would have to give in and respect her wishes. Worry was a weight in his chest, and he considered the comte's words again. She did not wish to be courted, but he hadn't been thinking of courting her, he reminded himself, and then sighed. He was an idiot. Perhaps he could see things in Aisling she wished to hide, but he was more than adept at keeping his own feelings hidden from himself. Likely because he was kidding himself, but like Barnaby said, a fellow ought to follow his dreams. He ought to *try*.

"How about that drink I mentioned?" the comte asked.

Sylvester nodded. "I think that's the best idea I've heard all day."

Chapter 6

If you cannot afford to lose, you ought not to gamble. The debt is due, and it matters not to me if the property has been in your family for ten generations or ten thousand. You proposed the bid; you lost.

Time to pay up.

—Excerpt of a letter from Ciarán St Just, Marquess of Kilbane, to an unfortunate opponent.

25th June 1841, On the London and Birmingham Railway.

"What are you smiling about?" Harleston asked Aisling.

She looked up at her brother and held up the piece of embroidery she was working on. It was a difficult piece, especially with the movement of the train to contend with.

"It's going well," she answered.

"Pretty," he said, with all the polite interest of an older brother, but he accepted her answer at face value.

It was a pleasing design, but not the cause for her smile, for she had been remembering the look in Mr Cootes' eyes when she had said, *Oh, have you been away? I had not realised.* Any other man would have scowled with annoyance at her rudeness, but his hazel eyes had sparkled with mirth. He'd been pleased with her for giving him a set down. He was undoubtedly the most peculiar man she had ever met. Her mouth turned up at the corners again and she scolded herself soundly. She must not think of him, must not believe he had any finer qualities or spin romantic notions about him, for they would not match reality. She had learned that lesson to her cost. Once, she had believed in the pretty façade, when what lingered just beneath the surface was cruel and disgusting. Her instincts were not to be trusted where men were concerned. Men were not to be trusted. They were best kept at arm's length, and the sooner everyone considered her an old maid, the better.

"The Comte de Villen is so very handsome," Cara murmured sleepily. The rocking of the train always made her younger sister doze off. "I hope he doesn't marry before I come out."

"Handsome is as handsome does," Aisling retorted.

"But he seemed nice," Cara protested. "He has kind eyes."

"Yes, and he changes his mistress as often as you change your gown," Aisling retorted.

"Aisling!" her brother snapped, staring at her in shock.

She bit her lip, realising she ought not to have mentioned mistresses before Cara. She ought to have held her tongue, or at least moderated her comment. But she feared for Cara and what would become of her if she did not learn what men could be. Aisling loved her brother dearly—he was a kind man and protective of his family—but even Harleston kept a mistress, though he would be mortified if he knew she had learned of it.

"I beg your pardon, Conor. Cara, I ought not to have spoken so."

"No, you ought not," Conor replied, staring at her with concern in his eyes.

It was an expression she saw there far too often, and in her parents' eyes too. They did not understand her, and they worried for her, and she wished they would not, for it made her utterly wretched. She did not deserve their concern. They sat in silence, with Aisling concentrating on her stitching until a soft snore from Cara announced she had fallen asleep.

"Why do you speak so of the comte?" Conor asked, keeping his voice low. "It is true the man has something of a reputation with the ladies, but I have heard no one speak ill of him, not even the ladies who no longer have his favour. Has he offended you? Made inappropriate advances? You must tell me, love, for I will need to do something about it."

Aisling blushed and shook her head. "No. I barely know him and… and he's always been very polite. Kind, actually," she added, for that was true, and she did not want Conor confronting the man.

"Then why speak of him so, as if you dislike him?"

Aisling gathered up her embroidery and began putting it away in the carpetbag she carried for the purpose. "I do not dislike him, only what he stands for. He uses women and then discards them. I do not wish for Cara to see a pretty face and believe that is all there is to such a man. I do not wish for her to be used and cast away, Conor. She must have her eyes opened. Society is cruel, and debutantes are so much sport for some men."

"That may be true of *some* men, but from what I know of Villen, I think you do the man a disservice. I think the women use him as much as he uses them, but more to the point, just who has opened your eyes to this behaviour, *deirfiúr beag?* For if anyone has—"

"No one," Aisling tsked, waving this away before he could pursue the notion. "I have eyes in my head, and you would be astonished what people will let slip in front of a wallflower. Oh, Conor, forgive me and my ill temper. I despise society, and it always puts me in a bad skin, but you can see as well as I can that Cara will be a beauty. She will attract attention in a way I never have, and we must prepare her for it."

"Mama will deal with that. She prepared you, did she not?" he said, apparently unconcerned.

Aisling swallowed. "She did. Of course, she did, but I worry for her. She is too innocent, too—"

Conor shook his head at her, his expression one of fond exasperation. "She's sixteen, love. Let her keep her innocence a little longer. Mama says she won't have her come out until she's eighteen, no matter how Cara protests. She has time yet."

Aisling let out a breath and nodded, forcing a smile to her lips, but she was not comforted. The season was not the only place that held unseen dangers, and sixteen was not too young for a girl to discover that to her cost.

26th June 1841, Trevick Castle, Warwickshire.

Holy mother of God.

Sylvester stared at the behemoth that was Trevick Castle in awe. He'd known Aisling's father was an earl, and a wealthy one. Of course he'd known. He'd known Trevick Castle was vast. He hadn't spent his entire life under a rock. She was above his touch. Yes, he'd known that too. Yet, he hadn't. Not in any real sense. He had not truly considered the family to which Aisling belonged. He considered it now.

"What is it?" Alana stared up at him impatiently. She had been a surprisingly entertaining travelling companion, and the journey had passed quickly. Now he wondered if he ought not to turn around and go straight back to Marcross.

"Nothing," he said, pulling himself together.

"Well, come along then!" Alana urged him, hurrying inside after the footmen who were carrying their belongings. The enormous place swallowed her up, and Sylvester shook himself out of his stupor and went after her.

"Alana!"

Sylvester looked up as Lady Cara flew down the stairs towards her friend. Another young woman followed her at a more decorous pace, and he guessed this to be Lady Violette, Aisling and Cara's adopted sister. Beside her was the earl.

"Mr Cootes, I must thank you for bringing such precious cargo to Trevick."

Sylvester regarded the man. His hair must have once been the vibrant red of his youngest daughter's, but it had faded somewhat, now touched with white at the temples. He had a warm smile though and appeared friendlier than Sylvester had expected.

"It was a pleasure to do so, my lord."

"Yes, he's hoping you'll keep me," Alana quipped, grinning.

"We might yet," the earl said, resting a hand on Lady Violette's shoulder. "We have been known to keep our favourite guests and not let them go. You might become part of the family if you're not careful."

"That does not seem a terrible prospect," Alana said, gazing about her in wonder. "Though Mama and Papa might have something to say about it."

The earl laughed. "I am certain they would. Now, the excellent Mrs Wilson here is our housekeeper and will show you to your rooms. I know she will have made the perfect arrangements, but if there is anything you need—"

"What the devil are you doing here?"

Aisling's furious voice rang out across the entrance hall, and everyone stopped to stare at her. The earl turned as well. Too late, Aisling realised her error. She blushed furiously, and Sylvester found himself torn between amusement and mortification on her behalf for the blunder.

"Aisling?" her father said sharply, regarding her with concern. "Is something the matter?"

"No, Papa," she said, though the words sounded choked, as if she'd forced them past her lips.

"I am afraid your daughter does not appreciate the finer points of my company, my lord," Sylvester said ruefully. "Indeed, she may have mentioned 'the most vexing man who ever lived?'"

"That does ring a bell," the earl replied mildly, looking between them with interest.

"Well, that's me."

If anything, Aisling turned a darker shade of scarlet.

"Perhaps I should go," he offered with a smile. "Alana is here safe and sound, and I can return to Marcross. I'll fetch her again when she is ready to go."

It was for the best, he told himself, though he was already regretting the impulse to be polite. Aisling looked so deliciously ruffled and out of sorts, like a wet hen. He wanted very badly to soothe her feathers, or perhaps ruffle them some more. He wasn't sure which.

"No. Wait."

Aisling was looking anywhere but at him, her hands clasped, the fingers so tight he felt sure she must be hurting herself.

"Of course, you m-must stay," she said, confirming it was she who had spoken. He had not imagined it. "Please forgive my outburst, Mr Cootes. I am afraid you took me by surprise. Mrs Wilson, which room have you given Mr Cootes?"

"The forest room, my lady."

Aisling gave a brisk nod, all business now. "Very well. If you would see to Lady Alana, I will escort Mr Cootes. If you would come this way, sir?"

Sylvester regarded her suspiciously. What was she playing at? She'd had the perfect opportunity to get rid of him, and she hadn't taken it. Too curious to object, he followed her up the stairs and along a wide corridor.

"Why didn't you let me go?" he demanded once they were out of earshot. "You could have been rid of me. That's what you wanted, isn't it?"

"Because it would have been horribly ill-mannered of me. My father was appalled by my rudeness as it was, and he was concerned. He'll want to know why I spoke to you so rudely."

"You mean to say you won't lie and tell him I insulted you?" he suggested.

She shot a furious glance at him. "Is this what you think of me? That I would lie to cover my own bad behaviour?"

"Easy, tiger," he said, holding out his hands in a peaceable gesture. "No. I don't think you'd do that, but I wonder what you will say, because I'm not sure you know yourself."

Her eyes flashed. "I assure you, Mr Cootes, I have no difficulty in knowing why you annoy me. You are a very annoying person."

Sylvester's lips quirked. "I try my best."

"In that case, you are most talented." She was striding through the corridors at quite a pace now, her skirts swishing, every line of her body taut with impatience. Why he should find her quite so beguiling, he could not fathom. It was like trying to befriend a hedgehog, no matter what angle one approached from a fellow got stabbed.

"I'm not as dreadful as all that, though. Am I, my lady? Be fair," he persisted, wondering if she was softening just a little. After all, she had let him stay.

She did not answer him, but opened a door and strode through it. "This is the forest room, so named for obvious reasons."

The enormous bedroom was lavish and somewhat overwhelming. The vast ceiling was a mid-green with mouldings in gold and the wall panels were filled with *tromp l'oeil* paintings that depicted woodland scenes with such realism that Sylvester wondered how he would close his eyes at night.

"I feel like a fox might savage me whilst I sleep," he murmured, staring about him.

He thought perhaps her lips twitched, just a fraction, but she did not laugh.

"One can only hope," she said sweetly. She strode to the door, clearly intent on abandoning him.

"I'm sorry," he said, before she could disappear.

She hesitated, suspicion glinting in her dark eyes, as though she sensed a trick. "What for?"

"For giving you a shock. You did not know I was coming, did you?"

She shook her head. "No. Probably my own fault. I expect Mama mentioned it, but I wasn't paying attention. A failing of mine, I'm afraid."

"A lowering thought," he said sadly. "I assumed one mention of my name would be enough for you to prepare to repel boarders."

She returned an impatient glance. "We are not at war, Mr Cootes. *Yet.* Trevick is a big place. With luck, we need not see each other for the entirety of your stay here with a little careful management. For example, this evening I shall plead a headache, so you might enjoy dinner with my family. If you could cry off tomorrow, that's two days gone already."

"Or… we could just be civil to each other and see what happens?" he suggested, wondering why she would go to quite such lengths to avoid him.

"You being civil is enough to make me want to break things. Preferably over your head," she said cheerfully.

"And this makes you happy," he pointed out with a smile, delighted to see her brighten up. Even if it was at the idea of doing violence against his person. "Look at how pleased you are at the thought of smashing things over my head. Perhaps we ought to give it a go? I'll risk it if you will. I have a remarkably hard head."

"*Thick* is the word you are looking for, but I think not. Now, I shall leave you to settle in before I really do have a headache. Enjoy a pleasant stay at Trevick, Mr Cootes. There is a deal of history and much to discover, but I don't expect I shall see you again."

She left, closing the door firmly behind her.

Sylvester stood staring at it for a long moment after she'd gone, quite unable to remove the stupid smile from his face. He had absolutely no intention of having a headache tomorrow evening, and he could not wait to see what she would do about it.

Chapter 7

Lady Elizabeth,

I should be most interested in taking an active interest in the new school. I fear I have spent too much of my life in idle and decadent pursuits and it would do me good to have a focus outside of my own shallow affairs.

I do not wish the school to bear my name, however, nor for anyone to know of my involvement if possible. I am certain we can think of a worthier candidate to give such an honour and get things off to a good start. Like naming a child, such a choice might influence character. We had best weight the possibilities with care.

—Excerpt of a letter from Lord Maxwell Drake, Earl of Vane, to Lady Elizabeth Demarteau (daughter of their graces, Robert and Prunella Adolphus, the Duke and Duchess of Bedwin).

26th June 1841, Trevick Castle, Warwickshire.

Aisling had been as good as her word and had not shown her face at dinner. Nor had he had any luck in tracking her down all day. She'd been right about the castle, however. Close to a thousand years old in parts, it was a fascinating place, and he could not pretend he'd been bored. She was never far from his thoughts, though, and he wished she had given him a tour of the place herself. It would have been far more entertaining to listen to her while they exchanged prickly comments and he could have admired the way her eyes glittered when she was vexed with him.

He could admire those pretty eyes now, however, for he had turned up at dinner instead of pleading a headache and she was not pleased. She was even less pleased to discover he was sitting beside her.

The meal was excellent, but not the lavish affair he might have expected of such a family or such a place. Indeed, the whole evening was as relaxed and convivial as the night before had been, with Aisling the only one not joining in the lively conversation.

"Marcross sounds a wonderful place, and it is always such a joy to see an old house come back to life," the countess said, her dark eyes shining.

The resemblance between her and her eldest daughter was marked. At least, they were alike in looks, but she was far more gregarious and outspoken than Aisling. Sylvester thought her lovely and had taken to her immediately, for she had a lively sense of humour.

"Do you remember when we restored the property in Ireland, Luke? My, but life was simple then, and so happy," she said, smiling at her husband wistfully.

The earl's expression was no less warm as he regarded his countess. "As if I could ever forget."

"It is something to take pride in," Sylvester agreed, meaning it, even though he was too aware of the fact that he worked *for* his brother. "And it feels good to return our childhood home to a place where my brother's family can be happy."

But it wasn't his. Not that he resented the fact. He was proud to work for his brother, and relieved to know Raphe was happy and settled. Yet, he wanted a place to call his own, too. Sadly, it would be some time before he could afford such a thing. Let alone a wife to live in it with him. Not that he was in any hurry for that, he reminded himself. The bachelor's life suited him very well, but the words rang hollow tonight and he emptied his wine glass, unsettled.

"Where do you live then, Mr Cootes? If Marcross is your brother's estate? Do you have a property nearby?"

Somewhat surprisingly, Aisling had asked, for she had barely spoken a word all evening. She watched him intently as she awaited his answer.

To his discomfort, Sylvester felt heat creep up the back of his neck. "My brother has generously given me a small cottage on the estate," he said, wishing the admission did not make him feel so hopeless. How could it not, though, when surrounded by a property of such grandeur, such wealth and power? Likely Aisling had said it to put him in his place, to remind him he worked for a living and had nothing to offer her, an earl's daughter. Well, it worked. His pleasure in the evening dissipated swiftly from that moment, and he excused himself early and retired to bed.

Sylvester was marching along the corridor that led to his room when Aisling stopped him.

"Mr Cootes."

He turned to see she had followed him.

"My lady," he said, for once wishing she'd left him alone.

He did not want to look at her now. She was exquisite in the candlelight, her dark hair framing her face, and the lovely gown she wore highlighted the curves of her figure. No doubt that one dress cost more than he earned in a month. Bitterness was a sour taste in his mouth, and he felt unaccountably angry.

"I wish to beg your pardon, for I believe I have caused you offense. It was not my intention."

"Wasn't it?" he said, unable to disguise his resentment.

"No!" she said, twisting her hands together, her dark eyes soft with concern. "I was curious, that's all, and there is no shame in your situation. My father was poor as a church mouse before he inherited the title."

Sylvester laughed, for her pity was even worse than her contempt. "Just to drum the point home," he said, curling his lip. He must get away from her before he allowed his pride to goad him into saying something unforgiveable.

"No, I… I did not mean it that way."

"Don't worry, my lady. I am well aware you are above my touch, and I assure you, you'll never have to endure anything as outrageous as a proposal of marriage. I'm no damned fortune hunter to go dangling after an heiress, no matter what low opinion you have of me. You interest me, that's all. I've offered to be your friend because I think you need one, but there's no more to it than that, so don't go thinking I'm pining away for the love of you or some ridiculous romantic nonsense for I'm not. We would not suit."

She stiffened and Sylvester realised his words had been too harsh, almost contemptuous. Suddenly he wanted to take it back, to beg her forgiveness, but his pride balked, and her expression suggested she would murder him no matter what the next words out of his mouth were.

"I am glad we have clarified the situation, Mr Cootes," she said, her voice cool. "For you ought to know that I should never accept you, even if you were as rich as Croesus. Good night, sir."

She turned and stalked away, head held high, and Sylvester cursed under his breath. *Bloody buggering bollocks*. Well, he'd made a right mess of that.

"Well done, Sylvester, excellent work. Now she really does hate you," he muttered, and let himself into his room.

27th June 1841, Trevick Castle, Warwickshire.

It was barely dawn as Aisling hurried away from the castle, heading towards the woods. She clutched her shawl around her to cover her bare arms. The day was already warm and would be hot soon enough, but there was a chill breeze if you were out of the sun. The grass was damp with dew, soaking her shoes, and the sun glittered upon cobwebs and sent dazzling colours across the sky, setting it aflame. She admired it for a moment, trying to find the peace that being back here usually gave her, but it eluded her today.

"Damn him," she said aloud, relishing the ability to swear out loud. She took a deep breath and let it out again. "I will not think of him. Not today," she promised herself.

Holding her skirts free of the damp ground, she hurried on, shivering as the cooler air of the woodland shut out the sun. She followed the familiar path, concentrating only on the ground beneath her feet, of the scent of decay and of life, of the rustle of the breeze stirring the leaves overhead.

The little cottage was well hidden if you did not know where to look, and as this was private land Aisling was assured of peace here. She knocked once and let herself in.

"Biddy, it's me."

"And who else would it be, child?" came the amused reply, the softly lilting Irish accent soothing the jagged edges of Aisling's temper. "And cross as a wet cat by the look of you."

Aisling hurried to embrace the woman who had been her nanny as a child and whom she loved as dearly as if she was her grandmother. "Not cross, only in need of some peace. London is a hellish place, and I am so happy to be home."

"Hmmm," Biddy said, her sharp gaze taking Aisling in and seeing her with far too much clarity. "And who is the handsome fellow staying at the castle, then? 'Tis nothing to do with him, this temper you're in, eh?"

"Well, he doesn't help matters," Aisling admitted, for what was the point of denying it? "You remember the annoying fellow I met at Christmas? Well, it's him, and he's worse than ever. I swear he is the most provoking man. He'd goad a saint into a temper tantrum."

"And you're no saint, *a leanbh,*" Biddy replied with a smile.

"No," Aisling replied, flopping down in a chair by the fire, which was lit despite the mildness of the day. "That I am not."

Biddy swung a large kettle over the fire and moved to take the chair opposite Aisling. She was a sturdy woman well into her sixties, her thick hair greying now, but she still exuded the restless energy of a far younger woman. "Why does the man aggravate you so, then? What is it about him that sets your hackles all on end?"

Aisling shrugged. "He has a knack for pricking at my tender places, and he seems to do it on purpose."

Biddy said nothing, but her expression was knowing and full of amusement.

"No!" Aisling huffed, defensive now.

"No?"

"No, he's not… he doesn't… He's just nosy! He's not interested in *me*. I assure you he made that very clear. He just thinks I have something to hide and is determined to know what it is. He says I can trust him," she added in disgust, folding her arms.

"And can you?"

"He's a man," Aisling said, drawing the words out slowly, as if that ought to be answer enough.

"Your pa is a man. Your brother, too. Ashton Anson is a man, and—"

Aisling rolled her eyes. "Yes, yes, I know! I know there are some good men out there, but they are few, and I'm not about to make another mistake."

Biddy sighed, shaking her head sadly. "You did not make a mistake, love. You were young and innocent and taken advantage of. 'Tis a different thing."

"Perhaps," Aisling allowed. "But that's not all of it, and you know that. He needs to stay away from me, for both our sakes. I don't… I don't want to hurt him too."

Biddy clicked her tongue, her next words sharp and impatient. "Child, you cannot punish yourself forever, and you ought not punish a man if he is truly trying to be a friend to you. The past is gone, stop biding there."

"And how do I know? How do I tell, Biddy?" Aisling demanded, frustrated now. "Men lie, and I've believed those lies. I don't trust my instincts anymore, and I certainly don't trust him."

The old woman stared at her hard, as if trying to make Aisling heed her words by sheer force of will.

"Your instincts are sound, and you ought to listen to them. You're not a child any longer. It is time to let the past go, love. Listen to that little voice in your head. Listen to your heart."

Aisling got to her feet. She had come here hoping that Biddy would sympathise and agree that Mr Cootes was an annoying presence and she'd be well shot of him. Biddy had little patience for most men herself. She had never married, refusing to become anyone's property, so to hear her defend the wretched man was infuriating.

"Ah, you're all at sixes and sevens," Biddy said, her expression softening and her smile only making Aisling crosser. "Reckon you know why, too. Don't fight it so hard, love. You like the annoying fellow, so why not enjoy it? Maybe he'll kiss you and make you remember how it feels to be a young woman again."

Aisling scowled, remembering Mr Cootes telling her in no uncertain terms that he hadn't the slightest interest in her romantically. Why those words had made her feel so much like weeping, she did not know, but they had, and ever since she'd heard them, she'd had no peace. She had not slept last night, hearing his scathing retort circling in her head until the early hours of the morning. The lack of sleep had hardly helped her temper and now she was, as Biddy had suggested, as cross as a wet cat. That she knew she was being irrational did not help a jot.

"I told you. He's not interested in me like that. He just wants to poke his nose where it doesn't belong, and I will not let him."

"So you say," Biddy said, with the singsong air of a woman who knew better.

Aisling gave a harrumph of frustration, kissed Biddy on the cheek, and snatched up her shawl, feeling even crosser than when she'd arrived. Her skirts swished as she strode out of the cottage, and she was well into the castle gardens before her temper subsided enough for her to slow her pace. She took a deep breath and told herself she was being ridiculous. Why was she so cross that a man she didn't even like wasn't romantically interested in her, when she hadn't *wanted* him to be interested in her in the first place? It made no sense.

She was still puzzling over this conundrum when she arrived at the large ornamental pond. It was a great circle with a fountain at its centre, and she usually found it a soothing place to be. Today, her nerves leapt as she saw Mr Cootes standing at the edge of the pond, gazing down at it as though he were looking for something hidden beneath the dark water.

Aisling hesitated, uncertain of what to do. She did not wish to speak to him after last night, but if she backed up and left, he'd notice. He'd think she was running away. Well, he'd be right, obviously, but she was damned if she'd let him know it. Deciding to just ignore the problem, she picked up her pace again, intending to stride past him with a nonchalant 'good morning Mr Cootes,' but not stop.

"Good morning, Mr—"

"Wait."

He moved the moment he saw her, moving to block her path. Aisling was so surprised that she took a quick step back and turned her ankle. She stepped again to steady herself and stumbled upon the low wall of the pond. With a gasp, Aisling fell backwards and shrieked as her backside hit the cold water with a splash. For a moment she just sat there, gaping up at him with her mouth open, the shock of sitting up to her waist in a mucky pond enough to stun her into silence.

Mr Cootes looked equally shocked. Thankfully he wasn't laughing, or things might have taken a turn for the worse.

"My lady," he managed, reaching for her.

Aisling batted his hands away. Anger morphed rapidly into abject humiliation, and she wanted to get away from him, wanted to cry, blast him. She never cried, not anymore, and yet this was the second time the impulse to sob had come upon her in his presence. Oh, how she hated him. *Loathed* him. The absolute beast!

Somehow, she got herself upright again and stared down at her ruined gown, which was now decorated with green pond weed. She swallowed hard. *No tears, Aisling. Don't you dare.*

"Aisling. I'm so sorry, I—"

"No," she said, shaking her head. "Not a word."

"But please… I must talk to you."

She shook her head again, determined to get away, though her sodden petticoats and skirts weighed a ton and clung to her legs, threatening to trip her.

"Aisling!"

He grasped her wrists and Aisling stilled, shocked by the sensation of his hands on her bare skin. His hold was gentle, and she could easily have pulled free, but the sensation of being touched by him had scattered her wits.

"I didn't mean it," he said, the words angry and brittle, as though they'd been torn from him against his will.

He looked a little wild. His hair was all over the place, as if he'd dragged his fingers through it several times over, and there was a slightly desperate look in his hazel eyes that made her stomach feel all skittish and peculiar.

"W-What?" she managed, for she was all in a muddle. He had his hands on her and… and she rather liked it. In fact, she didn't want him to let go and yet she was still so *furious* with him, and he was talking and… what was he saying?

"I didn't mean what I said. At least, I meant the part about not being a fortune hunter. I'm not. I don't give a damn for your blasted money, and I know I'm not good enough for you, and I do want to know what you're hiding, and… and I swear you can trust me, even if I'm just your friend, Aisling, but… oh, to hell with it."

He kissed her.

Aisling was too stunned to even close her eyes for a moment. She simply froze as he pressed his mouth to hers. He pulled back, such a startled expression in his eyes she almost laughed, until she saw anxiety there.

"I'm sorry, love. I didn't mean to… did I frighten…"

It was a moment of madness, perhaps only a desire to shut him up, but she lifted on her toes and pressed her mouth to his, stopping his words before he could annoy her. He obliged, kissing her again, tenderly now, with exquisite care. His lips were soft and warm and suddenly the kiss was not a kiss, but a dozen little kisses. Her eyes fluttered shut and, without conscious thought, her hand came up to grasp his neck as the other clutched at his lapel. She sighed, leaning into him, into his warmth and his strength as he let go of his hold on her, only to wrap his arms about her and pull her closer. She went, melting into his embrace as though it were inevitable, as though they'd both known this was the only place she could be all along. He teased at her mouth, parting her lips and deepening the kiss, and Aisling let him, without even a murmur of protest. She knew she *ought* to protest, ought to slap his face or find something suitable to hit him with, but… but….

He drew back, gazing at her warily, his chest rising and falling as if he'd been running for miles. Aisling blinked, staring up at him as whatever spell he'd cast over her dissipated and sanity returned.

"Oh, no," she said faintly, letting go of him like he'd burned her and stumbling away. "Oh, no, no, no. This is bad. Oh, this is very bad."

"Now, Aisling—"

"Don't," she said, holding up a warning finger. "Do not speak. Whenever you open your mouth, you only make it worse."

"It was only a kiss, love, and you kissed me too, I might add," he retorted, looking adorably rumpled and just as confounded as she felt. Wait. *Adorable?* Was she insane? Sylvester Cootes could not come close to adorable, even if he was smothered in kittens and fluffy bunnies and wrapped in a pink bow. That was it. She was losing her mind.

Aisling made a small sound of annoyance and stamped her foot. "No. Talking," she insisted.

Drat the man. Couldn't he hold his tongue? Like she didn't know she'd kissed him back. Oh, good heavens, she'd kissed him *back!* Another panicky sound escaped her, and she covered her mouth with her hand.

"Oh, come now, it's not that bad," he said, clearly affronted by her horror.

"Can't," she managed, shaking her head and stumbling away from him as her horrid wet skirts flapped about her legs and dragged at the bodice of her dress. "Can't," she said again, hauling the sodden material with her as best she could.

"Good heavens, what a drama you make of things. I wanted to kiss you, so I did. You liked it, so you kissed me back. It's simple biology. There's no need to take a hysterical fit over it."

"I am not hysterical," Aisling retorted, sounding just a wee bit hysterical.

"Well, you are soaked to the bone," he observed. "And it's going to take you an hour to get back to the house at that rate. Come here."

Before Aisling could inform him she had no intention of going anywhere with him, he swept her up into his arms. She gave a little squeal that made her sound like a five-year-old with ringlets and a pout rather than a grown woman, which did not help her temper. Oh, why did he always make her feel so out of sorts? Usually, she was a placid creature who bothered no one, but he turned her into a raving lunatic with a volcanic temper. It was most disturbing.

Rather than risk the hysterical fit he had accused her of, Aisling forced herself to suffer his attempt at chivalry with silent endurance.

"You're planning ways to murder me in my sleep, aren't you?" he said, glancing down at her with amusement.

Aisling struggled to hold her tongue, for the desire to ring a peel over him was far too tantalising, but she would not give him the satisfaction of arguing with him. He enjoyed it too much.

"I am sorry," he said again, and she heard sincerity in his voice. "For last night. You were right, of course. You offended me, which is ridiculous, but a fellow has his pride. I live in a small cottage on my brother's estate. I earn my living working as his estate manager and, though he is generous, it hardly makes me a fine prospect for any young lady. You hit a nerve, and I suspected you did it on purpose to put me in my place."

Aisling gasped, glaring at him. "You think I would do such a horrid thing? I was merely curious, that's all."

He nodded. "I realised that too late. You enjoy scolding me, but I have never known you to be cruel. Am I forgiven?"

She scowled, not wanting to forgive him. Things were far easier when she hated him.

He laughed, shaking his head as he studied her expression of consternation. "Don't worry, love. I'll give you another reason to be angry with me in short order."

"I am not your love," she objected.

"See?" he replied, his hazel eyes twinkling.

Aisling made a disgruntled sound but stole a glance at him once he'd turned his attention back to the path. He was too handsome, she decided, that was the trouble. *He* was trouble. His jaw was too strong – a warning of his stubborn nature, his hair was a dark gold and glinted in the sunlight, and his hazel eyes were warm and kind. Worse, his mouth… oh, his mouth was soft and looked always to be on the verge of smiling. Sylvester Cootes was a dangerous man, and she needed to keep away from him or she would turn into a brainless ninny all over again. She ought to know by now she was susceptible to handsome men and glib words. They made one feel important and pretty and as if they mattered more than anyone else in the world, and then they…. No. She would not think about that.

They were almost back at the castle now. Her skirts and petticoats alone weighed a ton now they were soaked through, but he carried her with apparent ease.

"You can put me down now," she protested as they arrived at the entrance hall.

"What, and see you spend the next half hour trying to drag those wet skirts up the stairs? I think not. I shall deposit you outside of your room."

She toyed with the idea of strangling him with his cravat. "You're very sure of yourself, Mr Cootes."

"High-handed," he agreed cordially. "You can hit me if you want to."

"Oh, may I? With something heavy?" she asked sweetly, and then blanched with horror.

Lord, what was wrong with her? She ought not to say such vile things, even in jest, but she had a wicked, violent streak that could not be trusted. Her stomach lurched, but he only chuckled, and the sound rumbled through his chest and into her, which was most disconcerting.

"Certainly, providing you kiss my bruises better afterwards."

Aisling blushed and began to struggle, and he set her down at once. "Well, you're only a few paces from your door. Honestly, I'm amazed I got you this far."

He was smiling at her, and Aisling did not know what to do, what to say to him, how to feel. She was in such a muddle and that frightened her, and she hated to feel afraid, had sworn she would never be afraid again. Anger rose, and that at least was safe. She could wrap herself in anger and protect herself from harm, from him. Though who would protect him from her? Yet she glanced up at him again to see concern in his eyes and her anger became a fragile, ethereal thing. Oh, drat the man!

With no idea how she ought to deal with him, Aisling settled on retreat, and fled to her bedroom without another word, slamming the door behind her.

Chapter 8

Dearest Kathleen,

I do understand truly, but you must see what a scare you gave us? You disappeared without a word and not for the first time, I understand. Your poor father was beside himself and I do not blame him for denying you the right to visit the school for a while. Your charitable impulses are to be admired, but not when they put your life at risk. The Seven Dials is not a place for a young lady without an escort.

You have a family who loves you. You must think of them if not of yourself. There is much that can be done to help the desperate people who live in such vile conditions without taking such hazardous chances.

I shall see you again soon once your father has remembered how to breathe again.

—Excerpt of a letter from Lady Elizabeth Demarteau (daughter of their graces, Robert and Prunella Adolphus, the Duke and Duchess of Bedwin) to Miss Kathleen de Beauvoir (adopted daughter of Inigo and Minerva de Beauvoir).

27th June 1841, Trevick Castle, Warwickshire.

Sylvester stared at the door Aisling had just slammed in his face. His heart was doing an erratic dance in his chest, and had been from the moment she had appeared beside the ornamental pond. He swallowed and let out a shaky breath, feeling the corners of his mouth tilt up.

He'd kissed her.

Some lunatic impulse had overtaken him, and he'd kissed her. Better yet, she'd kissed him. That was… that was too delicious for words. He had hoped, of course, but if she'd slapped his face and told him to go to hell, he wouldn't have been entirely surprised. Oh, but she had tasted sweeter than anything he could dream of, and the way she had responded to him, immediately and instinctively, made shivers run down his spine. He swallowed again, forcing down a laugh that threatened to make him look positively unhinged should anyone see him standing there, gazing at her door.

Sylvester made himself move away, albeit reluctantly, for he wanted to see her again. Now. This moment… even if she clearly did not wish to see him. The look in her eyes as she'd slammed the door had been unreadable, but he suspected the kiss had shocked her far more than it had him. He'd known he wanted to kiss her even if he hadn't wanted to admit it at first, but Aisling…. She was afraid, though apparently not of him, which was a relief. She would not bicker with him so delightfully if she were afraid of him, but she *was* afraid nonetheless. He suspected she still did not recognise, or refused to see, what was between them. Aisling did not know how to read the tension, and did not understand why he bothered her so. Not yet, at least.

He made his way back to his room, grinning inanely until he let himself back into the lavish chamber and reality reasserted itself. Reality was a miserable bitch, he decided, staring about at a room so opulent and luxurious he could not imagine what it had cost to furnish. He only knew he could not come close to this. Sylvester Cootes, estate manager, had no business going about kissing the daughter of an earl, especially as he'd not been invited to do so. What if she'd not responded? What if she'd complained to her father? What if her father had seen and wanted him driven from the estate at gunpoint?

He might have truly frightened her, and poor Alana would be mortified and heartbroken if she could not be friends with Cara, and he would have dragged Raphe into some humiliating scene as head of the family….

Sylvester fished about in his coat pocket for his flask and took a fortifying swallow, telling himself not to be so dramatic. She hadn't objected, and no one had seen. He'd know by now if they had. That did not change the facts, though. Aisling was out of reach, and he'd do well to remember that. Perhaps he ought to go home after all.

It was a thought he pondered for the next few hours, but he could not convince himself to leave.

Later that day, the countess invited Sylvester to take tea with her. Despite telling himself there was no way she knew about the kiss, and he was not about to be escorted from the estate by a legion of footmen, he was unaccountably nervous. He followed the butler, who had issued the invitation-command, to a small, sunny parlour that overlooked a rose garden.

The countess set aside the book she was reading and smiled warmly as the butler announced him, and Sylvester felt able to breathe again.

"Lady Trevick. This is a pleasure, thank you."

"A trial, more like. I can imagine you have been cursing me and wondering what the devil I want with you," she said, with such startling candour Sylvester could only laugh.

"No, I assure you—"

"Oh, pish. Sit yourself down and do call me Kitty. Lady Trevick makes me sound far too sensible and well-behaved, and I'm rarely accused of that, even now. Something I'm far prouder of than I ought to be, I know, but society is so dreadfully dull and opinionated. It's enough to give anyone the pip."

Sylvester blinked and sat as instructed, at a loss to know what to say.

"There, you see? I've shocked you," she observed with satisfaction. "I should get used to it, Mr Cootes. I am a terrible trial to my poor husband."

Sylvester opened his mouth to say something, thought better of it, and closed it again.

Lady Trevick grinned. "Milk and sugar?" she asked serenely as a footman laid a tray with an exquisite porcelain tea service on it before her.

"Milk, no sugar." He wondered what was coming next.

"Ah, sweet enough," she observed with a twinkle in her eyes.

They sat in silence while the lady made the tea just how he liked it and handed him the cup before seeing to her own.

"Do try the tea cakes, Mr Cootes. Our cook is a marvel and makes the simplest of pleasures into something quite decadent. I don't know what her secret is, but I should commit murder before I let anyone poach her from us, and they have tried."

"Really?" Sylvester paused with a tea cake in hand, diverted.

The countess gave a sigh of content as she bit into a cake and chewed, and he waited. "Oh, yes," she said, once she was free to speak again. "A wonderful cook is worth her weight in gold, and you'd never believe the lengths some people go to in their efforts to lure her away. Thankfully for us, she's loyal and has been with the family since the children were small."

"I imagine she knows a good thing when she has found it," Sylvester replied politely.

"Exactly," said the countess, wagging a finger at him. "Loyalty works both ways. We do all in our power to make sure she is content in her work and her life here is everything she could wish, and in return she dismisses other tantalising offers that promise the moon for the security and happiness she finds here. Good people, people you can trust, are scarce. But once found, they ought to be appreciated. Can I trust you, Mr Cootes?"

The ambush took him by surprise, and he needed a moment to rally. Perhaps he ought to have expected it, for he'd known the lady did not mince her words, but she had lulled him into a sense of security and now he felt a bit as if he'd had the rug pulled from under him.

"Yes," he replied as unease slid beneath his skin. Sylvester held her gaze and prayed he did not look as nervous and sweaty palmed as he felt. "Yes, my lady. You can trust me."

He'd kissed her daughter in the garden, and he wanted to do it again, but it wasn't a lie. He would never hurt Aisling, nor her family.

The countess stared back at him, so intently and for so long that he had to battle the urge to fidget under her scrutiny.

"Yes," she said with a nod. "I believe I can."

The vice that had fastened about Sylvester's chest released abruptly, and he let out a breath of relief.

"What are your intentions towards my daughter, Mr Cootes?" the lady asked, holding the tray of tea cakes out to him again.

Sylvester took one, prepared now for the kind of conversation this was going to be. "I have no intentions towards your daughter, other than that of a friend," he said, hoping she could not hear the bitterness and regret in his voice, for he did not wish for this lovely woman to pity him. "I am aware I have nothing to offer her, and I would never presume otherwise. My prospects are secure enough, but I must work to earn my keep and that's hardly worthy of an earl's daughter. I have no illusions, I assure you."

The memory of that kiss rose in his mind, calling him a liar, but he pushed it away. It had been a foolish dream, an aberration, a momentary loss of sanity. He would not let it happen again.

"You would be her friend?" she repeated, watching him intently.

"I would. In fact, the reason I stayed was because…."

He stopped, aware he could say no more even if he knew what the more was. If Aisling had secrets, they were *her* secrets. He did not know what they were, and would have no right to share them with anyone if he did.

"Because?" she pressed, and there was an edge to the word, a sharpness that made him believe she would be a formidable enemy if you thought to damage her children's happiness.

Sylvester hesitated, uncertain of what to say, and the countess saved him from stammering excuses by speaking first.

"Mr Cootes. I like you, and for that reason, I am going to throw caution to the wind, trust in your discretion, and be horribly candid."

Sylvester bit back a smile, for the lady had been nothing but candid since he'd stepped into the room.

"Something happened to my daughter. I do not know what, or even precisely when it happened, but something did, and she will not confide in us. I think perhaps it was a long time ago, but she is far too adept at hiding her feelings and pretending all is well. Yet Aisling is unhappy, and her unhappiness is eating away at her father and myself, for we do not know how to fix it."

"Yes," Sylvester said simply.

The countess let out a breath and nodded, and for a moment her eyes sparkled too brightly. He waited as she composed herself, picking up the tea cake he'd taken to allow her a moment.

"You must think me a dreadful mother, not to know something so important," she said after a long moment of silence.

"Indeed, I do not," Sylvester said at once. He knew something about bad parenting himself and he doubted this lady had made such mistakes. "I think Lady Aisling is a determined young woman, and far too proficient at keeping secrets."

The countess nodded, her smile tremulous. "That she is, and I think you are very kind, and that is the reason I have spoken to you about something so private. That, and because of how Aisling acts around you. She trusts you."

Sylvester choked on the tea cake.

"I beg your pardon," he croaked, once he could speak again. "But Lady Aisling *trusts* me? She doesn't even *like* me…."

Lady Trevick returned an indulgent smile. "She's rude to you, yes, and that is how I know she trusts you. Aisling rarely speaks to anyone outside of family and close friends. She rarely gives an opinion upon any subject outside of mundane chitchat, yet with you she seems ready to take up arms and defend her point to the death. She would never do that with a man she did not trust."

Sylvester conceded the point, having observed it himself.

"Will you help me, Mr Cootes? More to the point, will you help my daughter?"

Sylvester considered this for a moment. "My lady. You do me the greatest honour by putting your trust in me, and I would do anything in my power to help Lady Aisling, but I very much doubt she would ever confide in me. Even if she would, I will not pry her secrets from her only to hand them to you. I promise you, that if I can help her, I will, but it is her I help, not you. Anything I discover, any trust she puts in me, will remain with me and me alone."

"You promise? Even if you can never hope to marry her? Even if you do all the hard work only for her to find happiness with another?" the countess asked, her direct question proving she was far too perceptive for comfort.

Sylvester thought he really ought to be used to the way she hit you over the head with her rather brutal honesty this far into the conversation, but the question still stung. He reminded himself sternly that he enjoyed his bachelor status, and he wasn't ready to marry. Even if he had the funds and the position, he wouldn't be thinking about courting the lady. Yet, there was an unpleasant wrenching sensation in his chest.

"Even then," he replied, ignoring it. "I always keep my promises, my lady."

Lady Trevick smiled and reached out to pat his hand. "I knew I was right about you. I confess, my husband would be furious with me if he'd known what I intended to speak to you about, but Aisling is his little girl, and he is protective. I know she is a young woman, and a formidable one at that. You'll have your work cut out for you, Mr Cootes."

Sylvester smiled at that, thinking it was the first time she'd been less than forthright, for that was most certainly an understatement.

Chapter 9

Dearest Eliza,

I do understand that everyone worries, and I ought not to have disappeared as I did. I would not cause my parents or you any undue concern, and I will try to behave as I ought. I'm just not very good at being a lady. In all honesty I haven't the least idea what I am good at. I wish I did.

—Excerpt of a letter from Miss Kathleen de Beauvoir (adopted daughter of Inigo and Minerva de Beauvoir) to Lady Elizabeth Demarteau (daughter of their graces, Robert and Prunella Adolphus, the Duke and Duchess of Bedwin).

28th June 1841, Trevick Castle, Warwickshire.

There was to be a ride out the next morning to Kenilworth Castle and a picnic. A romantic ruin, Kenilworth's popularity had soared because of the popular novel about it by Sir Walter Scott. Sylvester was looking forward to the outing, though he wished it were only him and Aisling and did not include the trio of giggling girls. They were sweet-natured but inclined to make sheep's eyes at him, which made him uncomfortable. Aisling, however, had other ideas. They'd barely ridden a quarter hour before she complained the bright sunlight had given her a headache and she needed to return home. With a pained smile, she urged them to enjoy their day and promised to see them later.

"I'll escort you," Sylvester offered, not to be thwarted by the obvious ploy to escape his company.

"Oh, no! I wouldn't dream of it, though you are most gallant, Mr Cootes," she said, smiling prettily, though only he could see victory shining in her eyes. "I know the path like the back of my hand. I will be quite well."

"Don't worry, Mr Cootes, she has been riding this countryside since she was a small girl. She will be perfectly fine," Harleston said with a smile, and a knowing glance that suggested he believed his sister would be safer out of his company, whether or not this was a ploy.

Aisling looked triumphant, the wretch. "There, nothing to fret about. A cup of tea in the shade will set me to rights, I assure you. Enjoy your day, Mr Cootes."

She gave him a dazzling smile, forgetting herself for a moment before touching delicate fingers to her head as if the action had pained her. Then she turned her horse around and rode away.

Sylvester sighed, frustrated that a chance to speak privately to her had slipped away, but he had little choice but to carry on with the rest of the group. All his pleasure in the outing had disappeared with her departure, though, and he scolded himself for a fool. It wasn't her company he needed, he reminded himself. It had just been a perfect opportunity to discover more about her, about what she was hiding, that was all. He wasn't a besotted schoolboy, pining for the lack of her. He wasn't doing this for the pleasure of being with her, for the delight in hearing her scold him for annoying her. He *wasn't.*

They had ridden for perhaps another ten minutes when Sylvester's horse threw a shoe.

"Well, this is turning into an ill-fated outing," Harleston said with a sigh. "Shall I take her back for you, and you take my mount?"

"Oh, no. I'll walk her back. It's no bother," Sylvester assured him. He would far rather return to the house, and though he didn't much want to walk as the day was growing hotter, at least he might have time to speak to Aisling privately now. He smiled, thinking how cross she would be with him for coming home early.

"Do you remember the way?" Harleston asked, frowning.

"I'll find it," Sylvester assured him. He had a good sense of direction and was more than happy to wave off the rest of the party.

An hour later and Sylvester was regretting his blithe confidence. He'd taken a wrong turn somewhere and had lost his bearings. Pausing in the shade he took a moment to rest the horse and check her hoof again. All this walking about with a missing shoe would be doing the poor beast no good whatsoever. If she went lame because he couldn't find his way back, he'd never forgive himself. Muttering oaths as it was growing hotter and there was neither a soul nor a dwelling to be seen, he decided he'd head for high ground. The damned castle must be visible for miles around if he could find a vantage point to look for it. Sadly, he could see nothing but trees as the path meandered through woodland, and he had no choice but to follow it. At least it was cool out of the sun.

After another forty minutes Sylvester was trying to smother the disquieting sensation that he was walking in circles when he came upon a small stone cottage in a clearing. It was a tidy little place, obviously well-tended, and he was more than pleased to discover some evidence of life, even in such a forgotten corner. He stopped, staring at it. There was a well close to the cottage and Sylvester regarded it with relief.

"Help yourself."

He looked back at the cottage to see a woman standing there, watching him with interest. She was perhaps in her late sixties, her grey hair a mass of untidy curls about her face, and she had a robust figure. The woman folded her arms, watching him without apparent surprise or any unease, though few people must venture this way unless they'd become hopelessly lost.

"Thank you," Sylvester said, leading his horse to the well. He filled the trough next to the well for his mount before raising the bucket again and using the dipper to serve himself. The water was cold and sweet, and he was tempted to upend a bucket over his head, but he could feel the woman's gaze upon him still, considering.

"I got turned about," he said, gesturing to the path. "Which is unlike me. I usually have a good sense of direction, but I, er… can't see the wood for the trees." He offered her what he hoped was a charming smile.

She did not smile, but there was amusement glinting in her eyes.

"I mean, how can you miss a castle that big?" he added with a laugh.

"Are you hungry?" the woman said, turning to go back inside.

"Oh, no. I have no wish to…."

She looked over her shoulder at him before carrying on. "Nonsense. Come in. The cottage is cool, and you look like you could do with a few moments' peace."

Sylvester hesitated. He knew he must be close to the castle and, no matter how far he'd strayed, would certainly be on the earl's land, in which case this was a tenant, and he did not wish to be rude. Reluctantly, he followed the woman inside. He paused as he walked into what was obviously the main room of the house. It served as kitchen, dining, and living area, with everything neat and scrubbed and in order, much as the outside of the house had been. There were herbs hanging in bundles from the ceiling, and rows and rows of shelves lining the walls. On the shelves were jars, bottles, pots, and books, and… and Sylvester had the peculiar notion that he was Hansel and the cottage was made of gingerbread. He shook off the ridiculous idea and accepted a seat at the kitchen table.

"You're very kind, madam," he offered, watching her as she moved about the kitchen.

"Not at all, and call me Biddy. Everybody does. You are welcome here, Mr Cootes."

"You know me?" he said, a prickle of unease running down his spine.

The woman turned and laughed, reading his anxiety with apparent amusement. "I know everyone and everything that happens at the castle."

Those words sank in, and Sylvester told himself he was being daft for feeling so on edge. Then a feminine voice rang out from the front door.

"Biddy, it's me. I escaped the picnic, thank heavens. I didn't think I could bear another moment in that wretched fellow's—"

Aisling came through the door, tugging her bonnet from her head and smiling, looking more at ease and carefree than Sylvester had ever seen her before. That changed the moment she laid eyes on him.

"I was the children's nursemaid, Mr Cootes," Biddy said, a smile tugging at her mouth as she glanced between him and Aisling. "They often visit."

"What…?" Aisling began, her voice faint as she stared at him.

All the colour had drained from her face in an instant and, if he hadn't been so concerned she was about to swoon, Sylvester would have been deeply insulted. He leapt to his feet and reached for her, but she stepped back, swaying and sitting down heavily on the arm of the chair behind her.

"My horse threw a shoe, and I got lost," he said, aware he sounded stiff, but need she look so damned appalled at finding him here? He wasn't a fool. He'd known she'd been making excuses to get out of his company, but still.

"Your horse," she muttered, sending Biddy an accusing glance. As if she could have had anything to do with it.

Biddy shook her head, looking thoroughly entertained. "No," she said, holding up her hands.

Sylvester did not know what she meant by that, but Aisling only looked increasingly horrified. She stared back at him.

"How much farther did you ride after I left you?" she demanded.

Sylvester frowned, irritated by her question. "Ten minutes, perhaps."

"So, you were barely twenty minutes from the castle, your horse throws a shoe, and two hours later you turn up here?"

She was glaring at him and Sylvester did not know why.

"I got lost," he said again, annoyed now. Must she rub it in? "I'll admit I don't know how when I was so close, but… but I took a wrong turn and lost my sense of direction. Why are you so annoyed? It's not like I did it on purpose."

Aisling opened her mouth, but did not get the chance to reply.

"Of course you didn't. Now you eat up and you'll feel much better," Biddy said, her voice soothing as she set a plate of food on the table.

She ushered him back to his place and made him sit down again. There was bread and cheese and an apple cut into quarters, and she set a jug of ale at his elbow too before giving him a pat on the shoulder. The gesture was strangely reassuring, and he allowed his anger to dissipate. Ignoring Aisling and her obvious displeasure, he turned his attention to his plate, only now realising how hungry he'd been. He could hear the two women talking, an indistinct murmur, but he could make out the bewildered note to Aisling's voice and her old nursemaid's soothing responses.

Sylvester cleared his plate, drank the ale, and got to his feet. The women turned to look at him as he rose, Biddy's expression pleased for no reason he could fathom. Aisling's was unreadable, but she stood with her arms crossed, everything about her posture distrustful. Well, fine. If that was how she felt about him, she'd not have to suffer his company a moment longer.

"Thank you, madam, for your hospitality. I'm sorry to have troubled you. If you'll excuse me, I'd best be going. Good afternoon to you." He inclined his head to Aisling. "My lady," he said politely, and turned to leave.

"Wait," Aisling said.

He turned back to see her twisting her hands anxiously, her dark eyebrows drawn together in a frown.

"I… I'd best go with you, or you'll end up in Aberdeen."

"I am quite capable—" he began, only to see Biddy raise her eyebrows, giving him a *what the devil are you playing at* expression that made him swallow his words. What *was* he playing at? He'd wanted to get Aisling alone, hadn't he? It didn't matter that she didn't want his company. It wasn't for his sake, or anything to do with what he wanted. He'd made a promise to the countess to help, and he always kept his promises. He took a breath. "Thank you, my lady," he said, and though his pride stung, it didn't matter once they were walking back along the sun-dappled track with Aisling upon his arm. The horse ambled on his other side and the only sound was birdsong and the soft thud of hooves on the dirt path.

He stole a glance at Aisling. She hadn't bothered putting her bonnet back on, a scandalous oversight he was more than pleased by, for he could see her beautiful profile unhindered.

"Why were you so horrified to see me?" he asked, unable to put the question off a moment longer.

She gave him a scathing glance that might have provoked him if he wasn't so desperate to know the answer.

"Why?" he persisted.

A scowl tugged her eyebrows together, and he swore he would do anything to stop that being such a well-used expression. Aisling ought never be so worried and anxious and cross. She should have more reason to smile than to frown. He wanted very much to give her that.

"Aisling, please," he said, frustrated. "Won't you give me something? I only want to help you. I know... *I know* there can be nothing between us. You needn't worry that I'm going to try to seduce you or… or court you. I know I've not the least right to do so, even if I wanted to."

There was too much regret in those last words, but it was too late to take them back.

She was watching him now, those dark eyes so unfathomable.

"I don't want to trust you," she said, with such obvious honesty that his heart ached. Who had hurt her so badly to give her such a terror of putting her trust in anyone, or any man, at least?

"I know," he said, keeping his voice gentle. "But I wouldn't ever betray your trust."

Aisling stared at him for a long moment before looking away. "I've heard that before."

Sylvester nodded, unsurprised. "Your mother asked me to find out what is troubling you," he said, knowing it was a risk. "Your parents are worried about you. They know something is wrong."

She stopped in her tracks. "Mama… Mama asked *you*?" she said, staring at him in disbelief.

Sylvester nodded. "You cannot be any more shocked than I am, but she said she trusted me."

Aisling gasped and dropped his arm, taking a step back.

Sylvester quickly tethered the horse. They were on the edge of the woodland now, fields opening up before them, and the enormous castle dominated the landscape. How could he have been so damned close to it and not have known?

"Let me help you," he said, holding out his hands to her. "Talk to me."

"You cannot help," she said, her voice calm, resigned. "No one can help. There is nothing to help with. What is done cannot be undone, and some actions have far-reaching consequences, a price that must be paid. I accept that. I accepted that a long time ago."

"Well, I don't," he said, angry now. He took her hands and held on, trying to give her his assurance, his will to fight whatever was smothering the life from her. "You are suffering. I can see it, your family can see it. Hell, even that… that strange woman back there can see it. Stop running from it, Aisling. Stop running from me."

She shook her head and tugged her hands free. To his misery, he saw a tear overspill and fall, quickly followed by another. "I cannot. I am sorry. Please… Please don't follow me…."

He watched as she ran from him again, unable to follow her when she had forbidden it, powerless to help her if she would not let him in. What the devil was he to do now?

Chapter 10

I know what you did.

—Sent to Lady Aisling Baxter from an anonymous correspondent.

29th June 1841, Trevick Castle, Warwickshire.

"A party?"

Sylvester looked across the breakfast table to Aisling, who was white as a sheet and had exclaimed the words with the same enthusiasm as she might have announced, 'a plague of frogs?' Her mother nodded, avoiding Sylvester's eye. The countess appeared tranquil enough on the surface, but Sylvester could see the death grip she had on her teacup, and she risked snapping the handle if she didn't have a care. It was only the three of them for the moment, for none of the others were early risers. Aisling stared at her mama, her expression one of horror.

"Yes, dearest," Lady Trevick said, and Sylvester had the impression she was steeling herself for her daughter's response. "In two days. I know it's a lot of bother and upheaval, but it is expected of me to entertain, you might remember. Plus, it means employment for the locals and money spent on goods."

"Yes, yes, I know all that," Aisling said impatiently. "But you usually give your bigger parties during the winter months, when we are in town. You had dozens of entertainments this year. Isn't that enough? Why a summer one too?"

"For that reason. I've not done one for some time and now I mean to make amends. I think it is time you stopped using the summer to hide yourself away, too. Don't you, darling?"

There was a gentle yet implacable tone to the countess' voice that led Sylvester to believe she had not entertained during the summer months because of Aisling, because of this reaction.

"But so soon! You didn't even tell me you'd sent the invitations out. You must have been planning this for weeks, and—"

"And I didn't want you to worry about it," the countess cut in, her voice a mixture of sadness and frustration. "Whenever I mention a summer ball, you have a million reasons why I shouldn't hold one, yet you never tell me the real reason, Aisling. Tell me now, and I'll cancel it."

Aisling got to her feet, though they had only just sat down to breakfast. She looked ill.

"Oh, Aisling. Don't run off, you've not eaten a thing," the countess said desperately, gesturing to the untouched plate before her daughter. "Please, darling. Won't you talk to me?"

"I'm not hungry," Aisling said. "If you'll excuse me."

She hurried away, and the countess set down her teacup with trembling hands. She turned back to Sylvester, pleading in her eyes.

Sylvester hesitated and then snatched up a couple of slices of plum cake and wrapped them in a napkin before getting to his feet.

"Good luck," the countess said, giving him a sad smile as he hurried after Aisling.

She moved fast, he'd give her that. She was already outside when he caught up with her.

"Wait. Take this, at least."

She turned, frowning at him as he held out the napkin.

"If you're going to run away, you ought not do it on an empty stomach," he said, handing her the cake.

She unwrapped the napkin and sighed as she saw the cake. He watched as she wrapped it back up again. "Thank you, but I'm not running away."

"Yes, you are. You always run away. You run away from me, from parties, from life. Is that all there is for you now? Running and hiding?"

Irritation sparked in her eyes and Sylvester steeled his nerve.

"I never took you for a coward, my lady."

"I am *not* running away," she whispered, though he did not mistake the lack of volume for a lack of anger. Oh, she was furious with him. "And you know nothing about it."

"Then why not tell me?"

She laughed then, shaking her head. "Perhaps I should. Perhaps I should tell you everything, because if I did, you'd leave. You'd not be able to get away fast enough," she said bitterly, sneering at him, though her angry bravado only made his heart hurt.

"Is that why you don't want to tell me, because you think I'll leave? I wouldn't. I'm not such a feeble creature. Why not trust me?"

She stared at him, and he sensed her desire to do so, to throw caution to the wind and give him the truth.

"Aisling," he whispered, reaching out to touch her cheek but stopping himself from touching her. Her friend, he reminded himself. His hand fell and it was he who jolted in surprise when she took it, holding it to her face.

Her eyes fluttered shut, and she leaned into his caress. Sylvester stepped closer, savouring the feel of her skin beneath his fingers. *Please*, he begged silently, wishing he could carry the pain of whatever it was for her. He longed to pull her into his arms, to hold her and promise her he would look after her, that he would protect her and never let her go, that he would let no one hurt her ever again. That was not his right, though. All he could do was try to be her friend, her confidant. If only she would let him.

"I'm not who you think I am," she said, her eyes still closed. "You knew that from the start."

"Yes."

Her eyes opened and the pain there stole his breath. She nodded, and a tear slipped down her cheek.

"You were right. I'm not nice, sweet, shy Lady Aisling. I'm not nice at all. That's what you could see, isn't it? You knew it was a lie."

"What? *No!* No, that's not… I didn't see that at all. Only that you were hiding, love. Please…."

She shook her head, and her voice trembled as she let go of his hand and moved away from him. "I'm a bad person, and I've made dreadful mistakes. I… I did a terrible thing, and now I must pay for that, and that means being alone. That means not dragging anyone else into the mess I made. I'm sorry, Sylvester," she whispered. "I wish… I wish I could be what you want me to be."

"Aisling!" He reached for her, but she shook her head again, the look in her eyes forbidding him to follow, though he took a step towards her.

"Leave me alone, Mr Cootes," she said, and her voice was harder now, colder.

Sylvester cursed, watching her go as frustration and regret sat in his belly like a great lump of ice.

"I'm not letting you do this," he muttered to himself as she disappeared into the garden. "I'm not giving up on you. Even if you've given up on yourself."

Sylvester was determined to get some answers, but during the following days, Aisling avoided him like the plague, only appearing for dinner when he could not question her. At night he sat up, watching from his bedroom window. He didn't know what made him do it, but he felt certain he was right. At Christmas, he had seen Aisling leave Rowsley House in the dead of night, all alone, and eventually, she would do it again here. Why he was so certain he could not say, but that certainty sat in his guts like a lump of lead and would not let him sleep. Had she been meeting a lover? Was the man so unsuitable they only met in secret? Was he married? The questions circled his mind and, even though he knew it was jealousy that fuelled them, he could not fathom why she would creep about alone at night. He told himself he was being ridiculous and wasting a good night's sleep for no reason, but still he persisted. No matter how he reasoned with himself, he could not let himself rest, even though the castle was huge, and he could only look out over a small portion of the grounds. The chances of him seeing her leave were slim, even if he was right.

Aisling was hiding, though, and unless he discovered something solid that she could not deny, she would keep her secrets locked up tight and he could never help her.

It was well after one in the morning on the second night when movement caught his eye. If he'd not been on the lookout, he might have thought he'd seen a ghost, not that he believed in such nonsense. Yet the ethereal figure glided silently beneath the waning moon, her white nightgown catching the dim silver light as she hurried through the garden.

Sylvester stood, watching the path she took carefully, before hurrying outside and following.

She knew it was a risk with Sylvester in the house. He was too determined to play knight in shining armour. Aisling could feel his gaze upon her, sense his frustration and his desire to help. That much, she believed. How could she not when his sincerity shone from him? Yet he was a man, and he would not understand. Men never did. Even Biddy allowed that much, and she liked Sylvester. Aisling liked him, too. She liked him too much, liked bickering with him, and she wished he would leave almost as much as she wanted him to stay. There was no time for wishing and daydreams now, though. Mama had sent out the invitations weeks ago. The party was tomorrow, and now there was a prickling of danger beneath her skin. *He* would come. Even though he wasn't invited, he would come, and he would accuse her in public and there would be a great scandal, for she could not tell a barefaced lie. Mama and Papa would be shamed, and poor darling Cara would be ruined, and the family caught up in a scandal so profound it would take generations to live it down.

Why now? Why, after so many years, had that letter arrived? If someone knew what she'd done, why had it taken them so long to act upon the knowledge? Though she had no reason for certainty, instinct told her who her accuser was, and it was bad. Very, very bad. He would make her pay, of that she had no doubt.

There was no other choice. The moon was waning, and she must do it now or lose her chance.

Biddy had always taught her such work was best done out of doors, with the earth beneath your feet and nothing between you and the moon. Which was a pity, as it would be so much easier to do it in the privacy of her room, but she was too desperate to take a chance.

Though the day had been unseasonably hot, the night was chilly, more so down by the river's edge, where a sharp breeze caught at the thin cotton of Aisling's nightgown and made the hair on the back of her neck stand on end. Ignoring it, she got to her knees, facing east, and laid out a velvet cloth embroidered around the edges with gold thread. A large jar of salt came next. Aisling poured the salt and drew a circle counter clockwise around her. In her mind, she imagined a wall encircling her, protecting her from harm. She took four coloured candles from the small cloth bag she carried, setting them around the cloth and lighting them reverently, inviting each element into the circle. She let out a breath of relief, comforted by this familiar part of the ritual. In the centre, she placed a small saucer and then removed the black candle from the bag. Working carefully, she scratched the ruis and the straif runes into the base of the candle, and then wrote a name in the wax from the bottom of the candle, working towards the wick.

The crack of a twig snapping had Aisling sitting up with a gasp, her eyes searching the darkness. Far off, she heard the dreadful scream of a fox and shivered. She waited, her heart thudding, and the candle flames guttered in the breeze, but all was still again. Aisling fumbled in the cloth bag, hands trembling as they closed upon a tiny glass bottle. She pulled out the little cork stopper and poured a few drops of oil into her hands. The scent of spices and pepper warmed her, calming her nerves as she anointed the candle and set it down on the saucer.

Aisling took a moment to breathe, to remind herself of her intentions. She would cause no harm, not this time. This time, she only wanted to keep him away, to protect herself and her family. Focusing on her desire, she opened her eyes and lit the candle. She watched it take, watched the first drops of wax liquefy as the flame took hold.

Aisling closed her eyes again and inhaled deeply. She brought to mind the face of the man she did not want here, never wanted to see anywhere near her or her family.

"With the power of the elements living in me, your presence here will never be. No more harm will befall my blood. Get thee gone, be out of my sight, leave me in peace alone in the light. I name thee to banish thee—"

"Aisling!" Her name struck the night, smashing into her consciousness like a hammer breaking glass, and Aisling jolted in shock. Eyes flying open, she blinked, dazed and afraid, to see

Sylvester standing over her. He reached for her, hauling her up by her arms, oversetting the candle so that the velvet cloth caught the flame.

"*No*!" she cried desperately. "No! Oh, no, what have you done?"

She stumbled away from him, staring at the broken circle in horror.

"What the devil is this?" Sylvester demanded, glaring at the salt circle, at the candles, at her.

Aisling stared at him, wishing that for once in her life she could put her trust in a man who was not her kin, and not be disappointed. The energy that had fuelled her with hope, with this one chance to keep her secrets safe, drained away, leaving her hollow and fragile as glass. She swayed and her knees gave out, taking her to the floor. Her breath caught on a sob, and she tried to swallow it down, tried to hold it inside like she had held everything inside for such a long time, but she had no resources left, nothing left with which to fight it. The tears came then, and she could not deny them any longer. They had waited for too long.

"Aisling?"

Distantly, she heard him speak her name and admitted surprise that he had not fled from her, from what he had seen. Perhaps he would call a magistrate, have her taken up for witchcraft. They might not hang women for such crimes any longer, but it would still cause an uproar. There were still laws against it.

Strong arms gathered her up, and she only realised she was shivering with cold and distress as warmth enveloped her. He wrapped his coat about her and pulled her into his lap, rocking her like a child as she wept.

"All will be well," he murmured.

Gently, he wiped her eyes and cheeks with a handkerchief before pressing it into her hand. He sat stroking her hair, offering her comfort and security, though she did not know how long it would last. He was kind. She believed that of him now. Perhaps he was just offering her a moment of respite before everything fell apart.

"Nothing will ever be well again," she said dully, remembering her ruined spell, the invitations sent. The desperate inevitability of it all.

Sylvester held her, his arms a temporary shelter from the trouble about to rain down upon her. The promise of that shelter rang in his voice, his words, but she knew it could not protect her for long. "I don't understand, but you are going to explain it to me and whatever it is, I will help you. I promise, Aisling. I will do anything I can to protect you, but you are going to have to trust me. I always keep my promises, darling. Always."

She looked up at him then, blinking away tears and staring into his hazel eyes. Such sincerity dwelled there that her heart ached. She ought to have believed him earlier, but she'd not known how. Perhaps that made her a fool all over again. A fool who had put her trust in a wicked man and turned a good one away.

"What were you doing, love?" The words were tender, his expression calm, not full of suspicion or leaping to conclusions, but ready to listen to her.

"A… A b-banishing spell," she admitted, swallowing down a fresh burst of tears.

"Christ, you could have just asked me to leave," he said, hurt shining in his eyes.

"*No*! Oh, no, not you. I wouldn't… I-I don't want you to go," she said, clutching his lapels tight with both hands. "Not anymore."

He smiled at that, a crooked, one-sided smile that made him look boyish and pleased with himself. "You don't?"

Aisling shook her head and then laid it back against his shoulder. It was a nice place to be, in his arms. It felt safe, even if that safety was a lie. Sylvester was a good man, but when he discovered the truth, he would not want her. She could not blame him for that.

“Who then?” he asked, his arms tightening about her. “Who is it that frightens you so badly you turn to… to black magic?”

“It was not black magic!” she said, sitting up and staring at him. But she could not protest too hard, nor pretend she was innocent and had done no harm. “You think me a fool. You think it’s all a lot of nonsense. Eye of newt and bat wings. Don’t you?”

“I don’t understand it,” he admitted. “But I don’t think you are a fool. I do need you to explain it to me, though. All of it. From the beginning.”

“That might take some time,” she said with a weary sigh.

“We have all night,” he said, tightening his hold upon her. “And I’m not going anywhere.”

She leant into his warmth, resigned now. The circle was broken, her spell ruined, and the last night of the waning moon was drifting into morning. “I’m a witch,” she said, finding a little relief in admitting it.

“Biddy taught you?” he guessed, sounding remarkably sanguine about such a revelation.

She nodded. “Yes. Since I was just a little girl. You must not blame Biddy and accuse her of bewitching me, or some such nonsense, for it was the other way about.”

Sylvester took her hand, twining their fingers together.

“I don’t remember saying I was going to accuse anyone of anything,” he said mildly, and Aisling sighed.

“No. You didn’t, did you? Why aren’t you horrified and running away in disgust? Why are you still here?”

"I think you know why," he said, though he didn't meet her eyes.

Aisling pressed her lips to his cheek and he turned, staring at her with surprise.

"I'll never wash again," he said, grinning.

Despite everything, she smiled, feeling a swell of affection for the daft creature. He was still here. He hadn't abandoned her. *Yet,* murmured a spiteful voice in her head.

"So, Biddy…?"

Aisling nodded. "I saw her casting a circle, much as I was doing here, and she had no choice but to teach me, for I pestered and badgered her for weeks on end until she gave in."

"Your parents?"

She shook her head. "No one else knows."

He watched her steadily, and she sighed, knowing she must try to explain. "Mama knows I have knowledge of herbs and medicine, as she does, but she has never been interested in more than that. But I am. Women have so little power, Sylvester, but magic, that is ours. It's old knowledge, passed from generation to generation and it is nothing to be afraid of. It's worked for the good of all. I'm very good with herbs, medicinals. People come to Mama and to me as well as to Biddy for cures. I do good work with my skills usually, except… except it can be misused. I misused it because I was angry and afraid. I did a terrible thing and laid a curse, and I must pay for that. There is always a price. I wouldn't care if it was me alone who would suffer, but it won't be."

"So, this curse, it was against the man you were trying to keep away from here?"

Aisling plucked fretfully at the lace edging the sleeve of her nightgown. Fear stirred in her belly. If she told him he would know everything, know the worst thing about her, and what could a man do with such knowledge? She knew what some men would do, what one man had tried to do, to his cost. Sylvester said nothing. He just waited patiently, giving her time. She looked up to find he was watching her.

"Trust me," he said, cupping her cheek with one hand.

Oh, she loved his big hands, so warm and capable, and she turned into his touch, pressing a kiss to his palm.

"I won't let you down, Aisling. I promise."

She swallowed. "Very well, but it isn't about letting me down, Sylvester. It's about what I have done, and what you will think of me when I have told you. I could not blame you if you are disgusted, if you want to leave me to reap what I have sown. It's justice, after all."

"Let me make that decision for myself, love, eh?" he suggested, though she could see disquiet in his expression.

So be it.

Chapter 11

Cher Monsieur,

Have you been invited to Trevick? I hope so, for it seems an age since I saw you last. I bumped into Mr Godwin – quite literally – last week at a garden party. He nearly knocked me off my feet, though he was so mortified I could not be cross with him. I believe he was flustered as he was in pursuit of Lady Millicent, and she had a bevy of admirers about her, all demanding her attention. Personally, I thought none of them could hold a candle to Mr Godwin for he is such a kind man and so sweet natured. He looked very fine. Your hand at work, it appears. He sang your praises most enthusiastically. Indeed, I believe he has put you on a pedestal and means to do all in his power to make you proud of him.

— Excerpt of a letter from Miss Evie Knight (daughter of Lady Helena and Mr Gabriel Knight) to Louis César de Montluc, Comte de Villen.

30th June 1841, Heart's Folly, Sussex.

Louis sighed and folded the letter, putting it back in the pile before taking up another. He poured himself another drink and sat back, letter in hand, rereading, though he knew well enough what it said.

> *Oh, you'll never guess. I had my first proposal of marriage yesterday! Mr Cooper, of whom I spoke to you, asked to speak to Papa. It surprised me that Papa agreed to it, except I believe he knew I would turn the fellow down and thought I ought to speak to him myself. Honestly, it was mortifying. The poor man blushed and stammered so. I don't know which of us was the most embarrassed. I almost accepted him just to make it stop.*
>
> *I think I let him down gently. I hope he doesn't hate me now, but I only told him the truth, though I fear that I might have left him room to hope, which may not have been a kindness. I am far from ready to think of marrying anyone, though. I want to have some fun before I tie myself to a husband and a household. Goodness, how flighty I sound, but you know that is not what I mean. I just don't want things to change. Not yet.*

He stared at the words, wondering if he ought to be pleased by them or to despair. She did not want things to change. What did she mean by that? It was obvious she was not ready to marry. He wasn't a fool, and he meant to give her the time she needed, but….

Anxiety gnawed at his heart. Did she mean she did not wish for him to stop being her friend, because if she married another, their friendship would be over? Any husband would forbid her from such a close relationship with a man like him, even if he could bear to see her again if she married someone else. *Jamais!*

Never! That would never happen. If she did not marry him…. Fear made his guts clench, twisting into a knot and making him want to retch. He would have to go away, far away, and… and he did not know what. It wouldn't matter where he went or what happened to him if he couldn't keep Evie in his life. It would all be over. His one hope for the future snuffed out.

Merde.

He sat with his head in his hands, staring down at the words she had written without seeing them.

"Look what the cat dragged in."

Barnaby's cheerful voice snapped Louis out of his melancholy reverie, and he looked up to see the man himself guiding Lord Vane through the door. His lordship swayed gently, looking rather the worse for wear.

"Villen," he said, regarding Louis blearily. "Dreadful imposition. Throw me out if you want. Oh, er, and good evening."

Louis glanced up at the timepiece on the mantelpiece. "Good morning."

"Figured you'd still be awake. Don't you ever sleep?" Barnaby asked, eyeing the stack of letters on the table in front of him. Silently, Louis gathered them up and tied the ribbon back in place. "From a sweetheart?" Barnaby asked with interest.

Louis shot him a glance that made him quail, and Barnaby shook his head.

"No, no. Quite. None of my business." He moved closer to Louis and lowered his voice. "You don't mind if Maxwell here stays for a few days, do you? He seems a bit out of sorts. I know some fellows get blue devilled when in their cups, but he was maundering on about something or other and I didn't like to leave him alone. Not after… well, you know." Barnaby eyed Lord Vane with concern. The man had collapsed in the nearest chair, his long limbs arranged in an indolent sprawl, his heavy-lidded gaze fixed bleakly on the empty fireplace.

"You are too tender-hearted, Barnaby. That's your trouble, but no, I don't mind. There's room enough."

"Knew you'd say so," Barnaby said, beaming at him. "Told him so, too, but he didn't like to impose. Didn't have anywhere else though and the Fighting Cocks was full, and I wouldn't let a dog stay at The George. Frightful place. Took me an age to persuade him to come, though."

A soft snore emanated from their sleeping guest.

"He seems to have come to terms with it," Louis said dryly.

Barnaby stared at the sleeping earl with concern. "Fellow seems done in to me. I'd say he's been burning the candle at both ends, as he was always a devil for drinking and gambling, but I ain't seen him about at parties and the like hardly at all, and neither has anyone else from what I can gather. He just seemed a bit worn about the edges, if you get my drift."

Louis nodded, knowing exactly what Barnaby meant, for he felt the same himself, brittle and worn too thin, so that the tiniest spark would reduce him to ash in a matter of moments.

"So, how do you like your new house?" Barnaby asked, helping himself to a drink. "It's mighty grand, yet cosy, too, comfortable. Must have cost you a pretty penny to set it to rights. Last I heard, it was empty and had been for years."

"I like it very well," Louis replied as Barnaby came and sat at the table with him.

He was more than pleased with the house, though he had not bought it for him alone. If he were honest, he'd likely have bought it sight unseen once he'd discovered the house's name was Heart's Folly, but he'd never admit that to another living soul. Lord, but he was becoming dismally sentimental.

Evie did not know that he owned this place in Sussex yet, which would place her close to her parents, but not so close they could pop in unannounced at a moment's notice. It was a charming property, full of history, and in remarkably good repair, considering the previous owners had abandoned it, as Barnaby had said. Evie would love it, that much he was certain of. It would appeal to her romantic nature and love of history, and it was exceedingly pretty, quintessentially English.

For a moment, the image of her here diverted him, capturing his imagination, and it took him considerable effort to pay attention to Barnaby, who was speaking to him.

"When shall we go to Stratford then? There's the Trevick party, and Mrs Holland's garden party too. And we could spend a few days in Doncaster and have a flutter on the gee-gees."

"A what on the *what*?" Louis asked, frowning.

Barnaby laughed at his confusion. "Oh, sorry. Sometimes I forget you're French. A flutter on the gee-gees—a bet on the horses."

"*Mon Dieu,* sometimes your grasp of the English language makes my head hurt," Louis grumbled.

"Trevick," muttered a thick voice, and they looked over to see Lord Vane had woken up and was staring at them blearily. "I'm going to Trevick. Got a little place down there. Stay with me if you like."

"Oh, capital," Barnaby said with a grin. "Well, ain't that serendipity? Is that the word I want?" he mused, looking thoughtful.

Vane began snoring again.

"I believe it is," Louis replied, picking up his letters with care. "And I believe we shall remove to Stratford as soon as our house guest has recovered enough to make the journey without vomiting in the carriage. Good night, Barnaby, and please do not awaken me at some ungodly hour of the morning like you did today."

"It was half past ten," Barnaby protested with a laugh. "But I suppose you don't sleep until the sun's up, so I shall leave you be until midday. Word of honour."

"You are a prince among men, *mon ami*," Louis assured him, and took himself off to write his reply to Evie in private.

Sylvester was waiting for Aisling to explain herself, and though she just wanted to sit here with him all night, enjoying the feel of his muscular arms holding her close, that was a fantasy. There was to be no more hiding. Not from him.

She took a deep breath. "We used to have a big summer house party every year. And every year before I came out, I used to beg Mama and Papa to let me attend the ball. Every year I got the same answer: 'not until you are out in society.' Mama was determined that I have the freedom to grow up without thinking about husbands and marriage, and so she said I must wait until I was eighteen. She said that was time enough."

"But you were impatient," Sylvester guessed.

She smiled, nodding. "I was."

"What happened?"

Aisling stared down at the handkerchief he'd given her and traced the embroidered initials, SC. It was a boring design, and she wondered if he would like it if she made him some new ones. She smoothed out the rumpled cotton and folded it neatly. "We had a lot of guests staying at the castle in the weeks leading up to the ball. I was excited because it was nearly my sixteenth birthday, and I was determined that everyone should see how grown up I was. I hoped then Mama's guests might suggest I come out earlier than planned." She hesitated, glancing up at him.,

"There was a young man?" he prompted, for it was not so terribly hard to guess that much, was it?

Somehow that made it even more depressing, that she had done what so many foolish girls had done before and would continue to do until the end of time.

Aisling nodded. "I was utterly dazzled. He was eight years older than me and dreadfully handsome, quite unlike anyone I had ever met. I thought him dreadfully sophisticated and couldn't believe such a fine man would seek me out when there were so many beautiful women, and he could have had any one of them. He was always moving, full of energy, and he could not bear to sit still for a moment. I was enchanted by his lively mind, the speed with which he leapt from subject to subject and the interest he showed in everything. Especially in me. It was dizzying."

"You fancied yourself in love with him."

His voice was gentle, and Aisling gave a soft huff of laughter. "I was unforgivably naïve. My word, if only I could go back and give myself a hard shake and the benefit of what I know now. Mama had taught me the rules, as had my governesses. I'd had plenty of lessons instructing me on the proper behaviour for a lady. How not to get myself into situations I could not handle. Harleston and Papa had warned me, too, but I thought I knew better. I thought I was in love and that he loved me, that he would never hurt me. We met in secret, and he was so sweet, holding my hand and reading me poetry, telling me how lovely I was. He intimated that he wanted to speak to Papa after the ball and I assumed he would offer for me. In my head, I had our future all planned out, our honeymoon and where we would live. He knew I wasn't allowed to go to the ball, and so when he asked me to sneak out and meet him, I agreed, fool that I was."

"You were fifteen, Aisling. A child," Sylvester said, tucking a lock of hair back behind her ear. "Don't be so hard on yourself."

Aisling could not respond to his kindness, for she would cry and not finish what she had begun. "I put on my prettiest dress and my favourite perfume and made my way down here, to the riverside. He was waiting for me and at first it was everything I had dreamed it would be. He had set out a picnic blanket with candles all around it, and he'd brought champagne. I felt so sophisticated, sitting in the moonlight and drinking champagne with a handsome man who loved me wildly."

Aisling stopped, not wanting to say the rest, not wanting to speak the words that she had told no one before. Biddy knew the truth. Aisling had run to her afterwards, too ashamed to face anyone else, and she had guessed the next part. Aisling had never had to say it.

"What happened?"

There was a note to Sylvester's voice that she could not judge. It was anger, undoubtedly, but whether for her stupidity or for the man who had taken advantage of her, she could not be certain.

"I drank far too much champagne. He kept filling my glass, and I didn't protest, and then he kissed me. He kept kissing me and… and I let him…. I was aware it was going too far, and I asked him to stop, but he said I was a tease, that he'd tell everyone I'd led him on. He said there would be a dreadful scandal."

Aisling swallowed hard as nausea churned in her stomach.

"I had no choice then. I knew my parents would be devastated, that it would ruin Cara's chances of making a good match. I told myself to endure it, that it would be over and I need never see him again, but then he told me I must meet him again the next night. His voice was cold, and he treated me like I was nothing, like I was of no importance to him. I didn't understand why he was treating me so coldly, and I started to cry, but he just got angry with me, and I felt so stupid. When I told him I wouldn't meet him, he said if I didn't, he'd tell my parents I was a little slut. He said I was his whore now, and he'd use me as and when he wanted, and if I didn't let him, he'd tell everyone about me, about how easy I'd been. He said I'd led him on, and what had I expected to happen if I came down here alone with him?"

Her voice quavered, and she stopped talking. She would not allow herself to cry any more this night. She'd been a stupid little fool, and that was her own doing.

Sylvester was silent, his body stiff and unyielding, and Aisling glanced up at him uncertainly.

"I'm sorry," she said.

His dark eyes met hers, and she had the sensation he was wrenching himself from some far-off place to return to her. He swallowed, and when he spoke, his voice was rough and not entirely steady.

"Who?" he asked, that one word containing a world of rage. "You don't need to be sorry, Aisling, not for anything. He was a grown man, and you were innocent. He took advantage, and for that I'll make him sorry he was ever born. Tell me who it is. Give me the name of the bastard who hurt you, and I will kill him."

Aisling blinked back tears, struggling to get the words out, forcing her confession out into the open so that he might understand just how bad this truly was. "You c-can't do that."

"I can and I bloody will!" he said, the words no less determined by how quietly he spoke them.

"*No*!" Tears slipped down her cheeks, and Aisling shook her head, wishing it had been Sylvester she'd met that summer, wishing she'd not been such a reckless little fool. "You can't kill him, Sylvester, b-because I already did."

His expression might have been amusing if it weren't so appalling. He looked stunned, truly horrified, and Aisling could not remain in his arms a moment longer, though she wanted to. She wanted to cling to him and beg him for his forgiveness for the wicked thing she'd done, but she could not ask that of him. He might have raged about killing the man, but he didn't mean it literally. Even if he did, it would have been a duel, an affair of honour with both combatants armed and ready to take their chances. It had not been like that for her. She had acted without thinking, and her opponent had not stood a chance.

Regret clawed at her heart, a ragged thing by now after so many years of shame and sorrow that she had fought so hard to hide from the world. She was always hiding, always pretending. God, but she was sick of it. But some truths were too terrible to face. Aisling scrambled up and away from him, desperate not to see the revulsion in his eyes, that awful moment when the scales fell and he saw her for what she truly was.

She ran then, not looking back, not stopping when he called her, pleaded with her to stay. Because he could not mean it, he could not forgive her, nor ever care for her now. Not after the vile thing she'd done, not after everything she had become. She was ruined, she was a murderess, and she was a liar too. Good God, she'd once told her friends she didn't have a violent bone in her body and kept a straight face. What kind of creature could kill a man and say such a thing? What man could find anything to love in a wicked woman like that?

Chapter 12

Vane,

You seem to think there is some choice in the matter. I am afraid I must disabuse you of that notion. Get me what I want, or your private affairs will not remain private for much longer, and don't get it into your head to call me out. You know which of us is the better shot. I should hate to kill you, old friend.

— Excerpt of a letter from The Most Hon'ble Ciarán St Just, The Marquess of Kilbane to The Right Hon'ble Maxwell Drake, The Earl of Vane.

The early hours of the morning 30th June 1841, Trevick Castle, Warwickshire.

"Aisling!"

Sylvester pitched his voice low as they were close to the castle here, but he could see no sign of her. The gardens were a maze of paths designed to lead visitors on a meandering tour of the beautiful grounds, and Aisling clearly knew every inch of them, whereas Sylvester was quite literally in the dark. The thin sliver of moonlight had disappeared behind a thick blanket of cloud, and he could barely see his hand in front of his face.

He was desperate to see her, to reassure her he was still on her side. Her words had shocked him, there was no question of that. Yet somehow he still could not quite believe she spoke the truth, nor believe her capable of killing a man no matter how badly he had treated her. And if it really was true, *how* had she killed a grown man? And who the devil had it been? Surely someone would have noticed a dead man? Try as he might, Sylvester could not remember a young man going missing or dying in strange circumstances. Had she made it look like an accident? Had it happened that very night, in the heat of the moment? Or had she planned his demise? The questions circled his mind, and he felt he would go mad if she did not explain the rest.

As for her being a witch, well, he did not believe in magic. That was nothing more than a fanciful idea, but he would never insult her by saying it so brutally. He understood why she would want to believe it, why any woman would want a means to take control of her own life when there was no other option open to her. He was willing to believe such women had a knowledge of herbal law and natural remedies that ought to be respected, too, but more than that? No.

Finally, and after nearly falling on his face tripping over a huge terracotta plant pot, he made it back to the castle. There was still no sign of Aisling, though, and no matter how much he wanted to see her, to reassure her he meant to help her, he could hardly go to her room in the middle of the night and demand to see her. There was nothing for him to do but wait until morning and try to get her alone. Frustration and worry created an unhappy knot in his guts, but there was no other option. Reluctantly, Sylvester made his way back to his room, knowing he would not sleep a wink… not until he knew Aisling was safe and had put her trust in him.

Aisling leaned back against her bedroom door, fighting for breath, heart thudding so hard her ears were full of the rush of blood thrumming through her. She felt sick and dizzy. She slid to the floor and put her head on her arms. Oh, what was she to do?

I know what you did.

The words circled in her head, and a cold sweat prickled down her back. There was nothing for it. She must deal with this man, face what was coming head on, and do whatever she could to protect her family. The universe wanted its pound of flesh for granting her curse, and she must pay the price.

For a moment, she allowed herself to remember the comfort of Sylvester's arms around her, his anger on her behalf, and his promise to protect her. She wanted to pretend he still meant that now, even after discovering just how wicked she had been, but she would no longer live a lie. She had gone through the past years pretending that dreadful night hadn't happened, and hiding the awful consequences that had left a stain upon her soul. No longer. From now on she would face the truth only… only she did not think she could face Sylvester again. Not yet.

The ball was tomorrow night. She could avoid him for that long if she pretended she was unwell. It wasn't that unusual for her to stay with Biddy if she was poorly, and Mama knew the stress of the upcoming ball could make her ill. Biddy was a healer and Aisling's old nurse, and everyone knew how close they were. No one would think it peculiar if she spent the day there, and only Sylvester would know she was avoiding him. After she had faced her accuser and discovered what he wanted from her, she would tell Sylvester the rest and even he would agree there was nothing he could do to help her, assuming he still wanted to.

Then she would go away. She would hide herself somewhere her actions could not hurt her family or her friends. It wouldn't be so bad, she assured herself. She had been hiding ever since that night, anyway. A fresh start might do her good. She could reinvent herself, change her name…. A sob rose in her throat as she realised she was planning to tell more lies. So much for facing the truth.

God, but she was a coward. But how could she face the truth without hurting her family? How could she live with what she had done? But no matter how many times she asked herself that question, she never found an answer.

30th June 1841, on the road to Chessett House, Warwickshire.

Maxwell Drake, Earl of Vane, swallowed hard as the carriage rolled over a rut in the road and his stomach lurched. *Oh, God.* He would *not* puke his guts up in front of the comte. Too humiliating. Not that he was a stranger to humiliation, or to being entirely helpless and at the mercy of someone who owed you nothing and thought you were a waste of space. They'd not been wrong though, and Maxwell had done everything in his power to make amends for the harm he'd done. He'd had good cause to take a long look at his life and re-evaluate what was important. Getting murdered would do that to a fellow.

He ought to be dead. That he wasn't was damn near miraculous and he knew he had much to be grateful for. Mending his ways had included an end to womanising, gambling, and generally being a despicable arsehole. It had also included not getting off his head drunk. He'd been doing well, too, considering. But when Barnaby Godwin had found him, he'd been the wrong side of half a bottle of brandy and mired in melancholy.

"Not much farther now," Barnaby said cheerfully, and Maxwell smothered an uncharitable urge to tell him to shut up because he'd said the same thing an hour ago when they'd got off the train. It wasn't Barnaby's fault he'd allowed the past to catch up with him, to remind him what a disgusting human being he'd been until he was so wretched he'd fallen off the damned wagon. None of it was Barnaby's fault, nor anyone else's but his own.

Finally—praise be to God—the carriage rocked to a stop outside of his home. Chessett House was one of the smaller properties he owned, but it had become his favourite. A higgledy-piggledy Tudor building, the main and oldest part of the property was a two-storey high square block with a later L-shaped addition. The interior was splendid, designed with no expense spared, and yet it conveyed a homely, comfortable welcome in a way that none of the other grand houses he could claim as home did.

"Well," Barnaby said, staring about him. "I say, Maxwell. This *is* charming. Not at all what I was expecting, if you'll forgive me for saying so."

Maxwell winced inwardly, knowing exactly what Barnaby meant. In years past, he'd been a damned snob and ignored this lovely little gem of a house, preferring to spend his time at Vane Hall. That was a great mausoleum of a place which did the job of impressing visitors with its opulence and grandeur, whilst being impossible to heat and akin to living in a museum exhibit.

The comte nodded in agreement. "Barnaby is right. *C'est charmant,* Vane. Really, most beautiful."

Maxwell smiled, experiencing an unexpected sense of pleasure at his friends' enthusiasm. Not that they were his friends. They didn't know him. He didn't *have* friends, though that was something else he was working on. Perhaps one day, he might call them so if he didn't mess everything up.

"Please, call me Maxwell," he offered the comte, hoping the fellow might warm to him a bit more if he was less formal. "There's no ceremony here at Chessett House. I like to keep things simple. Someone once told me I needed to keep my feet on the ground and stop being such a pompous twat, or I'd get my arse burned by the sun. I've been trying to keep that in mind."

Both men stared at him in surprise and Maxwell wished he'd kept that particular bit of advice to himself. Then Barnaby gave a snort of laughter.

"Close friend was it?" he asked mildly.

The comte's lips twitched. "Only a close friend *could* say such a thing, I believe. And do call me Louis, if we are to relieve ourselves of the formalities."

Maxwell grinned, reassured. "Thank you. And, actually, more of a mentor than a friend, but it was sound advice, nonetheless. I did not behave well in years past and… I'm trying to put it behind me."

"If only it were that simple, my old friend."

A shadow fell over the entrance hall as a figure filled the doorway. Maxwell stiffened, recognising the slight Irish lilt softening the cut glass English accent all too well. He turned to see the figure of his oldest friend in the doorway. Except he and Ciarán St Just, the Marquess of Kilbane, had never been friends. They had drunk together, gambled together, cheated, whored, and caused havoc together until the world had learned to fear them, but they had never been friends.

"Gentlemen," Kilbane said, inclining his head towards Maxwell's guests, his strange violet eyes lighting with interest as they settled on Louis César. "Ah, and what fabulous good fortune befalls this weary traveller. As I live and breathe. If it isn't the angelic Comte de Villen. We meet again."

"My lord," Louis said politely. "You honour me."

"Oh, no. Not in the least, the honour is all mine. Like yourself, I consider myself a connoisseur and I have a great appreciation for beautiful things. The handsomest man on three continents, so society says. For once, I think they have the right of it. Sadly, I am considered too badly behaved to be beautiful. *I cheat at cards, you know,"* he added with a theatrical whisper.

Louis' lips twitched but he said nothing.

"Right ho, well. Perhaps we'll settle into our rooms, eh, Maxwell?" Barnaby said briskly, putting himself between Louis and Kilbane, though a fat lot of good that would do anyone if Kilbane decided to cause trouble. "Long journey and all that. Could do with forty winks before dinner, don't you think, Louis?"

"I do. Travel is so wearying, and dirty," Louis said, taking off his fine kid gloves and looking at them with distaste. "If you will excuse us, Maxwell, Lord Kilbane."

"Of course. Brandon!" Maxwell called for his butler. Brandon had been overseeing the unloading of their baggage, but thankfully the fellow returned with haste. "Show Mr Goodwin and Monsieur Le Comte to their rooms, please."

"And me, dearest Maxwell?" Kilbane murmured, a challenging glint in his eyes that boded ill, daring him to be anything less than civil. "Where are you going to put me?"

"Brandon, have Mrs Peterson make up another room for Lord Kilbane."

"At once, my lord," the man said, escorting Louis and Barnaby up the stairs, which left him alone with Kilbane.

The man lounged against the oak panelling, but his heavy-lidded gaze and indolent manner did not fool Maxwell. Kilbane appeared lazy, right up to the moment he struck, like a damned snake. He knew better than to let his guard down.

"Well, you have become a slippery fellow to nail down of late."

"I've been busy," Maxwell said with a shrug.

"Ah, yes. Busy polishing your halo. Did you actually die that night? For you have acquired a saintly aspect that I find most disturbing."

Maxwell met the man's eyes and did not look away. The only way to deal with Kilbane was to hold your nerve. The first sign of weakness, and he would find a way to exploit it.

"I am trying to make amends for my sins. That much is true. If you ever get close enough to meeting your maker, you may discover a desire for a second chance yourself, Ciarán. The sensation of your life blood oozing from your body on to the cold, hard ground has a marvellous way of focusing your attention on what's important, on what really has value."

Ciarán pursed his lips, looking bored as he tugged his gloves off and tossed them carelessly onto the table beside him. "It sounds dashed uncomfortable, I'll give you that, but really, Vane. Charitable works? Isn't that a little *de trop?* I adore a touch of drama and a delicious soupçon of irony, but really, your life is turning into some dull moral tale to be told to naughty children at bedtime. Surely the urge to do good has worn off by now?"

"Strangely, no," Maxwell replied, relieved to discover there was nothing Ciarán could do or say to tempt him back into his old ways. An even greater revelation was that he pitied Ciarán, for it would be hard to find a man who was more utterly alone in the world. He had no friends, no family, no one who would give a damn if he died, though there were plenty queuing up to help him on his way. He was not short of lovers, for he was handsome and wicked in equal measure and exuded a lethal charm that beguiled and entranced until you were entirely caught in his snares. But no one cared for him, no one trusted him, and with good reason.

Ciarán gave an impatient tsk of irritation. "Well, we both know it won't last. Eventually you will remember your soul is as black as pitch, for they tempered us in the same hellish furnace, you and I. But I can wait for your return to the fold. For now, I have other business. I do hope you have made arrangements as I requested."

"A request, was it?" Maxwell said darkly, wishing he knew what the hell the bastard was up to.

"Maxwell, do remember that I discovered your dirty little secret. I should hate for that to become common knowledge," Ciarán murmured. The light was fading outside and there was only one lamp lit in the hallway. It illuminated one side of Ciarán's face and glinted fiery sparks on the blue-black hair that curled about his face, making him look diabolically handsome, a creature from the depths of hell come to tempt mere mortals to sin.

"I'll kill you before I'll let you breathe a damned word, *old friend,"* Maxwell said, his voice low and threatening and meaning it.

Ciarán chuckled, pleased, and showing even white teeth. "Oh, I have missed you, Maxwell, and there's no need for such posturing. All I want is what I asked for, nothing more and nothing less. Do I have it?"

"Yes, damn you," Maxwell growled, hating that he had no other choice, and praying that whoever it was Ciarán had in his sights this time deserved what was coming to them.

Chapter 13

Miss Knight,

I shall be at the Trevick party and will look forward to seeing you there. For the next few days, Mr Godwin – whom you esteem so highly – and I are staying with Lord Vane at Chessett House. Mr Godwin also expresses a wish to lose some money at Doncaster. I shall oblige him, naturally.

Mr Godwin is generally flustered when in Lady Millicent's orbit, but you have the right of it. If she has the least bit of sense, she will ignore her prettier courtiers and the wealthy ones too. For Mr Godwin has that rarest of commodities, a kind and giving nature. Too many people mistake his kindness for foolishness, but I have seen enough of life to know the difference and value it for the rarity it is.

I wish he would not idolise me as he does however, but another disadvantage of being so open-hearted is to see the good in everyone. I hope he never has cause to regret such recklessness.

— Excerpt of a letter from Louis César de Montluc, Comte de Villen to Miss Evie Knight (daughter of Lady Helena and Mr Gabriel Knight).

1st July 1841, Biddy's Cottage, Trevick Castle Grounds, Warwickshire.

"Aisling!"

"You can stand there and shout until you're hoarse, young man, but you'll not see the child until she's ready to be seen." Biddy folded her arms, standing sentry by her front door.

Aisling had refused to see him since she'd run off last night and the ball was in a matter of hours. He did not think she was in any fit state to endure entertainments on a grand scale, and, if the preparations at the castle were anything to go on, it was indeed to be a lavish affair. He had to see her, to speak to her and reassure her—reassure himself—that things were not as dire as she thought. He still could not believe she had killed a man and, if she had, well, it had likely been an accident. Perhaps he had fallen and hit his head? That would explain there being no scandal or story about the murder of a young man. If so, her guilt was misplaced, and he could assure her of that… but it was an impossible task if she wouldn't even see him. By now Sylvester was beside himself with frustration and toyed with the idea of picking Biddy up and putting her to one side, but the idea of touching her was strangely unsettling, and he decided against it.

"Please, Biddy. I must speak to her."

"Ah, Lord love ye. You are a good man, Mr Cootes. I see that plain as day, but you've to give the girl some time. She'll be at the ball tonight, and she'll not run away without speaking to you, my word upon it."

"But she doesn't understand. She still does not believe I will—"

Biddy put a reassuring hand on his arm and shushed him. "Aisling struggles to put her trust in men, Mr Cootes, and I believe you know why that is, but I trust you, and she is getting there, I promise. Give her a bit of time."

Sylvester let out a breath and raked a hand through his hair, staring at Biddy, wondering just how much the woman knew.

"Enough, not all," she replied.

He blinked. "What?"

"You were wondering if Aisling had told me everything she told you."

Sylvester opened and closed his mouth, a shiver of unease skittering down his spine. But no, it was obvious what he was thinking. Aisling had revealed a secret to him. She must have told Biddy, and Biddy would know he was wondering if she knew it too. It was a simple deduction, nothing in the least bit magical.

"She needs help, and she needs protecting," he said, wishing he could convey a sense of urgency to this infuriating woman who just stood watching him placidly, as though there were all the time in the world and there was nothing out of the ordinary in this situation. But then, perhaps she only knew that Aisling had been ruined and cast aside. Perhaps she did not know that a man had died.

"He'll be just as dead tomorrow as he is today," Biddy replied, her expression remaining unchanged, her voice matter of fact.

Sylvester's mouth fell open. Very well. That time it had been creepy. He muttered a curse, staring at Biddy in alarm. "You know?"

Biddy rolled her eyes. “That she killed him? Jesus, Mary, and Joseph! Of course I know. Who do you think taught her the curse?”

He had the sudden forceful sensation they had plunged him into some bizarre fairy tale. Only he wasn’t certain if he was supposed to be the knight in shining armour or the hapless fool who gets murdered by accident and put in a pie. He told himself to stop being hysterical and concentrate on the matter at hand.

“Biddy,” he said, forcing his voice to remain even when he was on the verge of losing his damned mind. “What the hell happened? For the love of God, will you *tell* me?”

Biddy shook her head and Sylvester fought the urge to swear loudly and at length.

“I can’t do it, bless your heart. Even if I knew it all, it’s Aisling’s story to tell, and she’ll tell you the rest when’s she’s good and ready and not before. Now stop acting the maggot, run along and have yourself a nap before the party. You look done in. I can give you something to help you sleep peacefully if—”

“No!” Sylvester exclaimed in alarm before schooling his expression into something less anxious. She was just an old woman, he reminded himself. There was no such thing as witches. “No, thank you, Biddy. That won’t be necessary. Just… Just tell her I was here. That I’m here for her, and I always will be. Please.”

Biddy smiled, and it was such a delighted smile it took years from her and made something in his heart ease. This was a formidable woman, and she was Aisling’s friend. That was a good thing. She reached up and patted his cheek.

“I will. Now be a good fellow and get yourself some rest. I’ll look after Aisling. Don’t you fret none.”

There was really nothing else that Sylvester could do, so he had no choice but to leave and pray Aisling would change her mind and put her trust in him.

1st July 1841, Chessett House, Warwickshire.

Louis waited impatiently whilst his valet, Elton, fussed about, putting the final touches to his toilette. There was no point in remonstrating, though. The fellow would only sulk if Louis did not allow his creative flair to achieve perfection—in his valet's eyes, at least. Unlike Elton, Louis knew what hid behind the elegant façade facing him in the mirror, how much darkness lurked behind the mask, which was why he'd known at first glance that the Marquess of Kilbane was a dangerous man. Desperate men were always dangerous, and Louis recognised that particular brand of hopeless despair all too well. The kind that meant you did not much care if you lived or died. Boredom and power, damage and loneliness, that was a powder keg of explosive potential, and Louis had no intention of being the spark. Whatever Kilbane was up to, he wanted none of it, but he could not pretend he wasn't more than a little curious.

Elton picked up the sapphire stick pin for his cravat and hesitated before suggesting, "Perhaps tonight we might try the ruby and gold, monsieur, just for a change?"

Louis regarded Elton steadily. His valet sighed. "The sapphire then. It goes marvellously well with your eyes, I admit."

"I am a trial to you, Elton. Forgive me."

"Oh, no, never that!" Elton replied, looking horrified. "There're dozens of valets who would do me bodily harm to get this job. You're the most elegant man in the *ton*, and everyone knows it. It is a privilege to work for you."

"And such excellent work you do, Elton. Very nice, thank you."

Elton smiled, pleased, and then looked to his master as they heard a knock at the bedroom door. Louis nodded and Elton went to open it.

"Louis, help me with this blasted cravat, will you?" Barnaby grumbled.

Louis regarded the mangled affair hanging limply around Barnaby's neck and winced. Glancing at Elton he saw the fellow was twitching with the desire to put it to rights. "Elton, fetch one of mine at once, and attend Mr Godwin. There's a good fellow."

"At once," Elton replied with a sigh of relief.

Barnaby fidgeted as they waited for Elton to return, and Louis wondered how long it would take him to spit it out.

"What do you make of Kilbane?" he asked, which was quicker than Louis had expected.

They'd not seen the man all day, but his presence in the house was making poor Barnaby agitated. The man's self-appointed position as Louis' protector at once amused and touched him.

"As little as possible. Keep out of his way," Louis replied as Elton returned. He watched as his valet's deft fingers made short work of the cravat.

Barnaby huffed. "I'm not the brightest fellow, Louis, but even I'd deduced that much."

Louis smiled. Elton stepped back to allow Barnaby to inspect his work.

Barnaby stared at his reflection in surprise and flashed a grin. "Oh, I say. That's splendid. Thank you, Elton."

Elton preened, pleased with himself. "My pleasure, Mr Godwin. Will there be anything else, monsieur?"

Louis shook his head. "That will be all. Don't wait up for me tonight."

"Very good, monsieur. Have a pleasant evening."

Barnaby regarded himself in the looking glass again and reached to tweak his cravat. Louis smacked his hand away.

"Don't. It is perfect. Leave it alone."

"I don't like the way he looks at you," Barnaby grumbled, turning away from the mirror.

"Elton?" Louis asked mildly, though he knew well enough who Barnaby meant. His friend tutted impatiently.

"Kilbane!"

"Ah. Don't fret about Kilbane, *mon ami*. I suspect he has—how do you say—*d'autres chats à fouetter?"*

"Come again?" Barnaby looked at him blankly.

Louis pursed his lips, thinking. "Other fish to fry?"

"Oh, got you," Barnaby nodded.

"Oui. So stop fretting. In any case, I know how to handle our dissipated friend. I am no innocent virgin to be led to the slaughter, I assure you. I am not so easily seduced by a handsome face."

Barnaby blushed scarlet and Louis laughed, patting his shoulder. "*Mon pauvre ami.* I am a terrible trial to you. Come along and let us see if we can get Lady Millicent to dance with you twice."

Maxwell and Kilbane were waiting for them downstairs. Neither man looked entirely relaxed, though Kilbane's brooding gaze did a better job of hiding his tension than Maxwell, who appeared edgy and in need of a drink.

"The carriage is ready, my lord," the butler said, once they were all assembled.

Kilbane smiled, a slow, wicked smile. "Then let the fun and games begin."

1st July 1841, Trevick Castle, Warwickshire.

Aisling stared at herself in the mirror. Though it was hard to explain why, she was calm. Perhaps because she was so tired of living a lie, of waiting for someone to reveal the terrible truth. If it happened tonight, it might be a relief in some ways. Or perhaps it resulted from the ritual cleansing Biddy had helped her with. The scent of the herbs and perfumed oils she'd used still clung to her, rising with her body's warmth, quieting her agitated nerves. Biddy believed she could find her way through this evening. She had read her cards and told her Aisling held more power than she realised, and she clung to that belief.

Low voices pierced her thoughts, and she realised her maid had opened the bedroom door and her mother was here.

"Mama," she said, smiling and getting to her feet.

"Oh, Aisling. How beautiful you look." Mama put a hand to her mouth and blinked back tears before holding out her arms to her.

Aisling went into them and hugged her tightly.

"I'll crush your dress," she murmured, swallowing down the desire to cry.

"Never mind that. No one will look at me when you are standing there."

"Such nonsense," Aisling laughed, for her mother was a beautiful woman with a vivacious nature and a laugh that still turned men's heads.

"Are you well now, darling girl?" Mama asked, holding her at arm's length and studying her carefully.

She wasn't just asking about her absence today, Aisling knew. She took a breath.

"Not yet, Mama, but I think… I hope I will be. Soon."

Her mother's lips trembled, and she sucked in a breath. "Oh. Oh, that's… that's good. I'm so happy."

"Don't worry, Mama. I'm not a little girl anymore."

"No," Mama replied, her voice unsteady. "No, you are a woman, and a strong one, my darling. Only, I wish you would remember, you don't always have to be strong by yourself. I will always stand beside you with pride. No matter what, Aisling. We all would. No matter *what.*"

Aisling stared back at her mother, understanding what she was saying and doing her best to smile. She had known that, of course. Keeping secrets from them had been the hardest thing to do, but she had never believed her family would abandon her if they knew, or if she created a scandal. It would be far worse than that. They would forgive her, protect her, shield her, and defend her, and she would drag them all down into the mire.

"I will remember, Mama," Aisling promised, leaning in to kiss her cheek. "I promise."

Her mother nodded and took a deep breath. "Then I shall see you downstairs in ten minutes. Our guests will arrive soon."

Once her mother had gone, Aisling put on her shoes, pulled on her gloves, and headed for the door. She closed her eyes for a moment before her hand tightened upon the knob and allowed herself a moment to steel her nerves. Then she opened the door to discover Sylvester dithering in the hallway outside.

"Aisling," he said, his expression one of such concern that the tears she had not wept in front of her mother rose in a wave and she had to swallow hard.

"Sylvester." She ran at him in a most unladylike fashion and threw her arms about him, holding him tight. "You're still here," she whispered, for she had hardly dared believe he would be, that he would stay after everything she had told him.

His arms closed about her, holding her to him. "I won't let you down," he promised. "I swore I would help you, Aisling. That you could trust me. I would not say such a thing if I did not mean to honour it."

She looked up at him, drinking in the sight of his handsome face, and wishing as she had wished so many times these past days, that it had been him she'd met all those years ago, that he had been the one to whom she had given her heart and her body. But even the most powerful magic could not change the past.

"Kiss me."

She felt the surprise ripple through his body, saw his eyes widen.

"Please," she begged, feeling uncertain when he hesitated.

His hand cradled her face as he lowered his mouth to hers, and Aisling's nerves leapt the moment their lips touched. Oh, yes. *This.* She wanted this, wanted him. Aisling wrapped her arms around his neck and pressed closer, and Sylvester pulled away with a groan.

"No. Aisling. God, love, you're temptation enough to fry a man's wits, but your parents are waiting downstairs for you. I'd best not send you off all rumpled."

"I want you to rumple me," she admitted, smoothing a hand over his chest. She slipped it beneath his coat, feeling his heart hammering against his chest.

"Don't tell me things like that," he pleaded, his voice husky. "I swore to be your friend, Aisling."

"You can be my friend, but… I'd like you to be more than that."

He took a step away from her with a muttered curse, pacing and raking a hand through his hair.

Aisling's heart dropped. "Oh."

His head snapped up. "What do you mean, 'oh?'"

"Nothing," she said, to cover her embarrassment, though her cheeks were burning. "I thought… But that's silly, isn't it? Now you know everything about me—"

Before she could say another word, Sylvester closed the distance between them, hauled her into his arms and kissed her so hard her wits scattered in all directions. She whimpered as her knees threatened to buckle, and his arms firmed about her. His tongue plundered mercilessly, and his hands dropped to her hips, pulling her tight against him until she had no doubt of the effect she was having on him. Finally he pulled back, his eyes dark with wanting, his chest rising and falling too fast.

"Little idiot," he muttered, but with such affection, Aisling could only smile, though she wanted to weep. How could she have hated this man so much, have wanted so badly to get away from him when, all the time, *he'd* been the one trying to save her? "We need to talk."

He looked so worried for her, so determined to do whatever he could to protect her, that she nearly crumbled, but that wouldn't do. Not tonight. Tonight she must face up to the mess she'd made, to whoever thought they knew what she'd done. If she could make them go away, she would. If not… well, she'd cross that bridge when she got to it, but she could hurt no one else. Not even to keep her family's name from scandal.

"We do need to talk," she agreed. "But the guests are arriving now. After the ball. I'll meet you down by the river. Once everyone is gone."

Sylvester nodded. "If that's what you want, but I'm here, Aisling. I'm not going anywhere. If you need me tonight…."

Aisling smiled, buoyed by the realisation that her mother was right. She didn't have to do this alone.

She kissed his cheek, lingering there for a moment as he let out a shaky breath. "Thank you," she whispered, and hurried off to help her parents.

Half an hour later and Aisling's face was stiff from smiling and she was desperate for a drink, for her throat was parched. How strange that she had once longed to stand here with her parents as they greeted the endless parade of glamorous guests and now… and now she just wanted it to be over. Sooner or later, her accuser would be here, and she would face them, and now she was certain of that fact she could not wait to get it done. Yet friends and relations and neighbours came and went and….

"Monsieur Le Comte. How delightful to see you. I'm so glad you could come—"

Aisling heard her mother greeting Louis César, but there was a buzzing in her ears and her heart was slamming against her chest. A hazy sense of unreality settled over her, like when she had eaten those strange mushrooms that Biddy said would help her dream walk. There were three men with the comte and one… no… *no*… that was impossible. He turned then, his gaze meeting hers, and Aisling's blood ran cold.

"What is it?"

Louis turned to stare at Barnaby, who had asked the question. He, in turn, was regarding Maxwell. The Earl of Vane was staring at someone on the other side of the ballroom with a puzzled expression.

"Who is that?" he murmured, though he appeared to be talking to himself.

"Who do you mean?" Louis asked.

"That young woman?" Maxwell demanded, gesturing across the room.

Louis looked at the woman in question. She was slender, with dark gold hair, and an uncompromising, rather fierce expression. A handsome young woman, striking rather than pretty. Her nose was a little too big, her mouth settled in a rather mutinous pout, and her thick brows were drawn together, and yet these rather discouraging aspects came together to produce a face full of character. She would not be another dull, simpering debutante, that was for certain.

"I do not know the young woman, but I believe she is Miss de Beauvoir, the adopted daughter of the great scientist, Mr Inigo de Beauvoir," Louis said, regarding the earl with interest. "Why? You are interested in meeting her?"

Maxwell frowned. "No. At least… I don't know. Only she seems familiar."

"Familiar? Where from?" Barnaby asked, but Maxwell was already moving, towards the young woman as she walked through the crowd.

Barnaby looked to Louis and shrugged, his naturally jovial expression fading as Kilbane moved past them into the ballroom. "He's not supposed to be here. Did you see the Earl of Trevick's expression when he saw him?" he whispered as they also made their way through the crowded ballroom.

"I did, but it is not so easy to turn away a titled gentleman. Especially when there is the possibility of causing a scene." Louis inspected the crowd. He didn't much care what Maxwell and Kilbane got up to. He had two objectives this evening, to help Barnaby make headway with Lady Millicent and….

His heart did an odd little jump in his chest, a reaction he had become familiar with of late. But, oh, God, it had been so long since he had seen her. He smiled, unable to help himself as he saw Evie standing with Lady Rosamund Adolphus and another young woman he did not recognise. Evie was telling them a story, and her friend's attention was absolute. Her green eyes sparkled with mischief, and he could tell she was getting to the good bit for she was trying not to smile and failing, showing the dimples in her cheeks. Whatever she said next had her friends roaring with laughter as Evie looked on in triumph, pleased with herself for having entertained them. It was hard to breathe, hard to look upon her and want to be with her so badly when he did not know how long he must wait.

"Louis, do you think…?"

With difficulty Louis tore his attention from his beloved and turned to Barnaby, realising too late he was still smiling like a fool.

Barnaby was no longer looking at him, though. He had turned to stare at Evie in astonishment. He turned back to Louis, eyes wide. Louis' heart gave an uncomfortable thud.

"Oh," Barnaby said, a crooked smile appearing on his face.

"Barnaby," Louis said, uncomfortable now as heat crept up the back of his neck.

Barnaby only chuckled and patted him on the shoulder. "Don't be daft, old man. Shan't breathe a word. Upon my honour, I shan't. I say, though, she's a lovely girl. Can see why you're smitten." He beamed at Louis, who could only stare at him.

"You… You don't think…" Louis swallowed and rubbed the back of his neck, feeling ridiculous. "I'm not too… *old*?"

Barnaby gaped at him. "Good God, man, you're hardly in your dotage. You're the sort who'll still look good when you're eighty, you lucky blighter. She likes you, don't she? Best of friends, you said. Well, seems a good start to me, better than most have. What's a few years? Besides, she'll suit you nicely. Need a bit of looking after, I reckon, and she's the kind to dote on a fellow. Do you good, a bit of doting."

Louis swallowed and had to fight back the extraordinary urge to hug the fellow in public. What the devil was wrong with him?

"Be grand if we could get them both up the aisle, wouldn't it?" Barnaby said wistfully. "Still, your chances are better than mine."

Louis shook his head. "*Non*. She does not see me, Barnaby. I am her friend only, and I think I will soon lose my mind if I cannot change this."

"Really?" Barnaby said sceptically. "Reckon you ought to try harder then," he said, in a matter-of-fact tone.

"I…." Louis cleared his throat, feeling absurd, "I am afraid to. What if… what if she doesn't want me?"

Barnaby gave him a look of such sympathy and understanding Louis wished he'd kept his mouth shut. "Keep asking myself the same thing, old chap. There's only one answer and we both understand what it is. At least you'll know. You'll have tried, eh? Got to try."

Louis frowned, watching Evie from afar, and shook his head. *"Non.* She is too young, it's not time yet. She just told me the other day she is not ready to marry. I must respect her wishes."

"Well, fair enough," Barnaby said with a shrug. "Reckon you know more about affairs of the heart than I do, only… don't wait too long. Should hate some less scrupulous fellow to steal a march on you." His eyes lit up, and he elbowed Louis. "There's my lady. Tally ho, old man, best of luck to you."

Louis watched him go in consternation, very much aware that his pupil of the past few months had just turned the tables on him and given him some very sound advice.

Chapter 14

Father,

It is the ninth anniversary of your untimely demise, and I am raising a glass in your honour.

I am so happy you are dead. I should dance upon your grave, only I do not wish to dirty my boots. I do hope you are roasting in hell. No doubt I shall see you one day soon.

— Excerpt of a letter from Ciarán St Just, The Most Hon'ble Marquess of Kilbane, tossed into the fire.

1st July 1841, Lady Trevick's Summer Ball, Trevick Castle, Warwickshire.

Aisling stared down at the slip of paper in her hand and did her best to breathe. It seemed more difficult than usual, and she could only manage a series of short, shallow gasps. Somehow, she made it out of the ballroom and used the servants' passageways and staircases to cut across the castle without being seen. By the time she made it to the family wing, she had herself under control again. More or less.

She unfolded the piece of paper again with trembling hands.

Meet me in the library at 10pm. You know why.

The writing was bold and extravagant, that of a supremely confident man. Aisling closed her eyes and willed herself to remain calm. She had added a short note beneath the terse words, a brief explanation for Sylvester.

You can do this. You can do this. You must do this. There is a price to pay, Aisling. There is always a price. You knew that. You know it still.

She forced herself to move, to put one foot in front of the other. When she got to the end of the corridor, she waited until she saw a harried footman walking quickly with a crate of champagne.

"Excuse me. Browning, isn't it?"

"That's right, my lady," he said politely, though he was clearly eager to be on his way. No doubt someone would have his head if he didn't replenish the stocks.

Aisling lifted the piece of paper. This is very important, Mr Browning. "Find Mr Sylvester Cootes and give him this. Tell him I need him to come at once. It's urgent. Do you understand?"

Mr Browning blushed a little and gave a stiff nod, no doubt under the impression he was helping her arrange an illicit liaison, but she could do nothing about that now. He set the crate down and took the paper, tucking it into his waistcoat pocket. "Understood, my lady."

"Thank you, Browning. I rely upon your discretion."

"You may do so," he replied with a nod, before picking the crate back up and hurrying away.

Aisling listened to his retreating footsteps and then waited in the cool, dimly lit corridor. Words flitted in her mind, and she let them come, sending a prayer that she could find a way through this.

Moonrise above, earth spread below.

Protect me always from my foes.

Guard my loved ones, give me the power

To endure this fateful hour.

"Do no harm," she whispered aloud, clenching her fists. "Do no harm."

In the darkness, a clock chimed the hour, and Aisling made her way to the library.

"Monsieur!" Evie's eyes lit up at the sight of him and something in Louis' heart eased at the pleasure he saw there.

"Bonsoir, ma belle mademoiselle," he said, bowing over her hand. He raised her gloved fingers to his lips and pressed a kiss to her knuckles.

"Goodness, Louis, you are dashing tonight. Who are you trying to impress?" she demanded.

Louis sighed. "You, *ma petite,* as always."

Evie laughed and took his arm. "Whatever for? That's the wonderful thing about friends. You don't need to try so hard. Are you having a lovely time? I believe the entire world is here tonight. What a crush it is."

"Non, I have had a very dull evening so far, but now I think my luck has changed. You saved me two dances, I hope? You promised."

Evie grinned at him. "Papa isn't here, so yes. Of course I did. I don't *think* Mama will tattle on me."

"And if she does?"

"If she does, I shall endure another scolding, I suppose. I don't know why he worries so about you," she mused, shaking her head.

"Good Lord, if he knew how often we've been alone together and you, a perfect gentleman. Even when I was in my nightclothes. I almost told him about that the last time—"

"What? *Mon Dieu,* Evie!"

Evie stared at him and then gave a snort of laughter. "Don't look so horrified. What's the trouble? Afraid he'll force you to marry me?" She put her hand to her heart and adopted a tragic expression. "Good Lord, a fate worse than death!"

"Non!" Louis took her hand and clasped it in his. His heart had picked up speed and Barnaby's words rang in his ears. "I am not afraid of any such thing. Not in the least. Only that you not get into trouble with your father, whom you esteem so highly. I should not wish this for you, Evie, but… but as for marrying you, I should be—"

"Louis! How do. Are you having a splendid time?"

Louis cursed as the Marquess of Blackstone barged into their conversation and hooked an arm over his shoulder, leaning into him so heavily that Louis staggered. The wretched devil grinned inanely. He was half seas over already, damn him.

"Splendid," Louis managed through gritted teeth.

"Jules! Do go and drink some water. You're drunk as a wheelbarrow," Evie protested.

"No, *I* am drunk as a lord," Jules replied with offended dignity before saluting them both and staggering away.

"Daft creature," Evie said, laughing softly. "He'll have a dreadful hangover in the morning."

"One can only hope," Louis muttered.

The country dance being performed with some enthusiasm whilst they spoke finally ended and Evie consulted her dance card. "Our waltz is next."

Louis offered her his arm. He wished the rest of the world would go away, so he might have some peace to figure out how to make this work. He thought perhaps he would try for a little honesty to begin with.

"You look exquisite tonight, Evie."

She glanced up at him and smiled, dimples flashing. "You always say that," she said, as though he was just offering her the usual polite words.

"Because it is always true." He tried to hold her gaze, to get her to understand he did not say such things lightly, but she glanced away from him, refusing to take his words seriously.

"If I am, it's because of the beautiful dresses you design for me."

"I never said I designed them," he retorted, irritated that she would not heed him.

"You never said you didn't, either," she shot back, an amused glint in her eyes.

They found their place on the dance floor, and Louis took her in his arms. He saw Mr Hadley-Smythe watching as Evie put her hand on his shoulder, and did not like the look in the fellow's eyes. Barnaby was right. Whether or not Evie was ready to consider marriage, there were men enough here who would not wait for her. They would pursue her, persuade her, and if he was not careful, they might find their place in her heart before he could convince her to accept him. There was a fine balance between patience and respect and foolishness. Something must be done.

Evie glanced up at Louis as he led her into the dance. There was an odd tension about him this evening, a sense of restless impatience. Perhaps he was meeting someone here tonight, though if he had taken a new mistress she was at a loss to discover who it was, which was strange. No matter how discreet Louis was, the women always preened and whispered their secret behind fans and in quiet corners, eager to be the envy of their friends. Yet she had not heard so much as a murmur for months now. It was very odd. Perhaps he had finally met someone who respected his privacy, someone special. The notion niggled at her, an uncomfortable sensation like realising you had grit in your shoe and no opportunity to remove it. Probably just because he hadn't told her, and his secrecy vexed her. He always used to confide in her, but he had not done so for a long time, and that bothered her more than she liked to admit. Did he not want to be her friend any longer? Anxiety skittered down her spine and she gripped his hand tighter before she could think better of it.

His brilliant blue gaze settled on her, a question lingering there. *Are you well, ma petite?* She could hear the words without him even saying them. She smiled in response, telling herself she was being foolish. He still sought her out, didn't he? He still wrote to her several times a week, still scolded her if she didn't save him at least one dance. Of course he was still her friend.

"Evie?"

"Yes?"

"You *are* beautiful."

There was a look in his eyes that made her heart thud and she glanced away, giving a nervous laugh.

"You're very kind, monsieur."

"Non." He sounded annoyed now. *"Non,* I am not kind. You always say that, like it is in my nature to say meaningless things just to make people happy. Do you not know me at all? I am neither nice nor kind. I am the very devil, Evie, and *I* find you beautiful."

Evie's gaze snapped back to his, staring at him in shock. Whatever had got into him tonight?

He held her gaze and then let out a breath of frustration and looked away. The music swelled around them, and Louis spun her into a series of fast turns, leaving her breathless. His hold tightened upon her when she might have stumbled, guiding her effortlessly in the direction he wished her to go. For a shocking moment, her breasts pressed against his chest, the contact electrifying. Evie gasped. He loosened his grasp a little but was still holding her too close, heat blazing from his hard body. It lasted only seconds, but left her giddy, flushed, and bewildered.

Their waltz seemed to take forever, with her suddenly too aware of his masculine physique, of the scent of him, subtle and spicy and wildly expensive, of the unsettling look in his blue eyes. But the dance ended, thank heavens, and she curtsied to him, needing to get away and… and just *breathe.*

"Thank you for the dance," she said, forcing a smile, and was about to scurry away when he grasped her hand, setting it on his arm to escort her from the floor.

"You are angry with me," he observed.

Evie shook her head. She wasn't angry. She… she didn't know what she was, but it was disconcerting and frightening, which was why she needed to get away from him. Then perhaps she could puzzle it out.

He guided her from the dancefloor, out of the ballroom and onto the terrace. It was well lit and there were plenty of people out taking the air, but it was quieter than inside. Louis walked to the balustrade, and she let go of his arm, wanting to put distance between them, but he took her hand again. Evie glanced around, praying no one was observing them. What was he doing?

"Evie," he said, keeping his voice low. His thumb rubbed a slow circle against her palm, and despite them both wearing gloves, it elicited the most peculiar sensation beneath her skin. Her heart thudded uncertainly, and she glanced up at him, even though she was afraid to. Lord, but his eyes were so blue. Could an ocean really be that extraordinary colour? Oceans were treacherous places, weren't they? Oceans were full of wild storms that could pull you down, fathoms deep and she did not want to drown. Evie had always been afraid of risky situations, of doing anything reckless. She did not wish for an adventure but to stay safe at home and read about it in books.

"Don't you trust me, love?"

There was something in his voice, an aching sadness that she longed to soothe, but this version of Louis was unfamiliar and too dangerous. This was the voice of the man who could seduce any woman he wanted, and then walk away from her without a backward glance.

"Of course," she said lightly.

She had always trusted him, more than she trusted anyone in the world besides her family. Evie had told him her secrets, had put her faith in him, and yet there was a panicky sensation building inside her that told her things were changing and she did not want them to change. She did not want to lose her friend. Not ever. If she lost Louis....

Anxiety made her breath catch, and she pulled her hand free of his.

"The next dance is beginning. I am promised to Mr Price. Excuse me, monsieur. I will see you later."

She fled back to the ballroom, not understanding why she wanted to run from Louis when she could not bear the thought of not being with him. But the evening was too hot and noisy, and she was all in a muddle, and... and there was Mr Price and she owed him a dance. With relief, she allowed him to lead her onto the dancefloor and did not look back.

Chapter 15

Dear Bert and Pike,

I hope this letter finds you well, and that you received the parcel I sent. I know full well you would have shared most of it among those you consider worse off, but I hope you saved some of it at least.

Pike, have you been practising your letters? I will expect to see progress when next I visit. This evening I shall attend a very lavish party in a vast castle, the likes of which would make your eyes stand out of your head, and I shall tell you all about that, too.

It seems strange now, when I think how badly I longed to return to my rightful place in the world, but I miss you both. I am displaced, neither fish nor fowl, which is ridiculous. I am an earl, in a long line of noblemen, and yet after a few short months seeing the world through your eyes I am not the same man – thank God. I am blessed and cursed at once, for now I can make amends for the mistakes of my past, and yet I am all at sea. I do not know who I am any more. I feel like an imposter, trying to play the part of a good man when I know my soul is still black as pitch. Will it get better, do you think? If I keep playing the part, will that long forgotten decency I destroyed so thoroughly heal and repair until I am whole again? I hope so, even if I do not deserve it.

— Excerpt of a letter from The Hon'ble Maxwell Drake, Earl of Vane to Mr Burt Clump and Master Pike.

1st July 1841, Lady Trevick's Summer Ball, Trevick Castle, Warwickshire.

Aisling's hand trembled upon the doorknob as it turned, but she opened it and walked in, head held high, and then stopped in her tracks.

He was lounging in a chair, long legs stretched out in front of him in an indolent pose, a glass of liquor dangling causally from his fingers.

"Lady Aisling. So good of you to join me," he murmured. He got to his feet, the movement lazy but no less elegant for that. He grinned and executed a formal bow.

"What do you want?" Aisling said, her voice cold. "If you've come to cause trouble—"

"Trouble?" His eyes glittered with amusement, such a strange colour they were. Almost violet. "Whatever gave you that idea?"

She watched him watch her as she moved farther into the room, with the unnerving sensation she had stepped into some wild creature's lair.

The door flew open again with a crash, and Aisling gasped as Sylvester burst into the room. He took one look at the Marquess of Kilbane, and his gaze darkened.

"You bastard!"

Aisling gave a little shriek and leapt in front of him, her hands pressed flat on his chest. She knew she might as well try to hold back the tide if he didn't want to heed her, but he stilled, his gaze flying to hers.

"Why is he here, alone with you? Is he blackmailing you? What is going on?"

The desire to destroy something with his bare hands shone in his eyes. He wanted to protect her, to shield her from harm, and that made her heart ache.

There was a low rumble of laughter from the other side of the room.

"My, my, Mr Cootes. You *are* quick to leap to conclusions, and not very flattering ones at that. You've hurt my feelings."

"And why shouldn't I assume the worst where you are concerned, Kilbane?" Sylvester growled, the tension vibrating through him palpable. "Everyone knows what kind of man you are. A libertine and a scoundrel."

"Sticks and stones," Kilbane said softly, leaning one arm against the mantelpiece. He took a leisurely sip of his drink, his gaze never leaving Sylvester. "As it happens, you've got it all wrong, but then, I am much misunderstood," he added sadly.

Sylvester snorted in disgust. "I doubt that."

The marquess laughed and all the fine hairs on the back of Aisling's neck stood on end because she knew what came next. His languid gaze settled upon her and he smiled, a slow predatory smile that made her heart skittered behind her ribs. "Well, my lady, shall you tell him, or shall I?"

Aisling was almost grateful to him in that moment, grateful to get it all out into the open so Sylvester could finally know the entire story. He deserved that much if she could give him nothing else. She looked up at Sylvester to find his gaze upon her, waiting.

"His brother," she whispered. "I killed his brother."

Sylvester stared at her for a long moment during which she held her breath, waiting for him to leave, to see disgust in his eyes. But he reached for her. He took her hand and held on tight, and that connection seemed to be the only substantial thing in the room. She clung to it.

"My *older* brother, Richard St Just," Kilbane said pointedly, his expression mild. "The heir."

There was a prickling silence during which no one spoke. Kilbane moved to the decanter on the sideboard and filled his glass before glancing at Sylvester. "Want one?"

"No," Sylvester replied, though she suspected he wanted one very much. She certainly did, but she also declined when Kilbane raised a dark eyebrow at her.

"How much does he know?" he asked her, taking his drink and returning to his seat. "Does he know you're a witch?"

"I know," Sylvester said before she could answer, his voice firm, as if daring Kilbane to get on and make whatever threat he'd come to deliver.

Kilbane inclined his head, regarding her with interest. "You don't look like a witch," he mused. "At least, not the kind that appeared in the stories I read as a child. You're far too pretty. More like a succubus," he added with a wink.

"Shut your damned mouth. Unless you want to give me an excuse to shut it for you," Sylvester growled, his hand gripping hers so tightly it almost hurt.

"Such animosity." Kilbane tsked, looking reproachful. "What exactly have I done to deserve it?"

"You sent the lady a threatening note," Sylvester pointed out.

Kilbane pursed his lips and shrugged. "Was it threatening?" he queried mildly. "I only said that I knew what she'd done, and I do."

"What do you want from me?" Aisling said, sick of this dancing about. If he'd come to seek revenge, or blackmail her, she'd just as soon know about it.

Kilbane laughed, staring at her with delight. "My dear young woman, I want nothing from you."

"Then why the bloody hell are you here?" Sylvester demanded in fury.

Kilbane got to his feet, looking genuinely amused. "Why, to thank her, of course, and to take a look at the woman who destroyed such a powerful man. You may despise me all you like, Mr Cootes, and with my blessing, but rest assured, my brother was far worse. I am a mere babe in debauchery in comparison. Lady Aisling did me and the world, a great favour."

Aisling blinked at him, uncertain she'd heard him correctly. "To th-thank me?" she whispered.

Kilbane nodded and downed his drink in one large swallow. "Precisely that. I don't know how well you got to know my brother the summer he stayed here with you? He could present a charming façade when he wished to, I know. A talent we share. For your own sake, I hope you saw little more than the façade, though I assume something provoked you badly enough to want him dead. Not that I blame you. I despised him. He was a sadistic, evil bastard, and that's coming from *me*," he said with a wicked grin.

Aisling swayed, and Sylvester's arm went around her. "Sit down, love. You've had a shock."

She allowed him to guide her to a chair and sat down before her knees gave out. Sylvester straightened and turned back to Kilbane. "I want to know *precisely* what happened," he gritted out, and Aisling had the feeling he was holding onto his patience by a thread and would not endure much more.

Kilbane shrugged and went to pour himself another drink. This time, he filled a second glass and crossed the room, holding it out to Aisling. "Drink it up, child," he instructed.

Aisling took it, bristling a little at being called a child for they must be close in age, yet there was something about Kilbane that made him seem older than his years, a world-weary, cynical air of dissipation that hardened his handsome features and made her believe he could be cruel when he wanted. She didn't trust him an inch. A pity she'd not felt the same way for his brother.

He took the chair opposite hers and sat down, his sharp gaze never leaving her.

"I would like to know *precisely* what happened, too," he said pleasantly, arranging his long limbs in an elegant sprawl. "Do tell."

Aisling regarded him stonily. "I met your brother when I was fifteen, my lord. He's been dead these eight years. Why the sudden interest?"

Kilbane inspected his nails for a moment, as if deciding whether to indulge her, and then gave a despondent sigh. "Our family life was *not* a pleasant one," he said with a tragic air, and then gave such a beatific smile she knew he meant to unsettle her, and yet she could hear the truth in his words and suspected that was a monumental understatement. "I have not set foot on the family estate since my father died. It's a ghastly place and as I loathed my brother, I felt no need to call upon him after dear old Papa shuffled off. Even after my brother died, I could not bring myself to return to that be damned mausoleum. If I could be bothered to exert myself, I'd have the entire place torn down. Yet, my steward would nag and nag until I thought I would run mad. The tenants were revolting—well, as if I didn't know it. So, I went home, and discovered my brother's er… writings. His death was hushed up, of course. A tragic accident, and the staff are too terrified of me to breathe a word about what really happened."

"Writings?" Sylvester repeated, staring at him.

"You don't know how he died," Kilbane mused, regarding Sylvester curiously. "You know she was responsible, but no more. Interesting."

"Just get on with it," Sylvester snapped, folding his arms.

Kilbane turned to Aisling, refusing to be hurried. "You *told* him you killed my brother," he guessed.

Aisling nodded, and Kilbane's lips quirked into a smile. "Yes, Mr Cootes, my brother's *writings.* He kept a diary, but towards the end that did not seem to be enough for him, so he wrote upon the walls, the ceiling, and the floor of his bedroom. He scratched words into the furniture, even into the window glass. He filled every inch he could, and when he was done, he shot himself in the head."

"Oh, God." Aisling covered her mouth with her hand as nausea roiled in her stomach. She had only known the story put about by the family: a tragic accident whilst cleaning his gun. She'd felt sure that was not the truth, however, and here was the confirmation of her suspicions. It had been her doing.

"What on earth are you looking so wretched about?" Kilbane demanded in consternation. "You wanted him dead as much as I did, and he is. I'm inclined to dance a jig, but weeping seems rather ungrateful. Embrace your victories, I say, no matter how they came about. You don't know when you'll have another."

"W-What did he write?" Aisling stammered, ignoring his provoking words, wanting to know the truth as much as she wanted to run away and never hear it.

"*The witch killed me*," Kilbane said succinctly, watching her reaction.

Aisling felt the blood drain from her face and the room grew hazy. Well, there was no mistaking that then. Her doing. She'd murdered him.

"Aisling. Love. I'm here, it's all right." Sylvester crouched before her, cradling her face between his hands. She blinked and took a breath.

"Yes," she said. "Yes. I… I'm fine."

Sylvester stroked her cheek and then rounded on Kilbane, his tone furious. "If he wrote such things upon the walls of his bedroom, at *home,* how the devil is Aisling responsible for his death?"

Kilbane shrugged. "I never said she *was* responsible, only that I knew from reading his diaries, Richard believed it."

Aisling sat up, riveted by his words, staring at him. "You never said I *was*? What do you mean?"

"Yes, what the hell do you mean?" Sylvester demanded.

"Well, according to his diary, she put a curse on him in revenge for tricking her into losing her virginity," Kilbane said, looking thoroughly entertained by the idea. "And it couldn't have happened to a nicer chap. From what I can gather from his more lucid diary entries, she instructed him to go mad. My lady there told him that all the wickedness in his heart would consume his mind until he was a babbling lunatic. You must give me the exact wording, my lady. I'm desperate to know. Such a useful talent to have, and I don't blame you in the least for doing it, incidentally. I wish I'd thought of it years ago. It would have saved me a great deal of unpleasantness."

"Curses aren't real," Sylvester snapped. Aisling's gaze snapped to his, but he ignored her and yelled at Kilbane instead. "You mean to say all this time she believed she'd murdered the man for shouting angry words at him, when all along—"

"You think I'm mad." Aisling stared at him. "You think it's all nonsense?"

He turned back to her, clearly torn, but he took a breath and reached for her hand. "No, love. I do not think you the least bit mad, though his brother clearly was. I believe you may well have a gift for… for healing and the like, but… curses and magic?" He shook his head. "I'm sorry, Aisling, no. But this is a wonderful thing. Don't you see? The man was unstable, you're not responsible."

"My brother might not agree with you," Kilbane murmured.

Sylvester glared at him. "Shut your damned mouth. You'd have this young woman suffer more years of guilt, and for what?"

"No, I wouldn't," Kilbane retorted, though he did not look the least bit perturbed by Sylvester's anger. "I don't want her to lose a moment's sleep over that devil. I certainly haven't. He deserved everything he got, and more besides, but if it was a curse that did it for him, then I'm a believer. But perhaps I have a more open mind than you."

"An open mind?" Sylvester repeated in disgust.

Kilbane waved a nonchalant hand. "I will entertain the possibility of the curse doing for him, at least. Though I will admit my brother was not what you would call even-tempered. I had long considered him mad, dangerously so, for he seemed perfectly sane most of the time. Lady Aisling's curse, however, had a profound effect on him. Whether it contained genuine power and drove him to kill himself, or whether it was simply the idea working upon an already disturbed mind, I cannot say. I only know he's dead and I am here because I wished to thank the young lady he blamed in his diary. Mostly for making his last weeks on earth ones of absolute hell. I can only hope they are continuing on the other side." He smiled so sweetly that Aisling's blood ran cold. "To you, my dear," he added, raising his glass to her and taking a large swallow.

"This is nonsense," Sylvester said, shaking his head. He crouched down in front of Aisling. "You did not kill anyone, Aisling. Let me tell you how it went, shall I? The man treated you abominably, and you retaliated with angry words. Those words happened to be that of a curse you had learned, and you threw them back at him. Am I right?"

Aisling nodded. "You are right about the circumstances, Sylvester, but not about the curse. I saw the effect the words had on him, the terror in his eyes when he realised what I was. He ran away from me so fast—"

"I bet he pissed his pants," Kilbane said gleefully.

"Shut up!" Sylvester snapped. "Words can't kill people, Aisling."

"Oh, no," Kilbane sounded oddly sincere now. "No, no, Mr Cootes, I cannot let that pass. Words kill people all the time. Words can wound far more profoundly than any weapon if wielded by someone who knows where to strike. Believe me, I know."

"Had a lot of practice, have you?" Sylvester growled, glaring at him.

Kilbane's mouth quirked into a cruel smile, his eyes glittering. "More than you can possibly imagine, but then I learned from the best." His expression cleared, turning into something resembling fascinated wonder. "Could dear old Papa have been a witch, do you think?" he asked Aisling.

"What?" she stared at him, bewildered.

He snapped his fingers. "No, no, that's wrong, isn't it? He'd be a warlock. My God, I can see that, you know. When that bastard cursed you for stupidity or disobedience or whatever the hell it was, the pain of it could strike harder than any lash or fist, and I endured enough of both to know. I remember as a boy I'd far rather he beat me than reduce me to a quivering heap of flesh and bones with words."

He gave a visible shudder and sat back in his chair, rubbing his arms, a distant look in his eyes.

Sylvester stared at him in disbelief and then turned back to Aisling. “Come along, my lady. We’re leaving.”

“Oh, no. So soon? But it was just getting interesting,” Kilbane protested, pouting with disappointment.

Sylvester shot him a disgusted look and reached for Aisling’s hand, dragging her to her feet.

“No, wait.” Aisling tugged her hand free. She was so grateful to Sylvester for standing beside her, for not abandoning her and for trying to help, but she realised he had been placating her until now. He just thought she was a silly young woman living in a fantasy world. She knew better. “Kilbane. I am sorry. Your brother *was* cruel to me and hurt me deeply, and I was angry, but I never meant—”

Kilbane waved this away. “I really don’t care, sweetheart, so please do not indulge your bleeding-heart protestations of guilt on my behalf. Whether or not you did it, I am only here to satisfy my curiosity. What you do now is entirely up to you.”

He got to his feet and downed the last of his drink.

“You… You aren’t planning on blackmailing me?” she asked, rather dumbfounded.

He laughed and pulled a face. “Lord, no. How very provincial. No, no, if I indulge in blackmail, I prefer it to be more entertaining than this, and I believe I have wrung every ounce of enjoyment out of this little tête-à-tête.” He took her hand and bowed over it. “My lady sorcerer, it has been a delight, and you have my full permission to torment my brother in the afterlife to your heart’s content. Only, I beg you, do not try your hand at necromancy, for I really would have something to say about that. *Au revoir,* my darlings.”

He winked at them and sauntered from the room as if it had been a perfectly ordinary conversation.

"Christ," Sylvester said, watching him go with an expression of revulsion. "Thank God that's done."

Aisling nodded, feeling strangely numb. Kilbane had forgiven her, had even suggested that Richard had been unhinged and her curse was not entirely responsible for his death. He was certainly not distraught by his brother's demise, and it appeared she might have got off lightly if Richard had been as cruel and disturbed as Kilbane suggested. Remembering the cold-eyed devil who'd laughed at her distress that night, she was inclined to believe it. But then again, she wasn't certain she believed Kilbane was entirely sane, either.

"We'd best get back to the party, love," Sylvester said gently. "I'm sorry. I imagine it's the last thing you want, but we must not cause talk by disappearing."

Aisling nodded. She felt numb and rather exhausted and wanted nothing more than to be alone with her thoughts, but Sylvester was right. For now, she must put a smile on her face and pretend everything was perfectly fine. She'd had enough practise at that. So she took his arm and allowed him to escort her back to the ballroom.

Chapter 16

Dearest Torie,

I am so sorry to hear you are poorly. I shall come and visit you soon and bring some books to make you feel better.

Think of me this night, for I am attending the grand summer ball at Trevick Castle. I think Rosamund will be there too? I hope so for I will need a friendly face. I write this in haste, as I am waiting for the carriage to be brought around. It is the biggest event I have attended since I came out and I have a beautiful gown for the occasion. Mama cried when she saw me all dressed in my finery and so I must do my best to make her proud and keep my wretched mouth shut, though you know as well as I how hard that is. Especially when I must endure the snubs of all those who think me an imposter and not fit for the company of fine people. Actually, it's rather entertaining, seeing how fast people can move away from me, like they could contract a disease from the workhouse simply because I was born there.

Poor Hart suffers more than I do. He despises these events and avoids them whenever he can. Papa sympathises, I know, but even he admits Mama is right and that he must foster connections in this world, shallow and ridiculous though it is.

Oh, I how I wish I might escape this marriage mart and the sensation of being put up for auction, which is grossly unfair of me, for my parents would never force me to marry for anything but love. Perhaps tonight I'll meet a sensible man with a brain in his head who can converse about anything other than his blasted dogs, horses, or superior talents.

No, I don't hold out much hope either, but I must dash. Hart is bellowing that the carriage is here. Wish me luck.

— Excerpt of a letter from Kathleen de Beauvoir (adopted daughter of Mrs Minerva and Mr Inigo de Beauvoir) to Lady Victoria Adolphus (daughter of their graces, Prunella and Robert Adolphus, The Duke and Duchess of Bedwin).

1st July 1841, Lady Trevick's Summer Ball, Trevick Castle, Warwickshire.

Aisling endured for another hour before deciding she must escape for a while before the supper waltz. She did not feel like eating, certain the food would lodge in her throat and choke her, but she'd have to do her best.

Once she had slipped from the crowd, she made her way to the hidden balcony that overlooked the ballroom to catch her breath and see her sister. Mama had agreed to let Cara and her friends sit up here and watch the splendid affair, providing they were quiet and did not misbehave. From the mad giggling coming from behind the hidden door, they weren't being entirely successful. Yet the sound soothed Aisling's jangling nerves and it made her happy to hear the girls sounding so carefree and joyful.

She opened the door to the gathering and discovered the reason for their merriment.

"Aisling!"

Lady Catherine Barrington, known to all as Cat, would undoubtedly one day wear the crown of the most beautiful woman of the *ton*. She was a ravishing creature, even whilst navigating that awkward cusp between childhood and becoming an adult that plagued so many with unwelcome afflictions like greasy hair and spots. She was also strong-willed, full of mischief and devilry, and regularly gave her poor father heart failure. Not that anyone would ever dare put a foot wrong around her, no matter how lovely she became. The Marquess of Montagu was probably the most powerful, and feared, man in England, and only a madman would tangle with him. Whoever married his darling Cat would need to be an exceptional fellow to live up to her father's expectations. Aisling rather pitied the fellow, whoever he would be.

"Isn't it beautiful?" Cara said, staring at the whirling crowd dancing below with a wistful sigh. "Oh, Aisling, you are lucky. I wish I were out already. I want to dance!"

Aisling smiled at her sister, wishing that she would never grow up and come out and have to face this lavish world that was so glitteringly tempting on the surface but hid treacherous waters.

"Don't tell on me, Aisling," Cat pleaded, taking her hand. "I'm supposed to be in bed by now, and I will go in a moment, but it's so dull to miss out on all the excitement. Have you seen Mama? She looks ever so lovely."

Aisling hugged her and smiled. "Yes, I have, and she does. I won't tell if you go to bed when I leave. How's that?"

Cat pursed her lips, looking a little mutinous but gave a sigh. "Oh, all right, then. I suppose that's fair, but don't go yet."

Aisling helped herself to a glass of iced lemonade and sighed with relief as the girls huddled before the ornately pierced wooden window screen. They gossiped and exclaimed, pointing out people they knew and admiring the ladies' gowns.

"Who is that?" Cat demanded.

Cara shook her head, peering down through the gaps in the screen. "I don't know. Aisling, who is that fellow?"

Aisling moved towards the screen and a prickle of unease ran down her spine as she saw Kilbane moving through the crowd. They parted before him as though aware of a predator in their midst, everyone turning their gazes away from him and pretending to be having a fascinating conversation elsewhere.

"That's the Marquess of Kilbane," she said, watching him with unease. "He's not supposed to be here, for he wasn't invited."

"Why did Papa let him in, then?" Cara asked, glaring at the man.

"Because he's the kind to cause worse trouble if you deny him what he wants. Papa was hoping to avoid a scene. If he were a gentleman, he wouldn't have come."

"But why wasn't he invited?" Cat demanded, her blonde brows knitting. "That doesn't seem fair."

Aisling sighed. She could hardly tell the girls all about the marquess and his dreadful reputation… at least not in any detail. "Because he's a very bad man."

Cat made a scathing sound. “Kilbane is an Irish name. You know better than anyone that’s likely got more to do with it than any bad behaviour. After all, the Earl of Vane is here, and he’s supposed to be wicked too.”

Aisling looked at the girl in surprise. “It may be a part of it,” she admitted, for there was plenty of prejudice among the *ton* for anyone with Irish blood and it was a fair point, but she did not believe Vane had ever come close to Kilbane’s desire for scandal and vice.

“I don’t think it’s fair that he wasn’t invited,” Cat said crossly. “I would have invited him. Wicked men are always the most entertaining in books and—.”

“But not in real life! *Never* in real life!” Aisling snapped, wanting to shake the girl for her reckless words.

Cat looked up at her in shock, and Aisling took a breath.

“I beg your pardon, Cat,” she said, regretting how harshly she’d spoken, but a terrible sense of foreboding had prickled down her spine, making her breath catch. “But do not go getting the idea that men like Kilbane have any romantic qualities. He’s selfish and arrogant and immoral and… you *must* stay away from him.”

She knew at once she’d said entirely the wrong thing as interest lit the girl’s silver-grey eyes.

“If you say so, Aisling,” Cat murmured, but turned back to watch the marquess make his way through the ballroom alone.

Matilda Barrington, the Marchioness of Montagu, watched her husband as he adjusted his cravat with long, elegant fingers.

“If you keep looking at me like that, we will not return in time for the supper waltz and people will talk,” he said, his silver eyes glinting wickedly in the dim light.

Matilda hid a smile. "You've behaved quite badly enough already this evening, my lord," she said, endeavouring to sound cross with him, which was ridiculous. He knew damn well she was as besotted now as when she'd first met him, though she'd hidden it a good deal better in those days. "I don't know what gets into you," she added sadly.

There was a low chuckle that sent shivers prickling up and down her spine.

"Little liar," he murmured, and she jumped as she realised he was standing right behind her, his hands sliding about her waist and his warm breath fluttering over the back of her neck. "You know exactly what gets into me because you provoke me. You've always provoked me and you're doing it still."

Matilda grinned and leaned back into him, inclining her head to allow him another kiss. She sighed as he released her.

"You had best check on that she-devil of ours, or our little Cat will be up to no good, mark my words," he said, patting her bottom as she headed towards the door.

"I know," Matilda said with a sigh. "I am all for strong-willed, independent young women, but that child terrifies me."

A smile softened her husband's beautiful if austere face and she laughed, shaking her head. "How can you smile so indulgently when it's your fault? You've spoiled her. If anyone knew the terrifying Marquess of Montagu could be reduced to putty by a little slip of a girl, no one would ever fear you again."

He snorted with amusement. "Then you'd best never tell, darling. Give the wicked creature a kiss from me. I shall see you back in the ballroom in time for our waltz. Do not be late."

"I wouldn't dream of it," Matilda replied, waiting until he confirmed the coast was clear before she exited the dimly lit parlour.

She blew him a kiss and hurried off to check on their naughty daughter. She was making her way along the impressive long portrait gallery when she saw a tall, dark figure ahead of her. He made an elegant picture, standing regarding a family portrait of the Baxter family. Matilda knew the painting well, and it was a wonderful likeness of Kitty and her family.

The man was studying it so intently he did not appear aware of her presence. Matilda considered him as she drew closer, intrigued by the fascination in his eyes. He appeared thoroughly absorbed, as though he were looking upon a depiction of some distant foreign land, full of exotic mysteries, not a portrait of a happy family in an English drawing room.

"It's lovely, isn't it?" she said, curious why he looked so intrigued.

He stiffened at once and the curiosity in his eyes vanished, replaced by something harder and far more cynical. Her breath caught as he turned, for he was younger than she had first thought, but his expression was diamond hard. Glittering eyes looked her over, a strange violet shade of blue she'd never seen before, but it was unusual enough that she now knew who this was. The Marquess of Kilbane.

She had never seen him in the flesh, though she had seen his father, and she had heard much about him and his older brother. Her heart had bled for the two boys, so like her own sons. The eldest had died in murky circumstances, from what her husband had heard. This young man was of an age with her middle child, Thomas, yet he had never stood a chance. His father had been a despicable excuse for a human being and had delighted to turn his boys out in his own dissipated image. If rumour was to be believed, the old marquess had filled the house with whores and libertines since they were children and allowed his boys to run free among them. God alone knew what horrors they had seen or been subjected to. It was perhaps for that reason Matilda did not hurry away from him but stayed, her maternal instincts getting the better of good sense.

"It is lovely," he said, a smile flickering at the corners of his mouth. "I am just wondering which of them I fancy most. The countess is still a beautiful woman, and one must consider all the experience a more mature woman brings to the bedroom. She has a wonderfully naughty laugh. I think she'd be a great deal of fun. But then there's the earl, a handsome fellow. Such powerful arms. He looks like he might have a firm hand with badly behaved boys, don't you think? The daughters don't interest me, though they're pretty, I'll grant you, but virgins are too much bother. They have a disquieting tendency to weep afterwards. I'd far rather someone who knows what to do with what."

He grinned at her, and Matilda only smiled at him.

"I'm afraid you'll have to do better than that if you wish to make me blush, Lord Kilbane. I have two grown-up sons. I've heard all the rude words and I know when children are trying to goad me," she said gently. "I'm not easily shocked."

He tilted his head to one side, regarding her with delight. Black curls surrounded a devilishly handsome face, and she could only feel a surge of melancholy for all he was allowing to go to waste upon a life filled with debauchery and worthless pursuits. She doubted he was happy, doubted he knew what the word meant. His expression cleared, and she suspected he now realised who she was.

"Lady Montagu," he said on a breath of laughter. His heavy-lidded gaze roved over her with a provocative show of interest. "Well, well. I am honoured, my lady. I am almost tempted to exert myself to prove just how shocking I can be, and I *never* exert myself. Though I can believe your pretty feathers are hard to ruffle after so many years married to such a man. The *ton* fears him more than they do me, though perhaps for different reasons. I keep telling them they can only fall into sin if they *really* want to, if they put their heart and soul into it. Even I can't corrupt someone by simply breathing the same air. There must be an inherent desire to sin hidden somewhere in their souls… which I admit there usually is. But you must truly want to be a villain to do it successfully."

"I'm not sure that's true, or at least, that all villains wish to be so. Some have villainy thrust upon them."

He laughed at that, recognising the misquote. "I assure you, I was born a villain. With my bloodline it was never in doubt, though I like to think I have achieved far more than my due, considering my years."

He moved closer and Matilda was suddenly aware of the strength in his tall, athletic form. Kilbane might act the lazy aristocrat, but he was all coiled power, lulling you into believing he would not strike.

"How do you fancy making the evening more interesting?" he asked, his voice low and seductive.

Good heavens, but he was deadly! Matilda was not the slightest bit tempted, not with a beautiful and adoring husband of her own, but she could well understand how this man could cut a swathe through society, seducing anyone he put his mind to. Wickedness had its own appeal, as she knew very well.

"I don't think so, my lord. Even if I wished to—which I very much do not—my husband would feel the need to murder you slowly and painfully, and I suspect you would not enjoy the experience."

A slow smile curved over his sensual mouth, and he shrugged. "Well, you never know, but I would be happy for him to join us," Kilbane murmured, reaching out to touch a finger to her cheek. "I never learned to share my toys, but I could make an exception for him. Such a spectacular creature he is. Terrifying *and* gorgeous. Quite irresistible."

"He is indeed," Matilda said, feeling only regret for this damaged, beautiful man and all he might have been. "But I *am* the jealous kind, I'm afraid, and I should feel the need to murder you."

"Alas," the marquess said with a heavy sigh. "Such a disappointment, but life is full of such experiences."

"It is," Matilda said with genuine sadness. What might he have been if he had been her son? If he had belonged to someone who gave a damn? Though she knew it was madness, she reached out and grasped his arm gently. "You look tired. Why not have a brief respite from your dastardly ways and have an early night? Even villains need a day off."

He gave a bark of laughter, those strangely beautiful eyes shining with amusement as his sensual mouth curved into a cruel smile. When he spoke, his voice was hard and cold. "You think I can shrug off the role like a cloak, my lady? You don't have the slightest idea of what you deal with, though I should be delighted to show you."

Matilda nodded, knowing it was hopeless. He was too far gone to come back now, lost in the vile world his disgusting father had created for him. She wished the man wasn't dead so she could find a fitting punishment for him, but with luck, the almighty had that well in hand.

"Take care of yourself, Kilbane," she said softly.

He stared at her, frowning. He evidently hadn't expected that. Matilda patted his arm and walked away, sending up a prayer of thanks that her boys had never come to harm or fallen too far into darkness like that poor lost soul had done.

Chapter 17

Max,

Burt is sic. Plese come.

— Excerpt of a letter from Master Pike to The Hon'ble Maxwell Drake, Earl of Vane.

1st July 1841, Lady Trevick's Summer Ball, Trevick Castle, Warwickshire.

Sylvester searched the ballroom for the third time, but there was still no sign of Aisling. She had been understandably withdrawn since the strange confrontation with Kilbane, and he was uncertain of her mood. His own feelings were easier to read, relief that Aisling was not guilty of murder at the top of the list. There was no question in his mind. Even if what she'd said had precipitated the late marquess' descent into madness, she had merely spoken angry words in the heat of the moment. The vile man had got everything he deserved for treating an innocent so, and it seemed clear enough from what Kilbane had told them that his brother was already well on the way to madness. That Aisling believed all this nonsense she had learned from Biddy was more disturbing, but he did not know what to do about that. He would not lie to her and pretend he believed in curses or magic, yet he did not dismiss the possibility that much of what she believed was grounded in fact.

His feelings towards her specifically were not so easy to manage, though he understood them well enough. He was falling in love with her, much as he wanted to believe otherwise. It was stupid of him, and he needed to put distance between them as quickly as possible, before things went too far. After all she had suffered, the last thing he wanted was to hurt her if, by some miracle, she felt the same way. He knew that was unlikely, but she no longer seemed to loathe him, at least. He wished he were a wealthy man, or at least one with better prospects, but she was the daughter of an earl with a significant dowry and, though the admission hurt his pride, he was beneath her notice. The only reason she didn't have more men beating down her door was because she hid herself from society and kept everyone at a distance. Perhaps now the cloud over her head was gone she could heal and move on. He hoped so, even if he would not be there to see it. Melancholy swept over him, and he badly needed a drink.

To his relief, he found a waiter carrying a tray and snatched up two glasses before he headed out to the terrace. He downed the first glass of wine, wishing it were something stronger, and set down the glass before carrying the other with him to the balustrade where two men were leaning, staring down into the dark gardens.

"How do, Sylvester," Barnaby said, his expression gloomy. "I hope you are having a better evening than we are."

"What's amiss?" Sylvester asked, looking between him and Louis César, who looked as Friday faced as Barnaby did.

"Women," Barnaby said with a heavy sigh. "Lady Millicent has been besieged by a duke, a viscount, and a cit who could likely buy Derbyshire with his pocket change. I am outclassed."

"Then you're in good company," Sylvester replied darkly and mirrored their stance, leaning upon the balustrade and staring out into the darkness.

"The best," Barnaby said with a crooked grin, chinking his glass against Sylvester's and then Louis'.

"Must be nice to be titled and rich," Sylvester muttered before turning a quizzical gaze upon Louis. "Oh, and to look like a fallen angel. Bearing in mind, you are titled, disgustingly rich, and renowned for being the handsomest man on three continents, I find it hard to believe someone turned down your advances."

"Oh, well, it's—" Barnaby began only to make a strangled sound as Louis elbowed him. "Private," Barnaby wheezed succinctly, rubbing his ribs.

"Fair enough," Sylvester replied, taking a large swallow of his wine.

"Mr Cootes?"

Sylvester turned at once to see Aisling standing in the open doorway.

"My lady," he said, setting down his glass.

"Might I speak with you? In private."

"Of course." He hurried towards her, aware of Barnaby and Louis' murmurs of 'good luck.' Not that it would do him any good.

"Come with me," she said, guiding him back into the ballroom and out into a crowded corridor. Sylvester followed her, and she hurried along until they came to the long picture gallery. There were one or two people milling about, and she took his arm. "Pretend to look at the portraits," she whispered.

Puzzled, but willing to do as she asked, he regarded a large family portrait. It was a recent one, and the artist had caught the wary, haunted look in Aisling's eyes. She looked fragile and lovely, and his heart seemed to be squeezed within his chest. He wanted to be the man to take that look from her eyes, to protect her and help her find peace and happiness. He sighed.

"It's a good likeness."

"What?" she said absently, tearing her gaze from the couple who were just leaving the gallery. "Oh, yes, I suppose so. Come along, quickly."

She tugged at his arm, guiding him into an alcove and pressing her hand against a small square in the panel. There was a click, and a concealed door swung open. Sylvester looked at it and then at Aisling.

"There's a lot of hidden passages and rooms," she said, interpreting his look of surprise. "It's an ancient building. Come on."

Sylvester hesitated. As much as he wanted to be alone with her, he was not blackguard enough to think it was a good idea. "Aisling, I'm not sure—"

"Oh, do hurry," she said crossly. "Before someone sees."

The sound of footsteps behind them galvanised him into action, and he stepped through the opening, relieved to discover a lamp and tinderbox. He made quick work of lighting it before Aisling stepped through and closed the door behind her.

"It's this way."

Sylvester held the lamp aloft and followed her down the narrow corridor as it twisted back and forth, sometimes branching out in different directions. It was a maze with no defining features and he admitted himself impressed she knew the way so well. Finally, she stopped and opened a door, which turned out to be another hidden panel, this time leading into a small parlour. The room was dark, but the lamp gave out a friendly, warm glow that made it feel cosy and intimate.

Aisling closed the panelled door and Sylvester set the lamp down on a side table, wondering what she wanted to say. He waited as she turned to face him, but she seemed as uncertain as he was. She clutched her arms about her middle, staring up at him.

"I don't know whether to kiss you or hit you," she said at last, the frustration in her voice audible.

Sylvester laughed. "A common reaction, I fear, though the latter seems the most popular option."

"I can't imagine why," she grumbled.

"I'm sorry, love. I couldn't lie to you," he said, because it was obvious enough why she was cross with him.

"I don't want you to lie!" she exclaimed, her eyes flashing. "I just… It's been a part of my life for a long time, Sylvester, and… and I want you to keep an open mind."

Sylvester rubbed the back of his neck, uncomfortable with her demand. "If it means believing you are responsible for the death of the late marquess, I'll hold on to my scepticism. Thank you very much."

She frowned at him, shaking her head. "I have a lot to make up for, Sylvester. I did a wicked thing."

How he wished he could convince her otherwise, but she was determined to take the blame. He sighed, moving closer to her. Though he knew he ought not, he held out his arms to her, his heart giving a little skip of delight when she moved into them, seeking his embrace. She rested her head on his chest and he closed his arms around her as longing swept through him.

"You did not. You were hurt and angry and you lashed out. That man lied to you, used you and destroyed your innocence, and then treated you with callous disregard, never mind his attempt to blackmail you too. I do not believe you truly wanted him dead any more than you bear any responsibility for it. He made his own bed with a lifetime of wickedness, and you had the ill fortune to get caught up in it. That's all, love. You're a good person with a good heart. It's time to forgive yourself and move on. The best thing you can do is to live your life to the full, to be happy, and make other people happy along the way."

He looked down at her to find her dark eyes watching him. “That’s what Biddy said. She said he brought his fate down upon himself and I need to forget it.”

Sylvester smiled and reached to tuck an unruly curl behind her ear. “Well, then. You’d best heed our advice, eh?”

“Perhaps. I’m still annoyed you don’t believe me,” she said, though there was no anger behind the words, only a wistful note as she gazed up at him.

Desire stirred to life as his gaze fell to her mouth. *No*. She’d had a stressful evening, and he had nothing to offer her. The earl would laugh in his face if he dared to ask permission to court her.

“I know,” he whispered, unable to tear his gaze away from her beautiful face. She fitted him so well, her lithe body resting comfortably against his, her warmth sinking into him and making him want things he had no business wanting.

“But you are an honest man, Sylvester Cootes.”

He grinned. “To a fault,” he admitted wryly.

She smiled then and reached up to stroke his cheek. He closed his eyes like an indolent cat, drugged by her touch, wanting more, much more.

“It is strange how I wanted so desperately to be away from you, and yet you kept finding me. You found me in that tiny old bookshop when you’d never been there before, and then something brought you to Trevick, pushing us together again.”

“Alana, not *something*,” he said, feeling a little dazed as her gentle fingers stroked over his cheek.

“And then I did my utmost to escape you, and your horse threw a shoe, and you got lost and ended up at Biddy’s cottage.”

His eyes flicked open, and he gazed at her warily. “Just a coincidence, love.”

She shook her head. "The universe keeps throwing us together, Sylvester. At first, I was just too stubborn to pay attention, and then I disliked the idea on principle because… well, because you're so annoying. But the trouble is—you do bother me, just like you said. I admit it. You win. You bother me and annoy me and… and I like you very much, even when I want to shake you. I don't want to fight my fate any longer."

Sylvester stared at her. She liked him—*very much!* He bothered her, which was even better, and yet… he disliked the idea she thought there was some mysterious force at work. He opened his mouth to say as much, but she grasped the back of his neck and pulled him down, pressing her mouth to his.

Whatever words he might have spoken evaporated in a proverbial puff of smoke the moment her lips touched his. He might not believe in magic, or that she was a witch, but she enchanted him. She had cast a spell over him, and he'd been well and truly caught in her toils. Desire swept away all his good intentions in a burst of heat and need that caught him off guard. He held her tighter, taking control of the kiss and demanding more and more, wanting everything. He held her close to him, frustrated by too many layers of clothing. She made a soft sound that might have been pleasure or alarm, he wasn't certain, but it was enough to worry him and snap him out of the haze of lust that had claimed him.

Good God, a despicable man had already taken her advantage of her once. There was no way on earth he'd be guilty of doing the same.

"Christ, I'm sorry," he gasped, trying to move away from her. If he was going to claim any grasp upon sanity, he needed to put distance between them.

Aisling held on, refusing to let go. "Don't be sorry. Kiss me, again," she demanded.

Sylvester shook his head. "No. You don't mean that. You've had a difficult evening, that's all, and…."

She tugged at his neck again, claiming his mouth, and Sylvester groaned as she pressed closer to him. He wrenched away from her with difficulty and put a finger to her lips.

"Love, stop this. It's not really what you want."

"It is," she said, determination shining in her eyes. "I hated the entire experience with… with *him*, but when you kiss me, it's so lovely. I want to know how it is supposed to feel, Sylvester. I want to feel your hands on my skin, your body touching mine. I want you. Show me what to do."

Sylvester's brain melted.

"That's not a helpful thing to say when I'm trying to behave myself, Aisling," he managed, the desperate need to lay her down on the conveniently placed settee behind her warring with his desire to be a gentleman. He could not offer her marriage, not when he had no way of keeping a wife. He lived in a small cottage when her home was this great behemoth of a castle, and she was used to the finest things in life. The comedown would make her miserable and everyone would believe she'd married beneath her. They'd be right, too.

"I don't want to be helpful if you're going to deny me what I want," she said, with far too much honesty. Her clever fingers fell to his buttons, making short work of his waistcoat.

"Love, we can't do this," he said, though his heart was thudding with excitement and if his blood burned any hotter, he'd catch his clothes alight.

"Well, I can, so don't tell me you've forgotten what to do, or are you going to admit you're no good at this?" she asked, a provoking smile at her mouth. "Is it you that needs instruction?"

"No!" he retorted, even though he knew damn well what she was playing at. "I know very well what to do, I thank you, which is why I need to be the grownup here and make it stop."

"You? A grownup?" She burst out laughing, aggravating him so much it was a moment before he realised she'd pulled his shirt from his trousers. The feel of her warm hands on his skin made the point for him and he sucked in a breath.

"Christ!" he exclaimed. "Behave, Aisling! You don't know what you're doing to me!"

"Oh, I think I do," she said, laughing at his consternation. "I've long understood the mechanics of it. I just don't know how to get any pleasure from it, though I admit I'm enjoying this enormously."

He stilled then, staring down at her with his heart aching. Her first experience of physical pleasure had been anything but. It had been cruel and painful, and she was asking him to replace that memory with a new one. How could he deny her that? He knew how to bring her pleasure without fully consummating their relationship or risking a child.

"You truly want this?" he asked, studying her face.

She nodded, smiling up at him and he wondered how in God's name he could walk away from this, from her. He realised then why he was so reluctant to be intimate with her. It wasn't only a stubborn streak of decency, though he wanted to treat her with the respect she had always deserved. It was because he risked what little remained of his heart. If he did this, she would own him body and soul, for he could not give her what she asked without sharing his own heart with her. It would doom him to spend his days loving a woman he could never call his own, and yet he suspected it was already too late, so what difference would it make? He might as well have this much. But he would be honest with her first.

He cupped her face between his hands, staring down at her.

"Aisling," he said, his voice not entirely steady as his nerves leapt and his heart trembled at the idea of making himself vulnerable to her. "I want this, I want you, more than you can know. My God, love, you're so beautiful it's sometimes hard to breathe when you're close to me. I am in awe of your strength, of the courage with which you have endured the past years when you've been so frightened, and so alone. If I could, I would offer you the world, but I've not the world to give, love. I'm that despicable variety of gentleman who must earn his keep. I've no money, no home to offer you and even if I had both, I'm still far beneath your notice. You could marry an earl or a marquess, even a duke, and I—"

"Sylvester, what the devil are you on about?" she broke in, glaring at him. "I don't want a duke or a marquess or anything of the sort. I never have. I want *you*—and you're giving speeches. *Now*?"

She looked so outraged he didn't know whether to laugh or cry.

"Yes, love, because I can't stay. I can't offer for you as I should, as I want to do, and I don't want to be another man in your life who took something precious and then left you alone."

Her expression was fierce, but he could see beneath the bravado, see the too bright glitter in her eyes.

"Then don't," she said, her voice hard. Her fingers tightened on his shirt, holding tight. "Don't go. Hold on to me."

He shook his head. Usually he loved arguing with her, relished watching her eyes flash and the colour flame in cheeks as her temper rose, but he did not want to argue this point. This time, he had no choice. "How can I?" he whispered, stroking her cheek. "Your father would laugh in my face if I dared offer for you."

Aisling shook her head. "He wouldn't. Not if he knew, not if—"

"Love," Sylvester grasped her shoulders and gave her a little shake. "Be sensible."

Her stubborn chin jutted, and he recognised the mutinous glint in her eyes all too well. "Fine. But I shan't marry anyone else."

His stupid heart leapt at her words, and he gave a shaky laugh. "I can't ask that of you."

She glowered at him. "You didn't ask. I told you. You're the one I want. I won't have anyone else," she retorted, cantankerous as ever.

"So you did," he whispered, hardly daring to believe it. "Would you wait for me?" he asked, knowing he was likely only setting them both up for worse heartbreak in months to come, but she was wonderfully stubborn and he… he wanted her so badly he couldn't think straight.

"Yes," she whispered, her expression softening, her dark eyes glowing with happiness. "Yes, I would wait."

"I cannot make you promises this time. It's probably a forlorn hope," he warned her. "I am working hard to help my brother turn Marcross around and make it profitable, but… but I'll only ever be an estate manager, love. I've no rich relations to pin my hopes on. I'll never have a title…."

"Sylvester," she said, a note of impatience ringing in her voice. "Shut up and kiss me."

He couldn't fight it any longer. She was warm and willing and in his arms, and he wanted her with everything he had. He always had. Sylvester had wanted her from the first moment he'd seen her step out of the carriage eighteen months ago at Rowsley Hall. He'd known it then and had only been deceiving himself in the following months, pretending he wanted only to know what she was hiding. Well, now he knew, and wanting had become loving and needing and he was in a sorry state, and that was a fact.

"Lock the door," he said, his voice rough, for if he was to do this, he was damned if there would be any interruptions.

For once in her life, she obeyed him without question, and Sylvester shrugged out of his coat and waistcoat. She turned, leaning against the locked door, watching as he tugged his shirt over his head and cast it aside.

"You're sure?"

She nodded, her gaze travelling over him like a caress. His body tightened in reaction, his cock pulsing, impatient for her touch.

"Come here."

He almost smiled as she obeyed his command without a murmur of dissent, but then her hands slid over his bare chest and her touch was electrifying. Sylvester wrapped his arms around her and claimed her mouth, triumph surging through him as she pressed closer. Her hands glided up and down his back, sending shivers of pleasure cascading over his skin, and he needed to touch her. Now.

Though he did not want to stop, he broke the kiss, turning her around to undo the fastenings on her gown.

"Hurry," she pleaded, the word breathless.

Sylvester laughed and then cursed as his clumsy fingers fumbled over the ridiculous fastenings. There were too many of them, and the dim light in the room wasn't helping.

"Oh, do get on with it!" she pleaded, jittery with impatience.

"Well, if you'd hold still!" he complained, and then sighed with relief as the gown sagged and she wriggled it to the floor. She fidgeted some more while he undid her six—*six*—petticoats until there was an immense pile of white flounces at her feet. She turned back to him, grabbing hold of him about the neck, demanding he kiss her again. "So… impatient," he murmured against her mouth.

Breaking free, he swept her up into his arms before she could complain again and carried her to the settee. He sat down with her in his lap and encouraged her to move, so she sat straddling him. With relief he noted her corset fastened in the front, which made life easier, and he set to work, loosening the strings until she could cast it aside, leaving her in her shift, drawers and stockings.

Excitement thrummed beneath his skin, but he reminded himself of what was possible, how far he would go. He would not simply take as that vile creature had, the bastard. With his heart thudding a mad tattoo in his ears, Sylvester reached up and pushed the wide neck of the shift so it fell from one shoulder. She withdrew her arm and then did the same on the other side. Even in the dim light, he could tell she was blushing as she exposed her breasts to his hungry gaze. Tenderness swelled in his chest, and he wanted for her never to feel uncertain or ashamed or anything but loved and cherished ever again.

"You are so lovely, Aisling," he whispered, daring to stroke the impossibly soft skin with the back of his fingers. She shivered and closed her eyes. Gently, he eased her closer to him, aware of her sharp intake of breath as she settled against the hard ridge of his arousal.

"Nothing you don't want," he promised her, though his voice sounded cracked and uneven.

She nodded, bracing her arms on the back of the settee, leaning over him so that her splendid breasts were tantalisingly close to his mouth. He groaned and cupped the soft mounds, caressing and squeezing a little, toying with the delicate pink nubs at the tips which were making his mouth water with the need to taste them. Sylvester leaned in and caught one in his mouth, sucking delicately. Aisling jolted in his lap, inadvertently pressing her sex hard against his cock and sending a bolt of pure lust firing through his blood. He moaned and thrust his hips against her again, seeking more, and her breath caught. She clutched at his shoulders as he did it again, still suckling at her breast, grazing the tender bud with his teeth. Her hands moved to his hair, her fingers tangling there, holding him against her, as if he was fool enough to want to move.

She caught on quickly and was soon writhing in his lap, chasing her own pleasure as she drove him to the edge of sanity. If she kept this up, he was going to explode in his small clothes and he did not relish the idea of spending the rest of the evening damp and sticky. Removing them was an even worse idea, for his gentlemanly notions of what he could give her were fraying, and other, more urgent desires demanded he take control, take her and make her his own.

"Wait," he rasped, shifting her in his arms and laying her down on the settee. He moved over her, sliding his hand between her thighs and finding the slit in her drawers. She gasped as he discovered the soft nest of curls and delved deeper, parting her folds until he found the tenderest part of her and stroked. She cried out and arched beneath him, grabbing at his arms and staring up at him with wide eyes.

He grinned down at her, so happy something inside him shifted, settling into a new place, making room for the only woman who would ever fit in the space she had carved for herself in his heart.

"My, you look pleased with yourself," she murmured, breathless and a little indignant, though her mouth kicked up at the corners.

"With good reason," he said, staring down at her. "I am the luckiest man in the whole damned world."

She laughed then, her eyes shining with happiness, and his heart threatened to burst knowing that he had made her feel that way.

"Do you trust me?" he asked her, wanting to taste her so badly he was trembling with the need for it.

"You know I do," she said, those simple words breaking him when he knew what it cost her to put her trust in anyone. Those words were a gift beyond value, and he would treasure them always.

He leaned down and kissed her mouth tenderly, putting everything he felt into it. "Thank you," he whispered as he lifted his head, pleased by the dazed, unfocused look in her eyes. Moving down her body, he paused at points of interest, to lavish more attention upon her lovely breasts, the soft curve of her belly. He kissed and licked and gave tiny nips with his teeth until she was squirming beneath him. As he nuzzled into the soft skin at the apex of her thighs, her breath caught and held.

"Sylvester?" she murmured.

He smiled against her skin, the scent of her fogging his brain with lust. "Trust me," he murmured, before pressing his mouth to her dark curls. She gasped, and then squealed as his tongue traced the seam of that private place, easing inside to find the delicate spot that would make her moan and writhe and call out his name.

"Oh," she said, a note of surprise in her voice as he found the tender bud and teased it gently. "Oh. *Oh!*"

He licked her in one long sweep of his tongue, pleased by the shivering ripple of pleasure he sensed roll over her. So he did it again, and again, until she was wild beneath him, clutching at his hair, at the cushions of the settee, making soft sounds of pleasure, whimpering with need, until Sylvester was ready to come apart too without even touching himself or being touched. Finally she went still, holding her breath for a long, tense moment until she tumbled over the edge. She cried out, a desperate sound of delight as the climax rocked her. Sylvester held her hips still, gentling his movements as the crescendo ebbed, determined she should wring every last ounce of joy from this moment.

Finally she subsided, her breathing erratic, her gaze hazy and unfocused as she reached for him.

Sylvester shook his head. "Just… give me a moment," he rasped, trying to concentrate on not losing his mind.

"No," she said, her hands circling his arms, pulling him closer. "You didn't… You haven't…."

She blushed scarlet and Sylvester smiled at her, leaning down to kiss her mouth.

"That doesn't matter. This was for you, love."

"It matters to me," she said, stubborn to the last. Before he could protest, her nimble fingers were undoing the fall on his trousers, and he watched with his heart thudding dully as she freed him. His cock sprang forward, eager and demanding, and he damn near whimpered with gratitude as she curled her fingers around him.

"Show me," she said, staring up at him. "I want to do it right. You made me feel so… so lovely, Sylvester. Let me do this for you, please."

He made a choked sound and adjusted her hold on him. "All right, but it won't take long," he warned her, showing her how to stroke him.

"Like this?" she queried, a little clumsy at first, not that his body gave a damn.

She was touching him and, right now, that was all he needed. He closed his eyes, braced on his arms over her, trembling as he let go of the reins of desire he'd held onto so tightly. Her free hand stroked his flank, moved up over his belly to his chest where she toyed with his nipple, pinching lightly. That was all it took. His chest heaved, and a muted roar tore from his throat as the pleasure cascaded through him. He could do nothing but let it come, his body convulsing as her small hand possessed him, commanded him, and he spilled his seed in a hot splash across her stomach.

He tried to bring himself under control, to focus on her and assure himself she was not upset or disgusted by what had happened. When she finally came into focus, she was regarding him with a smug cat-in-the-cream-pot smile that put any nonsense of that sort to rest.

He collapsed beside her, utterly spent.

"I'll fetch you my handkerchief," he murmured. "In just a moment. Just… need a second."

She snorted and shook her head. "I can see to it."

He felt her get up and a moment later she returned to him, and he gathered her in his arms, holding her tight. She snuggled in close and the idea that he might never have this again made him want to howl with misery. He toyed with the idea of telling her parents he'd compromised her, but knew he wouldn't do it. Shaming her like that after everything she'd been through was beyond him, and besides, he could not bear for her parents to believe him a fortune hunter.

"We must return to the ballroom," she said, though he was relieved to hear the regret in her voice.

"Yes."

"I saved you the last waltz."

He perked up at that, propping himself up on one arm to look down at her.

"You did?"

She nodded, and he grinned at her. To his surprise, she reached up and traced the contours of his mouth, her expression so tender his throat grew tight.

"Handsome devil," she whispered.

"Aisling." He stared down at her, knowing he ought not to say it, not when he had no right to, but the words burst out all the same and he could do nothing to stop them. "I love you."

Her expression was one of surprise, and then her eyes grew misty, and her lip trembled.

"Oh, no, don't," he began helplessly. "Don't cry, Aisling. I—"

She gave a hiccoughing laugh and flung herself at him, holding on tight and peppering kisses over his face. Well, that seemed like a good sign, so he did not press her to return the words. She'd had emotions enough to sort through this evening without him demanding declarations of her. He was with her. She had trusted him with her secrets, with her body, and she wanted to wait for him. Aisling Baxter wanted to marry no other man but him, and if that wasn't a declaration, he didn't know what was. He gave her one last kiss and regretfully disentangled himself from her arms.

"Come on, my love. If we're to be in attendance for the last waltz, we need to be dressed or people might talk."

She gave a snort of laughter. "Ridiculous creature," she muttered, but with affection now, and he grinned at her.

"I suspect it's going to take longer to get you back into all those petticoats than it did to get you out of them, so get a move on."

"Yes, Sylvester," she said sweetly, rolling her eyes at him, and Sylvester decided this prickly, gentle, complicated, wonderful woman was the most perfect girl in the entire world, and he would do anything, anything at all to make her his.

Chapter 18

Pike,

Send for Dr Langley. Show him the card I gave you and tell him to send me any bills. With luck, I'll be with you before you get this, but I'm on my way. Tell Burt I'm coming as fast as I can.

— Excerpt of a letter from The Hon'ble Maxwell Drake, Earl of Vane to Master Pike.

2nd July 1841, Chessett House, Warwickshire.

"Must you go?" Barnaby demanded, wincing a little in the bright sunlight pouring through the windows of the breakfast room.

Maxwell nodded, accepting a cup of coffee from his footman. "I must, yes. A friend has been taken ill. Someone I owe a great debt to. I must return to London at once, but you may stay as my guests as long as you wish. My people will look after you."

"Oh, well, of course you must go in that case, and don't worry. We won't drink your cellars dry. Louis and I will be off to the races in a day or two, or at least that was the plan."

Maxwell laughed. He liked Barnaby a good deal, which was odd as he was the kind of good natured, if not terribly bright, fellow who'd have irritated him to no end in previous years. Now, he did not quite understand why that was, except that he'd been an arrogant, selfish bastard. Perhaps he'd disliked to see goodness or kindness in others, for it made him realise what a contemptible creature he'd become. He frowned, overwhelmed with the usual tide of self-loathing that swamped him when he remembered his past, all the terrible things he'd done, and the people he had hurt.

"Are they seriously ill?" Barnaby asked, his eyes filled with compassion, reading Maxwell's scowl with concern.

Maxwell shook himself out of his memories and paid attention to his guest. "I don't know. His… er… son, sent a note, but it had no details save that he was ill and to come quickly."

"A pity. I hope it's nothing serious. A false alarm, perhaps," he added with an encouraging smile.

"I hope so too," Maxwell said, hesitating before adding in a low voice. "Stay clear of Kilbane, won't you?"

Barnaby snorted and set down his coffee cup. "I'm aware I'm not the sharpest knife in the drawer, Maxwell, old fellow, but I ain't no flat. I know trouble when I see it, and Kilbane is trouble looking for a place to happen. Don't you worry, I intend to get Louis as far away from him as quick as I can. I'd talk him into leaving today, but likely we'll not see him stir before noon."

"Who won't stir before noon?" demanded a weary voice from the doorway.

Barnaby started in surprise. "Louis! Bless me. I did not expect to see you up and about at this hour."

Louis leaned against the doorjamb, shading his eyes from the bright daylight with a pinched expression. He was pale, with dark circles beneath his eyes, his hair was ruffled, and he had shrugged on a silk dressing gown over the clothes he'd clearly slept in, and yet still looked far more elegant than either Maxwell or Barnaby, who were properly attired for the day.

"Café, s'il te plaît," he murmured, his voice hoarse.

Barnaby tsked, shaking his head as he poured out another cup of coffee. "Now, I don't like to say I told you so, but I warned you not to start on the brandy. Said you'd suffer the consequences."

"Barnaby, the devil is using my head as an anvil, that is punishment enough without you scolding me too," he protested, moving reluctantly into the room and sitting down heavily in the nearest chair.

Barnaby put the cup of coffee into his hands and went to pull the curtain across to keep the sun from Louis' eyes.

"Better?" he asked.

"Marginally," Louis said with a sigh, sipping his coffee.

"Maxwell here is leaving us to attend to a sick friend, so we're to have the run of his house, but I thought we might leave anyway, soon as you're up to it, any rate? What say you?" Barnaby stared at his friend hopefully, his eagerness for them to be on their way and as far from Kilbane as possible, more than obvious.

Louis massaged his temples with delicate fingers. "I say I am liable to cast up my accounts if I get within ten feet of a moving carriage. Perhaps tomorrow."

Barnaby sighed. "Figured as much. Right ho."

"I hope your friend recovers, Maxwell," Louis said, looking very much as if it would not take a moving carriage to provoke such an eventuality.

"Thank you. So do I," Maxwell said, and got to his feet. He'd best oversee his packing. He was catching the early train and his luggage could follow on after, but he knew better than to leave such arrangements unsupervised. Worry knotted his belly as he wondered what was wrong with Burt. The old man was built like a whippet without a scrap of fat on his thin frame and had few reserves to call upon if he took ill. He was also a sly devil and tough as old boot leather. Maxwell knew he'd fight tooth and nail to stay alive and see young Pike grow up strong and happy. Not that Maxwell would let anything happen to the lad. If he'd had his way, he'd have moved them both out of London months since. He'd wanted to find them a place on one of his estates. When he'd suggested it, they'd looked at him with such abject horror it was clear it wouldn't happen. Perhaps now he could change their minds. Country air, away from London's filth, would do them the world of good.

Whilst he was there, he wanted to ask them some questions about his time with them. He only vaguely remembered any of it, having been out of his head with pain and laudanum, but he'd had the strangest sense of déjà vu at the ball last night. The young woman Louis had identified as Miss de Beauvoir had snagged in his mind, stirring a hazy memory. He hoped to God she was not someone he had wronged, she was too young for that, surely? Oh, please God, let that be true. His memory had snagged upon her though and insisted she belonged in the stews where he'd lingered in those months when he'd not known who or what he was. Yet what would a woman who was clearly accepted among the *ton* be doing running wild in the Seven Dials, of all places? It was a puzzle, and he did not like puzzles. He'd tried to speak to her several times last night, but all his efforts had been thwarted. The damned girl was like quicksilver, slipping away just when he thought he'd got her pinned down. He hadn't been the least bit sure if she'd done it on purpose or if she'd been unaware of him and it had just been bad luck.

He intended to find out.

10th July 1841, Trevick Castle, Warwickshire

Sylvester took one last look out of the bedroom window. The countryside as far as the eye could see belonged to the Trevick estate. The land was lush and fertile, well-managed, and made use of the most modern ideas, changing with the times, unlike many estates around the country. Sylvester had been grateful to the earl, who had happily shown him about the property and explained much of what they were doing to ensure the vast estate earned its keep. That was no simple task, yet for all the difference in size and budget, the same problems that the earl faced here beset them at Marcross, albeit on a smaller scale.

Trevick had seemed pleased with his interest and even appeared to like Sylvester. That was unlikely to continue if he discovered Sylvester was in love with his daughter, though. Despondency settled on his shoulders. He was leaving today, escorting Alana home, and then returning to Marcross. He ought to be grateful. He had a job, a comfortable place to live and a steady income, far more than he'd dared hope for until recently, when some days he'd not been sure if he could afford to keep his horse for another day or would have to sell it to pay his rent. Yet it wasn't enough, not if he was to win Aisling. He ought never to have agreed to let her wait for him, to give them both false hope when there was none. With a sigh, he walked to the door and closed it behind him. He did not want to say goodbye to her, not knowing when he would see her again.

"Oh, Mr Cootes. I'm so glad I caught you before you left."

Sylvester straightened and forced a smile to his lips as the countess called to him from down the hallway.

"My lady, I would not have left without bidding you goodbye and thanking you for your hospitality."

"No, of course not. I do you a disservice. You have been a delightful guest, and we have been so happy to have you here."

"You're very kind, my lady."

The countess drew level with him and reached out, taking his hands in her. "No. You are very kind. Mr Cootes. I have seen the change in Aisling these past weeks. She laughs more and seems to be regaining her sparkle. I do not believe I am wrong in thinking you have had something to do with this."

Sylvester smiled, pride and love and frustration bursting in his chest. "If I have, then I have never been more pleased about anything in my life."

"You are a good man, Mr Cootes," the countess said. "I don't suppose you would confide…?"

"If Aisling wishes to tell you, she will," he said, his voice firm. "She put her trust in me, and I will not break that trust, not even for you."

The woman's eyes sparkled, and she swallowed hard, but she nodded. "I understand," she said, her voice unsteady. "Well. I hope one day she will confide in me, only… I wish she had felt able to—"

"She loves you and her father, my lady, very much. It was not a distrust or fear of reprisals or any lack on your part as parents, I assure you. You have nothing to reproach yourselves for," Sylvester said firmly, interrupted the countess, for he did not wish for her to suffer any more guilt.

Aisling adored her parents and had given him every reason to believe they had been attentive and loving.

"Oh." The countess put her hand to her mouth, fighting tears, and Sylvester reached out and patted her shoulder, feeling extremely awkward. She made a choked sound, a laugh, he thought, which was a blessing. He was uncertain how to cope with Aisling's mother in tears. "You have relieved my mind. I have been so worried and upset and s-so guilty. Thank you, Mr Cootes. Thank you so much. I shall never be able to repay you."

Sylvester hesitated, wanting so much to ask but… she was hardly going to hand over her daughter's hand in marriage to him just because she was grateful.

"There's no debt to repay," he said gently.

The countess sighed and smiled at him, taking his arm. "I shall escort you downstairs," she said as Sylvester's heart sank. He'd hoped to take his leave of Aisling in private, but now that would be impossible. "I hope we shall see you here at Trevick again soon, Mr Cootes?"

"I hope so too," he said, brightening with the hope the lady might think to invite him. "I should be delighted to visit again."

"You will be returning to Marcross Manor to your brother's estate?"

Sylvester nodded, his heart turning over as he saw Aisling waiting for him in the entrance hall. Alana was there with Cara and Violette, the three girls hugging each other and whispering secrets. "Yes. Once I have delivered Miss Alana back to her parents."

"Well, we must wish our guests a safe journey, darling," the countess said, taking Aisling's arm.

Sylvester forced a smile to his lips, too aware of the quality of the countess' gaze. She was watching them closely. Perhaps she suspected Sylvester's feelings for her daughter. Well, he would do nothing to cause Aisling trouble, but would behave like a gentleman.

He took Aisling's hand in his and bowed over it, formal and excruciatingly polite. "Thank you for being such a charming hostess, Lady Aisling. You have made my stay here at Trevick a memorable one."

"The pleasure was mine, Mr Cootes," she said, and though he ought to worry, for fear her mother took note, he could not regret the depth of regard he saw in her eyes. "I hope we shall see you again soon."

"If fortune smiles upon me," he said, hoping she understood the words were not as light-hearted as they sounded.

"Goodbye, my lady, countess. Come, Alana, we must not keep the horses standing, and we risk missing our train if we don't leave now."

Moments later, they were on their way, and the enormous edifice of the castle disappeared behind a thick screen of woodland.

15th July 1841, Swan Hall, East Sussex, Kent.

Evie smothered a yawn as Rachel brushed her hair out with long, firm sweeps of the brush. It was soothing, making her sleepy after a long and lovely day. She was nineteen years old today and her family had celebrated with her. It had been an almost perfect day.

Almost, because she had not heard from Louis and, though she hated to admit it, for it made her sound very spoiled and ungrateful, it had taken the shine off her happiness. Usually he found a way to get her gift to her, even if he could not see her in person. She wondered if perhaps he had forgotten this year, though he had always given her such wonderful gifts in the past. Ruefully, she had to admit to herself it wasn't the gift she was missing, but his attention. She liked it when he made a fuss of her, liked being the centre of his attention. Not that she disliked the presents either, for he had such exquisite taste, always seeming to know what she liked better than she did herself.

Perhaps he really had found someone special, as she had suspected. She had nagged him for years to find himself a wife and settle down, for she knew he was lonely. Had he finally taken her advice? The idea made her stomach feel peculiar, a strange empty sensation like when the carriage rolled over a small hump in the road at speed and your belly dropped away. If he married, he might not be her friend as he was now. It would not be surprising if his wife did not like or understand their friendship, though she knew if she married, a husband would like it even less. Louis' beautiful wife might not see Evie as a threat after all, and Louis' wife would undoubtedly be beautiful, for he could have anyone he chose. But whoever Evie's husband turned out to be, he would not like a man as sinfully handsome as Louis to have such a close friendship with her.

Oh, bother. It had been such a lovely day, and now she was feeling all out of sorts. Evie scolded herself for being foolish and reminded herself of how very blessed she was. Mama had arranged a splendid family party, and Papa had spoiled her dreadfully as he always did. Her older sister Florence had come with Henry and their new son, Oscar, who was simply adorable. Evie had enjoyed playing auntie to her nephew and holding him in her arms had confirmed her hopes for the future. She wanted a big family, with lots and lots of children. A mad, chaotic, wonderful mess of a family who would cause havoc and noise and let her love them and organise them and make them happy. Perhaps, she thought sadly, if she had all that, she could come to accept the loss of her dearest friend.

Whoever she married must understand and support her in that endeavour, though. She could not choose a man who thought children should be seen and not heard, who thought the nannies should be responsible for everything and his children presented to him for five minutes before bedtime, all pink-cheeked and smiling.

"Shall I plait it for you, miss?" Rachel asked, setting the brush aside.

Evie shook her head and patted Rachel's arm. "No, thank you. I can manage. You can go now. I'm sure you must be tired, too."

"I am that, miss, but I'm glad you had such a lovely day. Happy birthday to you again."

Evie blew her a kiss in thanks and sighed as the door closed. Her bed was calling her and looked wonderfully inviting. She always slept better here at Swan Hall than in town, preferring the peace of the countryside and clean air. London was all well and good for parties and entertainments, which she enjoyed very much, but it was always a relief to escape it for a while, especially when the summer months made town so fetid and unpleasant.

Slipping off her dressing gown, Evie was about to climb into bed when a soft tap sounded upon the glass doors that led onto her balcony. She frowned, wondering if a cat or a bird could have made a sound like that, when it happened again. Perplexed, she moved to the door and drew back the curtains and had to smother a shriek of alarm in the instant she saw a man standing there, and then realised who it was.

"Louis!" she exclaimed, unlocking the door and opening it. "Whatever are you doing here?"

He grinned at her, holding out a prettily wrapped parcel. *"Alors, ma petite,* you did not think I had forgotten, surely?"

"Oh!" Evie gave a choked laughed, suddenly in the grip of a swell of emotion that made her eyes burn and her throat tighten.

"Evie?" he said, softly, frowning at her. *"Mon Dieu,* you *did* think I'd forgotten!"

She tried to smile at him, disconcerted to discover she might cry. Whatever had got into her, making such a silly fuss. Only she was so relieved to know he hadn't been too busy with someone else to think about her. Embarrassed now, Evie shook her head in reply and snatched the present from his hands, trying to grin and pretend that had been all she'd been concerned about.

He laughed softly and followed her into her bedroom, closing the door behind him. Evie paused as she sat on the edge of the bed, composed enough now to speak to him.

"You climbed up the house," she said in wonder, only now realising he was dressed all in black, like a burglar. The harsh colour suited him, making him look rather wicked. "Oh, Louis, you might have fallen and hurt yourself."

He gave her a disgruntled look and waved this possibility away with an arrogant gesture. "Don't be foolish. I climb like a monkey, remember?"

She laughed, nodding. "I remember, but please be careful."

"I promise, but now open your present."

He crouched down before her, his expression intent, his blue eyes gleaming with excitement, and she felt an answering tug low in the pit of her belly. Whatever he had bought for her was special, and he wanted to see her reaction to it.

Evie turned her attention to the box. It was square and shallow, wrapped in pale green tissue paper and tied with a dark green velvet ribbon. She tugged it undone, her suspicion that it was jewellery confirmed by the expensive-looking leather box she revealed. Except that would be most inappropriate and whenever would she wear it and… *oh!*

Evie blinked, staring at the necklace in consternation. She had seen nothing like it in all her life. No, that was not true. Duchesses and princesses wore jewels like this, and her wealthy father gave her mother such things on special occasions, too. All the same, it was quite out of the ordinary. The lavish necklace, composed of the finest, largest emeralds and diamonds she had ever seen in her life, sat on a bed of white silk and sparkled in the lamplight. Her breath hitched, her heart giving an uneven thud, and she forced her gaze up to Louis, though she was uncertain she wanted to. It was too much, too… overwhelming.

The quality of his gaze on her was not what she had expected. He looked uncertain, nervous even, and she did not know what to say, what to think, or how to feel.

"I wanted you to have something as beautiful as you are," he said, his voice low. "For once in your life, I wanted you to believe that I see you this way. You are exquisite, Evie, just as you are. I do not want you to change, but to be happy, and to know that there is not a woman among the *ton* who can hold a candle to you. I am not being kind. I am not telling you this because I want something from you. I am saying it because it is nothing but the truth, and I want you to believe it, to believe in me."

Evie could not speak, could hardly breathe. The jewellery box was a cool weight in her lap, and she did not know what to do with it, with the words he was giving her so earnestly, with the unsettling emotions crashing about in her chest.

"Do you like it?" he asked, his uncertainty audible in the question.

She made a choked sound which seemed to encompass the entirety of her vocabulary now and so she could only nod. For she did like it, she loved it, yet she could never wear it. Like the beautiful mechanical bird in a cage he had given her, she would have to hide it away and then… then what?

She wanted to ask him when and how he expected her to wear this impossibly lavish gift? What was she supposed to infer from it? It must have cost… she did not know how much. A king's ransom. It was the kind of present a rich man gave a wife or a mistress and she did not know what he was implying, but she was afraid. The question burned on her tongue, but she could not make herself speak it aloud, could not force herself to say anything that would change things between them because she did not want that. She wanted her friend and for things to stay as they were and… and she really was going to cry now. Then he would not think her pretty at all, for it would be ugly and awkward, and what on earth was she to do?

"Evie," he said, his voice snapping her out of her spiralling thoughts. "Don't look so frightened. I am asking nothing of you but to believe my words. You owe me nothing. This is my gift to you, because if I achieve nothing else in my life, I will make you realise your own worth, and you are priceless. *Joyeux anniversaire, ma petite."*

She felt the touch of his fingers beneath her chin as he raised her face and bent to press his mouth to hers. His lips only brushed hers for a moment, barely a touch at all, and yet her heart thundered, and her skin flushed, and she wanted to run away from him as badly as she wanted to make him stay. He did not wait for her to find her tongue, to unravel the messy tangle of emotions that were knotting up inside her and making her head spin with confusion. Instead, he straightened and walked away without another word, closing the door behind him and leaving as silently as he'd arrived.

Evie sat staring at the door for a long time afterwards, and if not for the fortune in jewels sparkling in her lap, she might have thought the entire scene a peculiar waking dream.

Chapter 19

Dearest Sylvester,

I hope this letter finds you well. God bless Biddy for sending it for me and for receiving those you send in return.

Do write and tell me more about Marcross and the work you are doing there. It sounds a magical place and I long to see it. You are quite wrong to cut short those parts of your letters. How can you think I would find such descriptions dull when you describe everything so beautifully and with such enthusiasm? I am glad you are happy in your work. It eases my mind to know that you have something that fulfils you.

I am working on a present for you and, if I say so myself, the embroidery is exquisite, quite the finest I have ever done. It pleases me to imagine you wearing it one day. I hope and pray that the day will come soon.

I miss you terribly, you dreadful man. I am well behaved and perfectly polite to everyone, and if I don't explode and have a temper tantrum soon, I shall run mad. But you are the only one who enjoys my displays of ill temper, and I need you to come and provoke me soon. When shall I see you again?

— Excerpt of a letter from Lady Aisling Baxter (daughter of Luke and Kitty Baxter, The Earl and Countess of Trevick) to Mr Sylvester Cootes.

12th August 1841, Trevick Castle, Warwickshire.

Aisling closed the door to Biddy's cottage with a sigh, shutting out the sound of gunfire as men took advantage of the 'glorious twelfth' and the opening of the hunting season. "Oh, I am so sick of that sound! Why must men go about shooting things?"

"It's in their nature, I suppose," Biddy said equitably. She was stirring a pot over the hearth and the pleasant scent of herbs filled the room.

At least here in the cottage, all was peaceful. Aisling crossed the room to kiss Biddy's cheek.

"What's that?" she asked, peering down into the cauldron with interest.

"My supper," Biddy replied, winking at her.

Aisling laughed and flopped down in a chair with a heavy sigh. Biddy looked up from the simmering pot and regarded her with sympathy.

"Instead of moping about, you could do something to bring him back to you. I know a sweet little spell that would do the trick."

Aisling frowned. "I promised myself I wouldn't practise magic anymore, Biddy. You know that."

Biddy clicked her tongue impatiently.

"It was your idea to deny myself something important as a sacrifice for what I'd done," Aisling pointed out as the woman scowled at her. "You said it would ease my conscience and bring balance back to my life, warding off any ill luck."

Biddy set the spoon aside and wiped her hands on her apron. She shook her head, still not happy about Aisling's decision. "I know that, but I thought you'd choose something more frivolous, like dancing or listening to music."

"It won't work unless it's something important. Besides, how am I supposed to do that?" Aisling demanded. "I think my parents might notice if I stop dancing next season or cover my ears every time the orchestra strikes up."

"I suppose," Biddy muttered. "But it seems a shame when you could just weave a bit of magic to bring the fellow back to you."

Aisling smiled. "You liked him."

The older woman shrugged. "Well enough. He made you happy again, which is a good recommendation. Still, I suppose there's nothing to stop me from doing it on your behalf."

"Oh, but that's cheating," Aisling protested, though the idea was an appealing one.

"Not if you don't know about it."

"But you just told me!" she exclaimed.

Biddy chuckled and put the lid on the big pot, swinging it off the flame. "Not when or where or anything. You don't know if I'll go through with it. Perhaps I shall wait and let fate take its course."

Aisling snorted and folded her arms. "Fate will see me as an old maid, Biddy. That's the trouble."

"Oh, no, *a leanbh.* Fate has other plans for you and that young man, of that I'm certain."

"Oh, Biddy, do you really think so?" Aisling said, hearing the note of desperation in her own voice. If anyone had told her at the beginning of the year that she would pine away, longing for Sylvester Cootes, she would have thought them stark staring mad. It was true, though. The wretched man had infiltrated her heart one maddening argument at a time, until she could not bear to think of her life without him in it. Yet he was determined to come to her father with better prospects than he had, and she could not conceive of how he was going to manage it.

She had almost confided in her mother, hopeful that she might take Sylvester's part as she had seemed to like him a good deal, but then Mama liked everyone. If her beloved could not think of some way to improve his fortunes soon, however, Aisling would have to take matters into her own hands.

"When are you going to stay with your friends in Sussex?" Biddy asked.

"What? Oh, at the end of the month," Aisling said absently, too consumed with thoughts of Sylvester to concentrate on the conversation. She was looking forward to seeing her friends, though, and she had a dare to accomplish too, though that was not something she was especially keen to think about.

As ever, Biddy seemed to know what she was thinking. "Will you complete your dare, do you think, then? Or are you going to make excuses?"

Aisling bristled. She might not be looking forward to it, but she wasn't such a feeble creature as that. "I'll do it!" she said stoutly.

Biddy grinned at her, looking far too pleased with herself.

"I'm glad to hear it," the woman said, chuckling, though Aisling could not imagine what she found so amusing.

At least she would see Evie soon. She needed a friend to confide in about Sylvester for if she didn't tell someone soon, she would burst. Feeling vexed and impatient, she wished Biddy a pleasant afternoon and made her way back to the castle.

23rd August 1841, Marcross Manor, Monmouthshire.

"Sussex?" Sylvester's elder brother, Raphe Cootes, Baron de Ligne, regarded him with a frown from his position by the French doors. A delicious little breeze whispered into the room, stirring the sultry air. It had been a long day, and the brothers had gathered, as was usual, in the library, one of the few finished rooms at Marcross to date. "Why the devil do you want to go all the way to Sussex?"

"Because I know the quality of these horses. They're the finest I've seen, and I know Lambert will give me a good deal because he owes me a favour."

"Oh, I remember Lambert," their youngest brother, Oliver, piped up, raising his head from the sporting journal he'd been perusing. "Big, jovial chap. His wife likes to stuff one with cakes whenever possible."

Sylvester snorted. "Not that you ever objected."

Raphe sighed. "All the same, Sy. It seems an awful lot of bother when the county is teeming with fine horses, and half of anything you'll save on the deal you'll pay out on accommodation and travel, and the time and hassle of bringing them…." He sighed. "I'm talking to the wall, aren't I?"

"No," Sylvester said, frowning, though he could not fault his brother's argument. It was a lot of bother, and he wasn't quite certain what had put this notion into his head, but something had, and he couldn't shake it. His gut told him the best horses were Lambert's, and they needed strong, reliable beasts to work the land. Lambert was a good man, he was trustworthy, and he was in Sussex. So, that's where he'd go to get them.

"I suppose there might be a detour to Trevick Castle on the way there?" Raphe asked, quirking an eyebrow.

Sylvester felt a familiar pain bloom in his chest and had to breathe through it. "No."

Oliver looked up again, his brows drawn together in concern.

"No?" Raphe repeated, staring at him. "Sylvester, don't go getting the fool notion I would begrudge you the time to visit your beloved, for I shan't. I'd far rather you go about the place with a spring in your step than the morose, woebegone face you've been showing the world of late. You're obviously pining for the girl, and I understand. Believe me, I do. But don't feel the need to trudge all the way to Sussex if you need an excuse to see her. I can spare you for a few days."

Sylvester sat down and put his head in his hands. "What's the point, Raphe? I shall have to go soon, but only to admit to her I can't marry her. She must forget about me and find someone else. It's the only option and I know it, but I've been putting it off because I can't bear to. I ought never to have allowed her to consider me at all. It was idiotic to think I could make it work."

Raphe moved to sit beside him, his big brother watching him with regret in his eyes. "Sy, don't say it. Surely, there's something we can do. Marcross is coming along nicely. I know it's hard to wait, but in a couple of years—"

"In a couple of years it will bring in a tidy income for you and your growing family, Raphe," Sylvester said, knowing he must say it because he could not hide from the truth a moment longer. "It can't support an estate manager who earns five times the going rate, and even then, I'd not be worth her notice. Don't you see? It's hopeless."

Raphe's eyes filled with sorrow, for he was no fool, and he would not recite platitudes when the truth was staring them in the face. "Perhaps I'd best call in at Trevick on my way home," Sylvester said, his voice bleak. "I can't ask her to waste any more time on me."

"Sy," Raphe began, reaching out to take his arm, but Sylvester shrugged him off.

"Don't be kind, Raphe," he said gruffly, heading for the door. "It's about the last thing I can stand right now."

And he hurried away, trying to figure out how a man was supposed to explain to the woman he loved with all his heart that he'd let her down.

25th August 1841, Swan Hall, East Sussex.

Evie flopped back on the bed with a sigh of relief. "Oh, I'm so happy you're here. It's been an age since you visited me," she said, grinning at Aisling as she settled beside her. Evie turned onto her side, leaning her head on her hand, her eyes wide. "Tell me everything," she demanded.

Aisling raised her eyebrows and did her best to look innocent. "I don't know what you can mean?"

"Little liar," Evie said with a smile. "But you don't have to tell me if you don't want to. I understand there are things you either can't or don't wish to share with other people."

"Are there things you can't share, Evie?" Aisling asked. Evie was always kind and understanding, but there was something in her words that made Aisling believe a similar dilemma troubled her friend.

"Of course. We all have our secrets, don't we?" she said, making light of it with a smile.

"Certainly, but you know you could trust me with yours, Evie. I'd take any confidence you gave me to my grave, I swear it."

Evie nodded. "I know that. I-I'm just in a bit of a muddle so it won't make any sense and… Oh, ignore me. I'm talking nonsense and, besides, I asked first."

Aisling laughed. "So you did, and perhaps if I tell you my secret, you will feel more confident in sharing your own, for you can trust me, I swear. Oh, Evie. I'm in love, and you'll laugh your head off when you realise who it is."

"Mr Sylvester Cootes, by any chance?" Evie murmured nonchalantly.

Aisling stared at her before snatching up a pillow. "Oh, you!" she exclaimed, batting Evie about the head with it.

Evie squealed and scrambled away, snatching up a weapon of her own and before long there were feathers flying. The two of them collapsed back on the bed, laughing and gasping and choking on the little fluffy tufts of down drifting in the air.

"I c-can't believe it was so obvious," Aisling grumbled, hugging her ill-used pillow.

"Darling, it was obvious from the start that he was besotted with you, and when Viv and I saw you together in April, we both felt it was inevitable."

"Well, you and fate knew better than I did, but you were right, and… Oh, Evie, I'm glad. I said he was annoying and provoking, and he is, but in the best way. He won't let me hide. He forces me to be myself and to be honest, and I cannot tell you how very liberating that is. I can say what I want and be as prickly and obnoxious as I like, and he still adores me." She could hear the wonder in her own voice and longing to be with Sylvester swept over her, making her sick with wanting him.

"What is it like, being in love?" Evie asked, frowning.

Aisling rolled over to regard her friend, whose gaze was intent, and she saw it was no idle question.

"It's lovely for the most part, but it hurts, too. I miss him dreadfully, and I worry he will never be able to offer for me. Not that I care how much money he has, but he does, and I want him to be happy, too. Half the time I'm wretched, the other half I'm walking on air. It's all rather a muddle, I suppose, but I think if it were easy, it might not be so worth fighting for."

Evie pondered this, staring down at the pretty embroidered counterpane covering the bed. It had been her nineteenth birthday present from Aisling. Blue silk roses climbed over a creamy lace trellis and Aisling had worked each one herself with painstaking attention to detail. The tiny caterpillar Aisling had hidden in one corner had delighted Evie, more so when she'd assured her friend that even beautiful things were imperfect and all the lovelier for it.

Now, Evie traced the petals of one of the larger flowers, her gaze remote. "Does it frighten you, to put your faith in him, to know he'll be your husband forever? How can you trust him to be what you need, to be faithful to you?"

Aisling considered the question and considered Sylvester. "No one can see the future, Evie. But I believe I see Sylvester, see the man he is, the man he wishes to be, and don't believe he would ever hurt me that way. I trust him because I love him, and part of loving is having faith, I suppose. I don't think you can have one without the other. Does that help?"

"I'm not sure it does," Evie said, laughing, though Aisling did not think she was joking. "Oh, never mind that. Though I am so happy for you, Aisling, but now… we have bigger things to think about."

"Bigger things than the man I want to spend the rest of my life with?" Aisling said, affecting a dramatic voice and pressing her hand to her forehead like some Gothic heroine falling into a swoon.

"Yes," Evie said decisively, clambering off the bed. "Rosamund and Kathleen will be here at any moment, and it's time to complete your dare!"

Aisling groaned and buried her head in the pillow, but Evie grabbed hold of her hands and began tugging. Aisling shrieked, laughing as pillows, counterpane, and her billowing skirts were all deposited in an untidy heap on the floor. "Well, if this is how you treat your guests…." she began, crossing her arms and trying to look annoyed.

"No, not my guests, silly, only my dearest friends," Evie said, giving her a saucy wink and running out of the door.

"Wait for me!" Aisling yelled, gathering up her skirts and feeling silly and childish, and altogether happy to be in her friend's company.

Chapter 20

Dear Pip,

Wherever have you got to of late? We've seen so little of you. The scandal sheets imply you are up to no good. Is it true? We all miss you.

I wish you would come and visit us again. It's been an age and I know Jules would love to see you, though he's too stubborn to suggest it himself. Shall we see you soon?

— Excerpt of a letter from Lady Rosamund Adolphus (daughter of their graces, Robert and Prunella Adolphus, The Duke and Duchess of Bedwin) to The Right Hon'ble Philip Barrington, The Earl of Ashburton (Eldest son of The Most Hon'ble Lucian and Matilda Barrington, Marquess and Marchioness of Montagu)

25th August 1841, Swan Hall, East Sussex.

"What are you up to, you wicked girls?" Lady Helena demanded, narrowing her eyes at Evie, Rosamund, Kathleen and Aisling. The four of them had their heads together, whispering, and had clearly piqued the interest of Evie's mama, who was playing cards with Aisling's mother and father and Cara.

"Something dreadful, I hope," Aisling's mother said, smiling at her warmly. Aisling blushed and bit her lip.

"No. Nothing," Evie replied, the picture of innocence.

"Don't believe a word of it," grumbled Mr Knight, looking up from the game of spillikins he was playing with his younger children, Felix and Emmeline.

At sixteen, Felix was at the awkward stage where he was growing at an alarming rate and was all long legs and arms. It was clear he had inherited his father's good looks, though, as well as his cutthroat desire to win, judging from the intense concentration on his face.

"It moved! Now it's my turn," Emmeline crowed in triumph, trying to elbow her brother out of the way.

"It did not!" Felix protested.

"Did too! Papa, you saw it move too, didn't you?"

Mr Knight cleared his throat. "I… er… I wasn't actually paying attention," he admitted sheepishly.

"Oh, Papa!" Emmeline looked like she would stamp her foot in annoyance.

"It's Evie's fault," he retorted. "She's plotting, and you know that always makes me nervous. How am I supposed to concentrate when she's plotting?"

"I am *not* plotting," Evie said, her expression one of righteous indignation, which was rich as they were plotting a way to get out of the house that night, once everyone had gone to bed.

"Hmmm," Mr Knight said darkly, before turning his attention back to the game.

"Well, we are going to bed now," Evie said, as the girls all got to their feet.

Mr Knight looked up again, deeply suspicious now they were retiring early.

Aisling smothered a grin, amused by how nonchalant her friends looked. She doubted it was fooling anyone, let alone Mr Knight. Still, they escaped, making their way up to Evie's bedroom, where they all huddled on the bed.

"Are you quite sure it's secluded enough?" Aisling asked for the hundredth time as butterflies danced in clogs around her belly.

"In the middle of the night?" Kathleen said, laughing. "No one is going to be walking around the lake in the middle of the night, Aisling."

"We will be," Aisling retorted hotly.

"It will be quite safe," Evie said, sounding confident that she had planned the whole thing perfectly.

"But it's awfully close to the village, and it's rather a long walk in the dark, too," Aisling said, wishing she'd pulled any other dare out of the hat than the one she had. Swimming naked by moonlight had to be the most idiotic dare she'd ever heard of. If she ever found out which Daring Daughter had written it, she would… well, she didn't know what, but honestly. She felt sick.

"It's not dark at all. There's a huge full moon out there. It's almost daylight," Rosamund said, peering out behind the bedroom curtains.

"Excellent, so any peeping Tom will be able to get a good look," Aisling muttered, folding her arms with a huff.

"Oh, stop looking so Friday faced," Kathleen scolded her. "We'll keep a sharp lookout. It will be fun. We've all hidden food, so we can have a midnight picnic too. I'm looking forward to it."

"Excellent. You can come swimming with me," Aisling said smugly.

Kathleen snorted and shook her head. "Not on your life. It's not my dare."

"Haven't you taken one yet, Kathy?" Rosamund asked her.

Kathleen shook her head. "No. Neither has Evie."

Evie blanched, glaring at Kathleen for bringing it up.

"Well, I think you three need to," Aisling said, folding her arms. "I don't see why I should suffer alone."

"What a pity we don't have the hat," Evie remarked with a heavy sigh, not looking remotely sorry.

"Well, perhaps I should write to Cat and tell her to send it down here." Aisling smirked at her, determined that they should suffer if she had to.

"Oh, no!" Evie looked so aghast at the idea Aisling relented.

"Well, you must all take one soon," she said with a huff.

Kathleen snorted and flopped back against the pillows. "I'd take three if it would mean I could avoid the season. It's going to be ghastly. I just know it is."

"Why?" Rosamund asked, looking indignant. "You've got us to keep you company. If we all must suffer through it, I don't see why you shouldn't."

"Oh, yes, it's a terrible ordeal when you're the daughter of a duke," Kathleen said, though there was no malice in her tone, and it was a reasonable observation. "You don't have to endure all the eligible men looking at you like you've got lice."

"Oh, surely, that's not true," Rosamund said in horror.

Kathleen snorted and put on a deep, drawling voice, intoning, "'Can you imagine marrying a girl like that, when you don't know her bloodline? Good heavens, her parents might have been *criminals*!'" She rolled her eyes, making light of it, but Aisling knew overhearing such a thing must have hurt her deeply.

"If anyone is rude to you, I-I shall stamp on their foot, or… throw a glass of punch over them," Rosamund said, her face flushing with fury.

Kathleen grinned and threw her arm about Rosamund, hugging her. "That I would pay to see. I tell you what, Ozzie. If you protect me from the loathsome toads that populate these events, I shall get Pip to dance with you."

Rosamund flushed scarlet. "Oh, n-no, Kathy, don't you dare ask him!"

"I shall," Kathleen said, a mischievous glint in his eyes. "For we all know you're pining for him."

"I am not!" Rosamund insisted, and then subsided with a huff when everyone gave her a pitying glance.

Kathleen leaned her head on Rosamund's shoulder and sighed. "It's so depressing, though, Ozzie. I don't care a jot about getting married and finding a husband, but I was so looking forward to dancing. But if the few events I've been to so far are any indication, I shan't dance at all."

"Jules will dance with you," Rosamund said, giving her a squeeze. "I'll make sure of it."

"And Pip would too," Aisling piped up, for Pip Barrington had a soft spot for Kathleen, regarding her in much the same light as his annoying little sister, Cat. "Well, if he ever shows up, I suppose," she added with a shrug.

"Monsieur Le Comte will too, I'm sure," Evie offered.

Kathleen blushed, shaking her head. "Oh, no. Evie, I don't think I'd dare dance with him. He's too… too much. Goodness me."

"Don't be silly," Evie said briskly, though her cheeks looked a little pink. "He's a man like any other, just prettier."

Kathleen and Rosamund snorted with laughter at that.

Evie clapped her hands, calling everyone to order. "Right, everyone had better pretend to get ready for bed. Remember, we'll meet by the fountain in the rose garden at midnight. Don't be late!"

Aisling pulled a face and didn't budge, so the girls came for her, tugging her by the arms until she got to her feet.

"Oh, I hate you all," she whined, while they all sniggered at her obvious reluctance, like the adoring friends they were.

25th August 1841, The Swan, Swanborough, East Sussex.

"They're a fine pair, Mr Cootes. Reckon you did right to come out and get them, even it causes a bit of aggravation getting them back."

Sylvester nodded at Davies, the head groom from Marcross, as they shut the stable door upon the two enormous beasts. The rhythmic sound of contented munching followed them, now they'd settled Sampson and Delilah for the night. The aggravation Davies spoke of had begun at once, for after some intense negotiating, Mr Lambert's wife had insisted they stay for lunch, which had been long and indulgent. Then they'd had the very devil of a time travelling the short distance to the inn, with Sampson throwing a shoe and an incident with an overexcited dog that could have ended badly. Thankfully, Delilah had behaved impeccably, though poor Davies had suffered a nasty nip on the ankle from the blasted dog. He'd been trying to get the idiotic creature out from under Delilah's massive hooves before she kicked it in the head, but the dog didn't seem to appreciate that. Getting the wound cleaned and bandaged had lost them more time and so they'd not arrived at The Swan until gone eleven. If they kept this sluggish pace up, it would take them three weeks to get home.

The landlord had muttered about inconveniences and folk arriving at a reasonable hour, but promised to rustle them up a decent dinner and some ale. Once they too had been fed and watered, Sylvester bade Davies a good night and was about to make his way up to his room when he glanced out of the window. It was a gorgeous night, warm and still, with an enormous moon that lit the countryside, glowing in the sky like a pearl.

Though it had been a long and trying day, Sylvester did not feel settled enough to sleep, so he let himself back outside and stood staring up at the moon. Was Aisling staring at that same moon? Likely there were letters waiting for him at Marcross, telling him what she was up to. An ache of longing bloomed in his chest and melancholy settled over him like a smothering blanket, dragging his spirits down. He could wish he were rich every day for the rest of his life, and it wouldn't change a thing. No matter how hard he worked, he'd never be good enough for an earl's daughter. Not when the very act of working set him apart and proved he was not a gentleman of leisure. He could never afford to keep her, not as she deserved to be kept. For the first time in his life, he felt just a tiny amount of jealousy for his older brother's title, but then the earl would consider a mere baron a comedown for Lady Aisling too. There was no other option but to return to Trevick on his way home and tell her the truth. He could never offer for her. It would break his heart, and he could not bear the idea of hurting Aisling, but he could not leave her to wait and hope for something that would never happen. That would be cruel, and he could never be cruel to his darling girl. Though he'd brought this all upon them himself. If he'd not wanted her so badly, he might have forced himself to stay away, knowing she was out of his league. He ought to regret that, but he was too selfish to do so. And he had helped her, at least. She was happier now in no small part because of him. Yet if he truly cared for her, he should hope she forgot about him and fell in love with someone else. He found he was not feeling quite that altruistic.

Thoroughly wretched, Sylvester walked aimlessly, following where his feet led him until the path opened up upon a lake. Moonlight sparkled upon the water as the glittering black surface reflected the huge silver orb above him. Not even a ripple broke the still surface and Sylvester turned as feminine laughter filled the night. There was a shriek and then a splash and Sylvester didn't stop to think. He tugged off his boots, stripped off his jacket and dived in.

25th August 1841, The Lake at Swanborough, East Sussex.

Aisling screamed, wishing she'd never heeded Evie, who thought it would be best to jump in off the little jetty and get it over with, rather than walking in slowly. Aisling had agreed, as it meant her nakedness would be covered quicker, but the water had been far colder than she'd expected. She gasped, treading water as her lungs drew in air, gasping to deal with the icy chill. Once the initial shock wore off, however, she discovered it was rather invigorating.

She was just wondering if she could persuade the others to come in with her when there was a large splash nearby. Before she had time to fret about what kind of creatures might lurk under the inky black water, powerful arms wrapped around her. A dark head emerged from beneath the surface, and Aisling's panicked brain remembered stories of kelpies and water gods. She screamed and struggled as the arms only held her tighter.

"It's all right, madam. I'll get you back to land, only don't squirm so, you'll drown us both!"

The irritated tone struck her as being terribly familiar, and Aisling stopped thrashing for long enough to stare at the mystical creature come to drag her down to the murky depths.

"Sylvester!" she shrieked, stunned.

"*Aisling*?" His glittering eyes were wide with shock. "W-What… H-How? I thought you were drowning!" he said, the indignation in his voice definitely familiar.

"I was completing my dare," she retorted, with as much dignity as she could, bearing in mind she was naked.

Screams came from the bank as her friends began wading in, intent on rescuing her.

"Put her down, you brute!"

"Take your hands off her!"

"It's all right. It's Sylvester!" Aisling shouted, and then wondered at herself, for she was wrapped around him beneath the water like pond weed and….

"You're naked," Sylvester croaked.

"Y-Yes," Aisling said, breathless with a combination of cold and the scandalous nature of this encounter. "That was the dare. To swim naked by moonlight."

Sylvester groaned and then darted a look at the bank where the girls were dithering, uncertain if Aisling needed rescuing. "This night is going to be burned into my brain for the rest of my days."

Beneath the water, his hands slid over her naked back, and Aisling shivered, pressing closer to him.

"Right," he said briskly. "You've swum naked in the moonlight. Now you'd best get out before I get ideas, or you freeze to death."

"What ideas? And it's August," she pointed out through chattering teeth. "Though I admit it's a bit nippy."

"We've got an audience, and it's August in England," he insisted, ignoring her question. "That does not discount the possibility of catching pneumonia. Come on. I hope you've thought to bring towels."

Sylvester hefted her into his arms and carried her out of the lake as her friends ran forward, wrapping her in a sheet to dry as he turned his back. Once they had her properly covered, they stood around her to protect what little remained of her modesty, staring at Sylvester in consternation.

"What are you doing here?" Rosamund asked, looking suspicious.

"I'm staying at The Swan and thought I'd go for a walk. What are you doing here?" he demanded of Aisling. "I thought you were still at Trevick."

"We're staying with Evie and her family at Swan Hall," Aisling said through her shivers. "Will you c-call on us t-tomorrow?"

"Only if you go and get dry at once!" Sylvester said, looking exasperated now. "You're freezing."

"I will if you promise!" Aisling said, grinning at him. Her heart felt lighter than she could remember. The sight of him was such a relief after missing him for so long she felt giddy and foolish and for the first time in what felt like forever, her future was full of hope. She was happy. That was this strange sensation bubbling up inside her. She had almost forgotten what it felt like, but she was happy and in love and it was all because of him.

"I promise!" he said urgently.

"And you always keep your promises."

"I do!" he agreed, half laughing, half desperate that she go and get warm. "Now go before you catch a chill!"

With a shriek, Aisling pushed through her friends and ran towards him, planted a smacking kiss on his lips, and then ran off giggling wildly as the other girls ran after her. Their laughter echoed across the fields, disappearing into the darkness and leaving no one in any doubt as to her mood.

25th August 1841, The lake at Swanborough, East Sussex.

"Oh, Luke!" Kitty pressed her hand to her mouth to smother a sob as she watched her daughter laughing riotously, running away from the lake with her friends. Mr Cootes stood there, dripping wet, a dazed smile at his lips as he watched them go, and she wanted to hug him for everything he'd done. Instead, she flung herself into her husband's arms. "Did you hear her? I told you so. Did you hear how happy she sounded?"

Luke considered this, his expression unreadable. "Bit of a coincidence that he turned up here. You really think she's in love with him?"

Kitty nodded, wiping her eyes as happy tears slipped down her cheeks. "I do, and he's such a good man, Luke. I know he loves her. He never betrayed her confidence, *and* he's made her happy. Oh! Aisling is happy again!" She was bouncing on her toes now, halfway between laughter and hysterical crying.

Her husband looked down at her, wiping away her tears with his thumbs. "She's been different these past weeks, so much more at peace with herself, and I'd have given every penny we have to hear her laugh again," he admitted.

"You just heard it," Kitty said, staring up at him. "And that young man is responsible, but he won't offer for her, Luke. I know he won't. He's too honourable to ask for her when he can't support her. Oh, please, darling. We must help them."

Luke sighed. "Is he a beneficial influence, though? I'm not mad about my daughter skinny dipping in the dead of night," he grumbled, though his stern tone did not fool Kitty for one moment.

"Oh, fustian. This was none of his doing and you know it. You saw what happened. He thought she was drowning and went to rescue her. Don't you remember dragging me out of the sea when we went looking for pirate treasure? She's my daughter through and through, and it's exactly the sort of daft scrape she ought to get into. She always used to before… well, before something changed her. Besides, it was her dare. She had to complete her dare, didn't she?"

Luke smiled down at her, adoration shining in his eyes. "Yes, Kitten, and looking at poor Mr Cootes, she has enchanted him the same way you did me. Are you certain you've no fairy blood in your veins?"

Kitty laughed, hugging him tightly. "What if I have? *I've found you, and you've found me, and so… we shall be together, and never alone again.*" He kissed her then, as he always did when she reminded him of the words she'd given him so very long ago. "I want this for Aisling, Luke. Help that poor boy. *Please,*" she whispered, clinging to him.

"Anything for my tricksy fae," he murmured, giving her one last kiss before escorting her back to the house.

Chapter 21

Dearest Biddy,

Was this your doing? If it was – thank you! Thank you, thank you, thank you!

— Excerpt of a letter from Lady Aisling Baxter to Old Biddy Burke

26th August 1841, Swan Hall, East Sussex.

Sylvester dragged a deep breath into his lungs. His chest felt uncomfortably tight, as did his cravat. He tugged at the wretched thing as he strode up the elegant driveway to Swan Hall. Unsurprisingly, it was an impressive residence. Mr Knight had built it for his wife, Lady Helena, upon whom he doted, and it boasted every modern convenience, including indoor plumbing. Mr Knight had gone himself to view the Tremont Hotel in Boston, which was the first hotel of its kind to offer water closets and baths. Naturally for a man of his wealth and ambition, he'd immediately gone about building his own luxury hotel in London. It had been an instant success, adding to an already prodigious fortune. Swan Hall was surprisingly restrained compared to the opulence of that establishment. Likely his wife's influence, for Lady Helena was widely recognised as the personification of good taste.

The sight of the beautiful building and the elegant, well-tended gardens surrounding it did little to soothe Sylvester's mood. This was one of Knight's smaller properties, a mere summer getaway, and the sort of place he could only dream of offering Aisling. Men like Mr Knight and the Earl of Trevick might as well exist on another planet, they were so far from anything he could compete with financially. Misery welled up inside of him, making his footsteps drag as he got closer to the house, closer to saying farewell to the only woman he would ever love. How was he to bear it?

He gave his card, hat, and gloves to the butler and waited in the elegant entrance hall. Brisk footsteps sounded upon the marble floor and Sylvester looked up, surprised to see the Earl of Trevick striding towards him.

"Mr Cootes," the earl said, his expression unreadable, though he did not appear surprised to see him. "I'm glad you're here. I've been wanting to have a word with you."

Panic darted through him as Sylvester wondered if the earl had got wind of his tendre for Aisling, or perhaps last night's folly, but… surely not? Still, the fellow did not look as though he wanted to disembowel him and display his head on a pike, so maybe it was something unrelated?

"My Lord Trevick. A pleasure to see you again."

"Hmm," murmured the earl, looking him up and down and making Sylvester want to tug at his cravat again. He had the strong urge to check his cuffs weren't fraying or dirty, but he stood the scrutiny as best he could without fidgeting. The earl sighed. "I suppose you'll do."

"Do, sir?" Sylvester queried.

"What do you know about drainage?" the earl demanded.

"Er…." Sylvester stared at him for a moment.

"Well?" Trevick asked, one eyebrow raised in imperious enquiry.

Sylvester rallied, forcing his startled brain into action. "Oh, well, quite a lot, actually. We've just done a great deal of drainage work at Marcross and—"

For the next hour and a half Sylvester was cross-examined about drainage, crop rotation, foot and mouth, his views on the best method of dealing with turnip beetle, and the efficacy of the single horse skeleton harvest cart. By the end of this interview, his brain felt like mush, and he had the oddest notion there was some significant part of this conversation he was missing.

"Hmmm," the earl mused, regarding him with intelligent blue eyes. "Mr Cootes, I am in need of an estate manager for Trevick. The fellow I have now is a good sort, but should have retired five years since. I'm tired of fighting him over every new method or piece of machinery I wish to introduce. It's high time I pensioned him off, and I'm in the market for someone young and hardworking. Someone with an interest in all that is modern. Do you think that could be you?"

Sylvester stared at the earl, dumbstruck.

"Well, sir?" Trevick demanded, impatient now.

"My lord, I… I am honoured by the offer you make me truly, but… but I am working for my brother at present, and—"

The earl nodded, waving this away as a mere trifle. "And you'll need time to find him a suitable replacement. That's no problem, though I understand your younger brother is well qualified to take over. Is that right? Of course, you'd need some financial inducement, so I'm prepared to be generous."

The earl named an outrageous yearly sum that made Sylvester's head spin.

"B-But that's far too much," he protested, stunned.

Trevick's eyebrows rose. "Aren't you worth it?"

"I don't think anyone's worth that much," Sylvester said frankly.

The earl regarded him for a long moment and then chuckled, clapping him on the shoulder. "Well, there we might have to beg to differ, for anyone who can make my daughter happy so that I might have the pleasure of hearing her laugh again is damn near priceless to me."

Sylvester stared at him and then frowned. "Lady Aisling asked you to give me a job," he guessed, his pride rearing up. "My lord, much as I appreciate the offer, I cannot accept."

"Why not?" Trevick demanded, his blue eyes narrowing.

Well, there was nothing for it but to tell the man the truth, to put all his cards on the table. "Because I'm in love with your daughter, my lord, and I would do anything to be in a position to offer for her, but as I cannot do so, I do not think it wise to spend so much time in her company, and—"

"What the devil do you think I'm offering you this job for, if not to give you the means to marry her?" Trevick asked, shaking his head. "And Aisling knows nothing about it, I'll have you know. You may blame my countess, though."

A ringing noise sounded in Sylvester's ears, and he had the oddest sensation of floating, not quite certain if he was awake or dreaming.

"Marry…. For Aisling…. You're… for me?" Sylvester stammered, aware that hadn't made the least bit of sense, but the earl seemed to get the gist of it.

"Yes, lad. My wife had got it into her head that you're the only fellow who can make Aisling happy, and I was told in no uncertain terms I had better make it happen. I hope you've not been getting any daft notions we would marry the poor girl off to some doddering old duke, for heaven's sake? I've been at the receiving end of such machinations myself, and I'm damned if my daughter will suffer the same way. So, then. Was Kitty right? Of course, the ultimate answer will rest with Aisling, but assuming this is what she wants, can you make my daughter happy?"

Sylvester nodded dumbly before realising that probably wasn't giving the man the best impression. He stood a little taller and squared his shoulders. "Yes, my lord. I believe I can. At least, I shall try my damndest. I swear I shall."

Trevick nodded. "Excellent. We'll expect a wedding early next year, then. That will give you time to put things in place at Marcross and learn the ropes at Trevick. Oh, there's a very nice manor house that goes with the position, of course. Not a vast property, and needs a bit of work, but just the thing for newlyweds. Puts me in mind of my first place with Kitty," he added with a wistful smile. "Though that was in Ireland, of course. Lovely place. You might like to honeymoon there. Aisling loves it."

In something of a daze, Sylvester allowed the earl to guide him back to the house, aware he had a stupid smile on his face and quite unable to do a thing about it.

15th February 1842, Trevick Castle, Warwickshire.

"You may kiss the bride."

The rather pompous vicar's voice rang out across the church, but Sylvester was still gazing at her, unmoving, he looked dazed. He'd looked like that a lot over the past few months, though she didn't blame him. They were both too deliriously happy to believe their luck.

"Sylvester!" she hissed, widening her eyes.

"Oh!" Snapping out of his abstraction, her new husband hauled her into his arms and kissed her with a thoroughness she did not think the vicar was expecting. When he finally released her, Aisling avoided the man's gaze, certain she would snigger at the first glance of his disapproving face.

Sylvester grinned at her, a smug, boyish grin of delight that made her heart turn over.

"Well, wife, you've done it now. I can bother you to my heart's content."

Aisling sniffed as she took his arm and stuck her nose in the air. "Just see that you do," she said airily, as he escorted her back down the aisle.

Once outside, their friends and family bombarded them with rice, until Aisling felt certain she'd be picking it out of her hair for days.

"How much longer until I can be alone with you?" Sylvester whispered in her ear, his warm breath tickling her neck and making her shiver.

Aisling blushed and attempted to look cross. "We've got the wedding breakfast to go yet," she said sternly, though she was likely the most impatient of the two of them. Try as she might over these interminable months, she could not overwhelm her husband's innate sense of decency. Though she now had a very thorough knowledge of kissing and a few other wicked pleasures, he had drawn the line at making love to her. She had protested that she was not a virgin, so such constraints ought to be forgotten, but Sylvester had become quite cross. In his view, she deserved all the respect and patience due to her. She had been rushed into things the first time around. This time he wanted her to have time to be wooed as she ought to have been, to be entirely certain of and confident in her decision, and nothing she could say would shake him.

She had to admit to being glad of it now. The anticipation, as tormenting as it had been, made this day something special, to remember for reasons beyond their vows, as important as they were. This feeling was reinforced as she saw the look in his eyes and had to turn away before she flushed scarlet. He had certainly waited long enough.

The wedding breakfast was small and intimate, at Aisling's request. Their families were here, as were all the Cadogans, including the Earl of St Clair and his wife, Harriet, one of her mother's closest friends. Aisling smiled as she noted Sylvester's brother, the baron, fussing over his heavily pregnant wife and arranging cushions for her back. Greer smiled up at him beatifically, glowing with happiness. Aisling's breath hitched, an unexpected prickle of tears in her eyes. She had thought she would never have that for herself, not after everything that had happened. The dream of a husband who loved her, a family, was something she had mourned, never expecting to be granted such blessings after all that she'd done. Except that Sylvester had made her see that she'd been innocent, a child manipulated by an older man with evil intentions. She had reacted out of fear and hurt, not with malice aforethought, and whether or not her words had caused a man's death, she must forgive herself for it.

"Aisling? Darling, what is it?"

She turned, her husband's handsome face blurring behind a sheen of tears, but she could still see the worry in his eyes.

"You're not having second thoughts?" he asked with a soft laugh, though she heard the anxiety lingering behind his words.

"Idiotic creature," she said, and then burst into tears, throwing her arms about his neck. "I'm j-just so h-happy," she sobbed.

Sylvester gave a choked laugh and held her close for a moment before picking her up.

"Time to go," he said decisively. He kissed her nose, and she laughed too, tears still streaming down her cheeks. "My wife is overcome by her great good fortune in gaining such a wonderful husband and needs to retire," Sylvester announced to their families with great seriousness.

"Oh! You devil!" Aisling said in outrage, smacking his shoulder, and then she grinned at him. "But I can't deny it."

She kissed him, to the delight of everyone watching, who whooped and cheered.

"Please enjoy the rest of the celebrations, but we shall bid you a good day."

Sylvester inclined his head in farewell as Aisling gave a regal wave, and he carried her off.

15th February 1842, Between Trevick Castle and Heathcote Manor, Warwickshire.

Sylvester looked down at Aisling, tucked into the crook of his arm as the carriage took them the short distance to their new home. They were going to be here for the next ten days before leaving for Ireland to enjoy their honeymoon. Kitty had warned them it would likely rain for the entire time, which suited Sylvester admirably. He had no intention of letting Aisling out of their bed, if at all possible. He had been heroically patient in his estimation, but a fellow had limits and he'd certainly reached his.

"Your brother told me you had absolutely no need to go to Sussex in search of horses," Aisling said, giving him a narrow-eyed stare.

Sylvester shrugged, knowing she was returning to the same old argument. Not that he minded. He adored arguing with her. "Yes, I did. They were especially good ones, and it was an excellent deal."

"Biddy made you come to me. She bespelled you."

"Pfft." He made the dismissive sound with the soul intention of seeing the sparks fly in her lovely dark eyes. It worked.

"So, you just *happened* to be staying at the Swan at the same time that I was staying at the Hall, and you just *happened* to be walking past the lake in the middle of the night?"

"Yes," he said, his tone decisive. "Nothing but a coincidence."

He bit back a grin. She was going to burst if he kept this up.

"And going to the bookshop when you'd never been there before, that wasn't fate?"

He shook his head, wondering if she would try to shake him. She looked like she wanted to. "Coincidence."

"Your horse throwing a shoe, and you getting yourself lost when you were a stone's throw from the castle?"

A shiver ran down Sylvester's spine and, despite himself, he had to agree there were a lot of implausible coincidences, but arguing with her was just too delicious. He'd never admit to it. "A strange coincidence, but a coincidence nonetheless."

"Argh!" She threw up her hands as she did every time they had this conversation.

Sylvester chuckled and leaned down to kiss her nose. "I am a terrible trial to you, love. I know it."

She huffed at him but kissed him back before relaxing into his arms and settling against him more comfortably.

"I told Mama and Papa," she said after a long moment, glancing up at him.

Sylvester let out a breath of relief. He had tried to persuade Aisling to tell her parents what had happened to her all those years ago, but she had been reluctant, and he hadn't wanted to press her.

"I'm glad," he said, stroking her cheek and marvelling at how soft her skin was. She snuggled closer, her hand tracing the exquisite whitework embroidery on the elegant waistcoat she had made for him.

"So am I, though I wasn't at first. Oh, Sylvester, they were so devastated and furious on my account. We sat up all night and cried buckets. Papa said it was a good job the fellow was dead, and I rather believe him. My father is a gentle soul, but I think he might truly have done the man serious harm if he were still alive. They blamed themselves, of course, which is why I didn't want to tell them but… but it's all right now. I feel better. They know the truth and I feel like… Like I have laid it to rest, and I can move on. A fresh start. You were right. I ought to have told them years ago."

Sylvester smiled at her. "Ah, love. You're going to have to get used to me being right. I always am, you know."

She rolled her eyes at him, which was what he'd intended. He did not wish for her to be sad on such a joyful day.

"I think you mean you will need to get used to me being right. For *I* always am," she retorted, a sparkle of mischief in her eyes that made his heart feel like it might burst. Aisling was happy.

He'd helped her chase away the past and that shy, unhappy girl who hid in corners was gone for good. His wife was full of life and naughtiness, and he was going to delight in provoking her for the rest of his days.

Chapter 22

Monsieur,

I write this in haste, as the house is in chaos. We are leaving. Papa has taken it into his head that we shall do some travelling, though he won't tell me where. Last night I was accepting invitations for the coming week and this morning I am told to cancel everything. He's behaving most oddly and will not tell me where we are going or for how long, but I think we will be absent for some months. I have tried asking Mama, but she just smiles and tells me it's for the best.

I do not understand what is happening. I think they've both gone mad. They won't listen to reason. I don't want to travel or miss the season. I am sorry to leave for so long without saying goodbye properly, but they give me no choice. When I get the chance, I will try to write to you again, but I think it may be difficult.

— Excerpt of a letter from Miss Evie Knight (daughter of Lady Helena and Mr

Gabriel Knight) to Louis César de Montluc, Comte de Villen.

15th February 1842, Heathcote Manor, Warwickshire.

Aisling squealed with laughter as Sylvester swung her up into his arms and carried her over the threshold of their new home. It was a handsome red brick building built in the previous century, and Aisling loved its symmetry and elegance. More than anything, however, she loved the man in whose arms she was carried, the man who had made everything right again, as impossible as that had seemed such a short time ago.

"Put me down before you hurt yourself," she protested as he headed for the staircase.

"Hurt myself?" he retorted indignantly. "Are you casting aspersions about my manly physique, wife?"

She snorted, holding onto his neck. "No, only about your good sense. Sylvester, I'm too heavy."

"I've carried you before, sodden skirts and all," he pointed out, ignoring her and carrying on up the stairs.

"And whose fault was that?" she demanded.

"Yours."

"*Mine*?"

"Of course it was your fault."

"You pushed me in," she said indignantly.

"I did no such thing. You tripped over your own feet."

"I would never be so clumsy." Aisling stuck her nose in the air with a disdainful sniff, even though he was right.

"That was the first time you kissed me," Sylvester mused, turning to push open the door to their bedroom.

"You mean you kissed me?" Aisling corrected him.

Sylvester shook his head, setting her down with care. "No, I don't."

"Oh, yes, you do! You kissed me first. I distinctly remember that—"

His mouth covered hers, and Aisling sighed, relaxing into his embrace as his arms went about her. He kissed her thoroughly, his tongue teasing and caressing as a pleasant warmth simmered beneath her skin.

"I did kiss you first," he admitted, when he finally drew back. "Most intelligent thing I ever did in my life."

"I kissed you back," Aisling admitted, sliding her arms about his neck.

"I know." He grinned at her, his hands at her waist as his hungry gaze skimmed up and down her body. "This is a beautiful gown, love."

"It is," she agreed, not taking her eyes from him.

"Take it off."

"Yes," she murmured, not moving, but gazing up at him. Lord, but he was handsome, and all hers. A sense of possessive pride swept over her, and she felt quite giddy with wanting him.

"Lord, don't look at me like that, love. I'm dying here as it is."

"Like what?" she murmured, as he turned her around and began undoing the fastenings on her gown with deft fingers.

"Like you want to eat me in one bite."

"Mmm, one bite," she said with a happy sigh.

He leaned down and nipped at her shoulder. "As many bites as you like. We have all the time in the world now."

All the time in the world and yet she fidgeted impatiently as he divested her of her gown and the endless layers of petticoats and corset. Finally, he lifted her shift over her head, and she was standing in only her stockings and garters.

"Turn around, Aisling," he said.

She did as he asked, astonished that at this of all moments, she didn't feel the slightest bit shy. Not with him. But she never had with him. He made her bold and brave, and let her be entirely herself.

"Sylvester Cootes, you lucky dog," he murmured, a smug grin tugging at the corners of his mouth.

"You're wearing too many clothes," she pointed out, her skin prickling with anticipation as his heated gaze roved over her.

"We'll deal with that in a moment. Come here, wife," he demanded, pulling her into his arms.

Aisling squeaked as cold buttons and his watch chain pressed against her warm skin, but he covered her mouth with his, smothering her indignation. His hands glided over her, caressing tenderly, and soon she was so overheated she was certain anything metal would melt against her. Sylvester pulled back with a tortured groan.

"Help me," he demanded, tugging wildly at his cravat.

Aisling laughed, starting on his waistcoat buttons as he threw the cravat aside and shrugged off his coat, dropping it to the floor. She tried to pull his waistcoat off his shoulders as he hopped on one foot to tug off his boots. He cursed as he lost his balance and nearly landed on his backside, just hitting the edge of the bed instead. Aisling tugged at the boot for him and cast it aside, where it landed with a dull thud. She reached for the other one, tugged that off too, then she pulled at his trousers as he lifted his hips and pushed from the top, and the absurdity of their eager haste had her giggling like a maniac.

"Are you laughing at me?" he protested, disappearing as he tugged his shirt over his head.

Aisling stumbled back as his trousers and smallclothes came free, and suddenly, he was sitting there in all his naked glory. The laughter died in her throat, and she stared for a long moment before shaking her head.

"No. Not laughing." She took in powerful shoulders and muscular arms, the light dusting of hair on his broad chest that arrowed down, directing her gaze to that most masculine part of him. Aisling sighed. "You are beautiful, Sylvester."

He smirked, not above preening a little. "Glad you noticed. I can't hold a candle to you, though, my gorgeous wife. Come here now, before I go mad with wanting you."

She did not need a second invitation and ran to the bed, tumbling into his arms. He rolled her onto her back, kissing her as his hands explored new territory. He let out a sigh of pleasure as he traced the curve of her breast.

"God, you're lovely," he whispered, his hazel eyes dark with desire. "You're not worried, are you? Frightened? I won't hurt—"

Aisling pressed a finger to his lips. "Foolish man. You would never hurt me. I trust you. Make love to me, Sylvester. Show me how it's supposed to be."

To her surprise, his eyes glittered with emotion, and he bent his head to press a soft kiss to her mouth. "I love you," he whispered. "With all my heart. I think I have loved you since the first moment I saw you, stepping out of the carriage at Rowsley Hall the Christmas we first met. I think that's why I was so awful to you, because I was so bloody overwhelmed. But I do love you, and I'll never stop, either. You're mine now."

Aisling opened her mouth to reply, but he did not give her the chance, stealing the words with another deep kiss. So she showed him instead, by giving him everything she had, holding nothing back.

His lips trailed down her neck, making her shiver as he pressed kisses along her collarbone and the hollow at the base of her throat. She gasped as he nuzzled against her breasts, capturing a nipple in his mouth and suckling. Bursts of sensation radiated from the place where his mouth worked, arrowing directly between her legs. She was all liquid fire, already damp and throbbing with need. He knew she needed his touch though, his hands skimming down her body to ease between her thighs and stroke. Clever fingers sifted through the coarse curls to the delicate place beneath, and caressed her there.

She cried out, arching her hips, seeking more, and he lifted his head, taking her mouth again and kissing her, sweet and tender at first and then deeper as his fingers slid inside her and her body convulsed, squeezing around him as pleasure rolled through her in waves. But this was the easy part, giving herself over to his touch. Though she had meant what she'd said, she was still a little nervous, anxious that she would not enjoy what came next. Her only experience had been painful and harsh, and though she trusted Sylvester entirely, she feared she might be too badly damaged by the experience to—Aisling gasped, her breath catching in her throat.

"I'm sorry," he groaned, bracing himself above her. "I'm sorry. I couldn't wait any longer. I didn't… Christ, Aisling. Did I hurt you?"

She blinked up at him, stunned, and then wrapped her legs about his hips. "Do it again," she demanded.

Moving slowly this time, his gaze locked upon hers, Sylvester withdrew and pushed back inside her.

"Oh!" She gave a startled laugh, entranced by the feel of him inside her, filling her. It was absurdly intimate and so… so right.

"Yes?" he asked her, his voice hoarse.

"Yes. Yes, please," she whispered.

He dropped his head to her shoulder with a groan. "Oh, thank God."

From there it was easy, so easy to love him, to stare up into his face and know that this man was the one who would always see her, see exactly who she was, and love her for all of it. Aisling braced her feet on the mattress, arching her hips up, wanting more, wanting everything. His hands clasped her backside, lifting her, moving deeper until he touched something inside her that made the world shatter around them. She clung to him, sobbing with the force of sensation and emotion, overwhelmed as she spun out into the darkness, knowing he was there with her as his body jerked in her arms. He made a harsh sound, fierce and primal, and Aisling laughed, delighting in the fundamental joy of their union.

He collapsed on top of her, still inside her, and Aisling held onto him, holding him in place when he would have rolled to one side.

"No, stay," she said, still breathless. She reached up and held his face in her hands. "Stay with me."

"Always," he whispered. "Always."

She slept then, waking sometime later with Sylvester wrapped around her, her back to his chest. He murmured words in her ear that she did not hear but understood all the same. She agreed sleepily and he took her again, slow and quietly this time, building her pleasure with languid caresses until she was quivering in his arms, ready to tumble into bliss the moment his hand slid down between her legs and drove her over the edge with him. The night passed like that, sleeping in each other's arms and waking to rediscover their joy in each other all over again.

"I'm destroyed," Sylvester murmured as the sun rose outside their bedroom window, his voice drowsy and heavy with pleasure. "I'll never leave this bed again."

Aisling snorted and turned to look at him, leaning on his chest and toying with the coarse, dark hair there. "Well, we have nine more days until we need to leave for Ireland. I think everyone was hoping to see us again before we leave, though."

Sylvester shook his head. "You'd best not, love. They'll be shocked when they see the poor, frail husk of a man you've made of me with your insatiable demands upon my body."

"*My* demands?" she retorted, indignant. "You're the one who keeps—"

He moved, and suddenly she was flat on her back, his big, warm body covering hers, his interest in continuing their lovemaking unmistakable.

"Who keeps what?" he enquired politely, his eyes full of mischief.

She narrowed her eyes at him. "Sylvester Cootes, I think you have misled me. You're a very bad man."

He chuckled, and the sound rumbled through her in the most delicious way. "Shall I show you just how bad I can be, my little enchantress?"

"Yes, please," she said with a sigh, pulling his head down for a lingering kiss.

He obliged her with enthusiasm, drawing back sometime later to observe the devastation he'd wrought.

"I love you," she murmured, dazed and sated and quite blissfully happy.

"Well, why wouldn't you?" he asked, quirking one dark eyebrow. "I bother you dreadfully. Everyone else knew you were head over ears for me, even if you didn't."

"Dreadful creature. You're horribly conceited," she said fondly.

"But you love me," he pointed out.

"Yes," Aisling sighed. "Now get on and show me how bad you can be. You did promise."

"So I did," he agreed, and Sylvester always kept his promises.

Next in the Daring Daughters series…

To Dare the Devil

Daring Daughters Book Eleven

Their mothers dared all for love.
Just imagine what their daughters will do…

Neither Fish nor Fowl…

Kathleen de Beauvoir does not know who she is. Adopted by loving parents when only hours old, she has a wonderful family, including an irascible older brother, and a place in her parents' hearts that is never in doubt. Yet she doesn't fit in. Her father is a brilliant scientist, but she has no aptitude for the subject. Her mother is a dynamic whirlwind of a woman who can claim the Duke and Duchess of Bedwin as kin, and Kathy is not at ease among the *ton*. Even with friends at her side, it is hard to be comfortable among people who regard her with suspicion, who believe her blood may hold unknown qualities that could taint the purity of their family line. Good heavens, her actual parents might have been *criminals*! Unfortunately, Kathy does not help her situation, overburdened as she is with a wealth of opinions, a habit of speaking before thinking, and an impulsive nature.

Her first season is bound to be ghastly.

A Devil on the Road to Redemption…

The Earl of Vane has a well-earned reputation for being selfish, arrogant, cruel, and despicable. He has made an enthusiastic study of vice and dissipation for most of his adult life until someone decides he's gone too far. Stabbed and left to die in a filthy alleyway, Vane realises his mistakes too late, but a quirk of fate and charity he has no right to claim gives him a second chance.

An Unlikely Alliance…

When Kathy recognises this man is the one she helped raise from the dead, she calls in the debt he owes, finding her own sense of purpose in the school he is funding to atone for his sins. Kathy is in no doubt of what kind of man the Earl of Vane is, having heard his fevered confessions of wickedness. However, she cannot be certain such a man can ever truly change, no matter how many schools he funds or how much she wants to believe it possible.

A terrible secret…

Vane's memory is still hazy following his attack, and it takes some time and a chance encounter for him to remember the girl who helped tend his wounds, though her sharp tongue left more of a mark than her care.

A wicked past is not so easily erased, though, and as Vane dares to hope for a future with a woman he knows he does not deserve, he discovers the path to redemption is harder than he could ever have imagined.

Pre-Order your copy here:

The Peculiar Ladies who started it all…

Girls Who Dare – The exciting series from Emma V Leech, the multi-award-winning, Amazon Top 10 romance writer behind the Rogues & Gentlemen series.

Inside every wallflower is the beating heart of a lioness, a passionate individual willing to risk all for their dream, if only they can find the courage to begin. When these overlooked girls make a pact to change their lives, anything can happen.

Twelve girls – Twelve dares in a hat. Twelves stories of passion. Who will dare to risk it all?

To Dare a Duke

Girls Who Dare Book 1

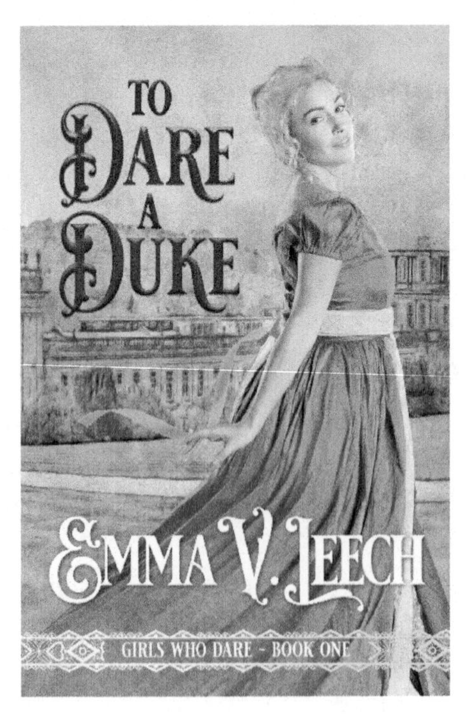

Dreams of true love and happy ever afters

Dreams of love are all well and good, but all Prunella Chuffington-Smythe wants is to publish her novel. Marriage at the price of her independence is something she will not consider. Having tasted success writing under a false name in The Lady's Weekly Review, her alter ego is attaining notoriety and fame and Prue rather likes it.

A Duty that must be endured

Robert Adolphus, The Duke of Bedwin, is in no hurry to marry, he's done it once and repeating that disaster is the last thing he desires. Yet, an heir is a necessary evil for a duke and one he cannot shirk. A dark reputation precedes him though, his first wife may have died young, but the scandals the beautiful, vivacious and spiteful creature supplied the ton have not. A wife must be found. A wife who is neither beautiful or vivacious but sweet and dull, and certain to stay out of trouble.

Dared to do something drastic

The sudden interest of a certain dastardly duke is as bewildering as it is unwelcome. She'll not throw her ambitions aside to marry a scoundrel just as her plans for self-sufficiency and freedom are coming to fruition. Surely showing the man she's not actually the meek little wallflower he is looking for should be enough to put paid to his intentions? When Prue is dared by her friends to do something drastic, it seems the perfect opportunity to kill two birds.

However, Prue cannot help being intrigued by the rogue who has inspired so many of her romances. Ordinarily, he plays the part of handsome rake, set on destroying her plucky heroine. But is he really the villain of the piece this time, or could he be the hero?

Finding out will be dangerous, but it just might inspire her greatest story yet.

To Dare a Duke

Also check out Emma's regency romance series, Rogues & Gentlemen. Available now!

The Rogue

Rogues & Gentlemen Book 1

The notorious Rogue that began it all.

Set in Cornwall, 1815. Wild, untamed and isolated.

Lawlessness is the order of the day and smuggling is rife.

Henrietta always felt most at home in the wilds of the outdoors but even she had no idea how the mysterious and untamed would sweep her away in a moment.

Bewitched by his wicked blue eyes

Henrietta Morton knows to look the other way when the free trading 'gentlemen' are at work.

Yet when a notorious pirate bursts into her local village shop, she can avert her eyes no more. Bewitched by his wicked blue eyes, a moment of insanity follows as Henrietta hides the handsome fugitive from the Militia.

Her reward is a kiss, lingering and unforgettable.

In his haste to flee, the handsome pirate drops a letter, a letter that lays bare a tale of betrayal. When Henrietta's father gives her hand in marriage to a wealthy and villainous nobleman in return for the payment of his debts, she becomes desperate.

Blackmailing a pirate may be her only hope for freedom.

**** **Warning**: This book contains the most notorious rogue of all of Cornwall and, on occasion, is highly likely to include some mild sweating or descriptive sex scenes. ****

Interested in a Regency Romance with a twist?

A Dog in a Doublet

The Regency Romance Mysteries Book 2

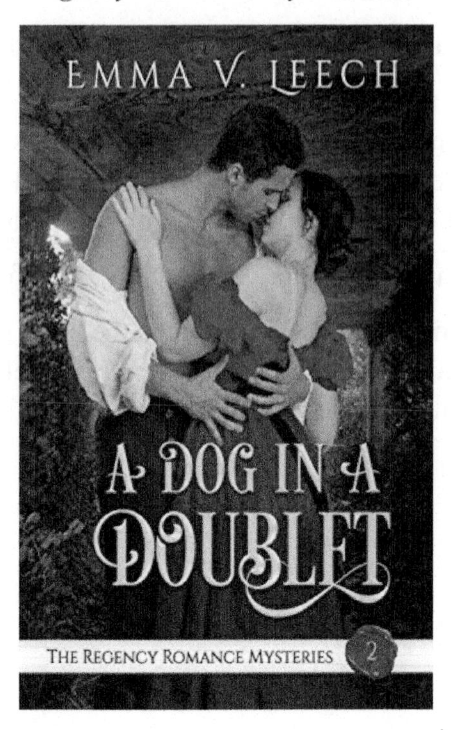

A man with a past

Harry Browning was a motherless guttersnipe, and the morning he came across the elderly Alexander Preston, The Viscount Stamford, clinging to a sheer rock face, he didn't believe in fate. But the fates have plans for Harry whether he believes or not, and he's not entirely sure he likes them.

As a reward for his bravery, and in an unusual moment of charity, miserly Lord Stamford takes him on. He is taught to read, to manage the vast and crumbling estate, and to behave like a gentleman, but Harry knows that is something he will never truly be.

Already running from a dark past, his future is becoming increasingly complex as he finds himself caught in a tangled web of jealousy and revenge.

A feisty young maiden

Temptation, in the form of the lovely Clarinda Bow, is a constant threat to his peace of mind, enticing him to be something he isn't. But when the old man dies, his will makes a surprising demand, and the fates might just give Harry the chance to have everything he ever desired, including Clara, if only he dares.

And as those close to the Preston family begin to die, Harry may not have any choice.

A Dog in a Doublet

Lose yourself in Emma's paranormal world with The French Vampire Legend series.....

The Key to Erebus

The French Vampire Legend Book 1

The truth can kill you.

Taken away as a small child, from a life where vampires, the Fae, and other mythical creatures are real and treacherous, the beautiful young witch, Jéhenne Corbeaux is totally unprepared when she returns to rural France to live with her eccentric Grandmother.

Thrown headlong into a world she knows nothing about she seeks to learn the truth about herself, uncovering secrets more shocking than anything she could ever have imagined and finding that she is by no means powerless to protect the ones she loves.

Despite her Gran's dire warnings, she is inexorably drawn to the dark and terrifying figure of Corvus, an ancient vampire and master of the vast Albinus family.

Jéhenne is about to find her answers and discover that, not only is Corvus far more dangerous than she could ever imagine, but that he holds much more than the key to her heart …

Now available at your favourite retailer.

The Key to Erebus

Check out Emma's exciting fantasy series with hailed by Kirkus Reviews as "An enchanting fantasy with a likable heroine, romantic intrigue, and clever narrative flourishes."

The Dark Prince

The French Fae Legend Book 1

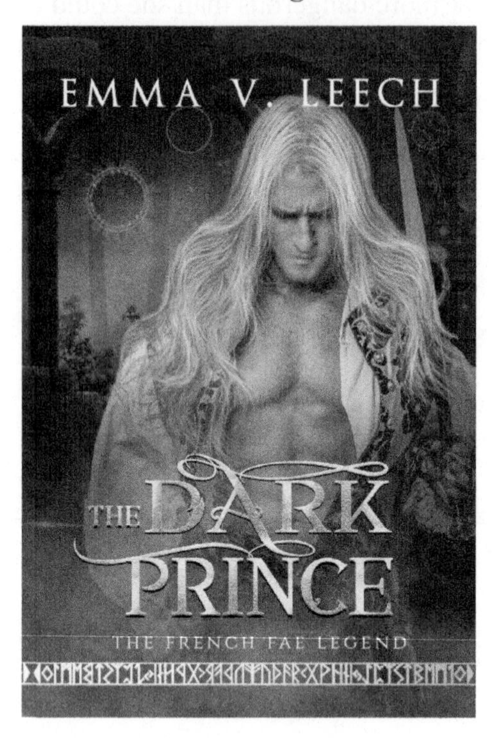

Two Fae Princes

One Human Woman

And a world ready to tear them all apart

Laen Braed is Prince of the Dark fae, with a temper and reputation to match his black eyes, and a heart that despises the human race. When he is sent back through the forbidden gates between realms to retrieve an ancient fae artifact, he returns home with far more than he bargained for.

Corin Albrecht, the most powerful Elven Prince ever born. His golden eyes are rumoured to be a gift from the gods, and destiny is calling him. With a love for the human world that runs deep, his friendship with Laen is being torn apart by his prejudices.

Océane DeBeauvoir is an artist and bookbinder who has always relied on her lively imagination to get her through an unhappy and uneventful life. A jewelled dagger put on display at a nearby museum hits the headlines with speculation of another race, the Fae. But the discovery also inspires Océane to create an extraordinary piece of art that cannot be confined to the pages of a book.

With two powerful men vying for her attention and their friendship stretched to the breaking point, the only question that remains...who is truly The Dark Prince.

The man of your dreams is coming...or is it your nightmares he visits? Find out in Book One of The French Fae Legend.

Available now to read at your favourite retailer

The Dark Prince

Want more Emma?

If you enjoyed this book, please support this indie author and take a moment to leave a few words in a review. *Thank you!*

To be kept informed of special offers and free deals (which I do regularly) follow me on *https://www.bookbub.com/authors/emma-v-leech*

To find out more and to get news and sneak peeks of the first chapter of upcoming works, go to my website and sign up for the newsletter.

http://www.emmavleech.com/

Come and join the fans in my Facebook group for news, info and exciting discussion…

Emma's Book Club

Or Follow me here…

http://viewauthor.at/EmmaVLeechAmazon

Facebook

Instagram

Emma's Twitter page

TikTok

Can't get your fill of Historical Romance? Do you crave stories with passion and red-hot chemistry?

If the answer is yes, have I got the group for you!

Come join me and other awesome authors in our Facebook group

Historical Harlots

Be the first to know about exclusive giveaways, chat with amazing HistRom authors, lots of raunchy shenanigans and more!

Historical Harlots Facebook Group

Printed in Great Britain
by Amazon